KATE STERRITT

love my way

Editing by Lauren McKellar - www.laurenkmckellar.com
Cover design by Marisa at Cover Me Darling - covermedarling.com
Formatting by Tami at Integrity Formatting - integrityformatting.wixsite.com
Proofread by Tricia Harden

DEDICATION

To Lauren McKellar.

*Thank you for your friendship
and supporting me throughout this journey.*

I couldn't have done it without you.

PROLOGUE

EVEN WITHOUT SEEING her face, I know that the woman standing at the water's edge is desperately sad. Her back is to me and her shoulders are slumped, perhaps heavy with regret. It kills me to know I am partly to blame, and for that reason alone, it's impossible to look at her. Leaning against the rough trunk of the tree, I close my eyes. My life will forever begin and end with her, and I'm unable to witness her heart breaking.

Standing still is no longer an option, so I begin to pace. Is she still waiting for him or has he already left? Fear pools in my veins at the uncertainty. Above all else, I want her to be happy. If this is too hard, I'll have to walk away again. I let out a long breath, frustrated by the whole situation.

Emerson Hart is the love of my life. Unfortunately, I'm not the only love of hers. And therein lies the problem.

PART
one

CHAPTER

1

~ Present ~

"CONCENTRATE, EMERSON!" MY boss's voice thunders across the kitchen, bouncing off the stainless-steel surfaces. "Those cakes aren't going to bake themselves."

Carrie Singleton, the owner of Carrie's Cupcakes, is a perfectionist, a task master and an astute business woman. Her short fuse and booming voice make Gordon Ramsay seem like a shrinking violet, and a long line of apprentice cake makers have run for the hills because of it. I've been working here for three weeks now, and some days I think she might want us to be friends. Some days. Not today.

"Sorry, Carrie," I reply.

She's cradling her planner in her left arm and making notes. Glancing up, she looks at me over the top of her glasses. "You're due at the Holland residence at midday."

"I know." I smile confidently at her. "I won't let you down."

"You'd better not. Sarah is a very important client."

"I know," I repeat, mindful of keeping my tone professional.

When she's gone, I struggle to refocus. I've lost count of all the jobs I've had since moving to Melbourne shortly after finishing high school, but this one is a definite step up from my previous one—selling insurance for a sleazy broker. I lasted two days before I was back online searching for something else. Despite my lack of tertiary education, I'm a fast learner and will try my hand at almost anything. Keen for a change of pace, I'd answered an ad for a job in a cake shop in one of the city's most exclusive suburbs. Carrie's Cupcakes is located amongst trendy cafes, a handful of expensive homeware shops, and a small art gallery I've yet to visit. The leafy streets create a beautiful village atmosphere, and it isn't difficult to understand why houses around here command such high prices.

Carrie was desperate for help at the time and hired me on the spot. When she fired her cake decorator on my second day, I was thrown in the deep end, where I managed to swim with a surprising degree of flair. I've not set foot in the shopfront since and spend my days with fondant and food dye.

For the time being, I'm content, and that's the best I can hope for these days. With that thought in mind, I pack the cupcakes into their box and head off.

The hot summer sun beats down on me, warming my bare arms. A light sheen of sweat beads across my forehead as I carry the box of fifty cupcakes with great care. Walking up the sandstone path towards the imposing front door, my arms ache from the weight of the box. The chocolate cakes inside with white fondant and black polka dots look elegant and chic, even if I do say so myself.

I manage to push the intercom button with my elbow, and when no one answers, I try again. Still nothing. Sighing, I balance the cupcake box precariously on one hand, then try knocking.

I think I hear a woman's voice coming from inside, but I can't be certain.

"Hello," I say, moving closer to the door.

When I get no response, I test the large, brass handle and find the door eases open. "Hello?"

The foyer is opulent, but the expensive décor isn't intimidating in the way I've come to expect in the clients' homes I've been to so far. I breathe in the inviting citrus scent wafting from the candles burning on the wooden entry table. The artwork hanging on the wall above the table is hard to miss, and I immediately recognize it from an art history book I studied in high school. It's Monet's *Woman with a Parasol.* Our teacher told us this beautiful painting of Monet's first wife and his eldest son was early evidence of his focus on light and colour over line and shape. It impacted me when I was a teenager, but seeing it in person, even if it's a replica, is startling and I quickly divert my gaze.

"Can I help you?"

My eyes snap halfway up the staircase to where an elegant woman sits with her arms wrapped protectively around her legs. She's dressed in a white linen shift dress, her expensive-looking heels pushed tightly together. She pushes an errant strand of golden hair behind her ear and takes a deep breath. Her eyes are rimmed with red, and mascara has made smudged rivers down her cheeks. I am definitely intruding on a private moment and it's uncomfortable.

"Hello, Mrs Holland," I say. "I'm Emerson from Carrie's Cupcakes. I have the cupcakes you ordered. If you tell me where they should go, I can be out of your hair in no time."

Without saying a word, she places her hands on the carpeted stairs, pushes herself up, then descends with effortless grace.

"I was expecting one of my sons," she says when she reaches the bottom. "I'm sorry you caught me like this." Her bottom lip quivers as the words tremble out.

"Please don't apologise," I say sincerely.

She nods and gives me a sad smile. "The kitchen is this way." Her heels click as she walks across the tiles.

I follow her past the staircase, through an archway, and down a hallway leading to an expansive kitchen.

"Where would you like them?" I ask quietly. She appears so fragile that I worry she might break if I say the wrong thing.

"Oh. Yes." She points to the far corner of the kitchen where there's an open door. "Just in there. Anywhere you can find a free spot is fine."

I make my way across to the walk-in pantry and carefully set the cakes down on the bench. After giving them a quick once-over, I head back to the kitchen and see Mrs Holland just outside in the adjoining courtyard.

She's sitting at a large outdoor table covered in a white cloth. Vases filled with lemons make a line down the centre of the table and are surrounded by fresh flowers.

"Excuse me, Mrs Holland," I say, standing at the door. "I'll be heading off now." I'm not sure if she heard me. Her shoulders shake ever so slightly, her body wracked with silent sobs.

"Are you okay?" I realise it's a stupid question, but it's all I've got.

She looks up at me with tear-filled eyes. "Will you sit with me for a while?" she asks, her voice hoarse. "I'm sure my son will be here soon, but I'd really like the company."

"Sure," I reply, hesitantly sitting down on the plush cream cushion. "I'm sure Carrie won't mind if I'm out a little bit longer."

She nods, wiping her eyes with a pale pink handkerchief she pulled from a pocket in her dress. She then pours two cups of iced tea from the jug on the table and hands me a glass. "There is something strangely familiar about you," she says eventually. "I don't know why, though, because I'm sure we've never met." She studies me, and I don't really know what to say to that. "The moment I saw you, I felt like I knew you already."

I take a sip of tea. "I've had quite a few jobs so maybe you've seen me somewhere before."

She stares into the distance. "Possibly. I can be a bit vague these days."

Neither of us say anything for a minute or so, and I can tell she's completely lost in her thoughts. I glance at my watch, wondering if Carrie thinks I've gotten myself lost. Shifting in my seat, I decide to break the silence and perhaps find a way to make my exit. "Are you having a party?" I ask.

"I have a charity afternoon tea here today," she replies.

Nodding, I wrack my brain for something else to say, conscious that this poor woman's eyes are brimming with unshed tears.

"Do you want to talk about it?" I ask cautiously.

She shakes her head. "Not really." A few tears spill from her striking green eyes.

As much as I want to leave, I decide I'll just sit with her until her son arrives. "Do you live here alone?"

She nods. "My husband died from a heart attack."

"Oh my goodness. I'm so sorry. When?"

She takes another deep breath and meets my gaze. "Ten years ago. You probably thought I was going to say last week."

I shake my head. "Grief has no time limit."

She nods and gives me an appreciative smile. "We were looking forward to enjoying our golden years, but then . . ." She pulls out her hanky and dabs at her eyes. "I know this house is far too big now, but I can't bear to sell it. This is *our* house, and I can't imagine anyone else living here." More tears slip down her cheeks. "I'm sorry, Emerson. You are just here delivering cupcakes, and I'm unloading on you."

"It's totally fine," I reassure her.

"Some days, I'm okay and the pain feels manageable." She blows her nose with her hanky. "But other days, like today, it all just feels unbearable."

"I'm so sorry for your loss, Mrs Holland."

"Please call me Sarah," she says, shrugging. "Ten years." She shakes her head. "I can't believe a whole decade has passed, and I'm still grieving as if it was yesterday. I think maybe some losses are impossible to recover from. It doesn't seem to matter what you do or how hard you try to move on, the pain is too great and your mind doesn't allow your heart to heal." She looks at me through bleary eyes, and I wish there was something I could say or do. "I lost the love of my life, and I don't know how to carry on some days."

I chew the inside of my cheek, deliberating whether I'm in any way equipped to offer anything of value, then say quietly, "I think you just have to keep treading water, hoping each day it becomes slightly easier to stay afloat."

Her eyes soften. "My son, Josh, gave me something years ago that helped me stay afloat. He took his father's death the hardest and has always been the most concerned about my welfare." She cocks her head towards the open French doors. "Can I show you what he gave me?"

I nod. "Of course."

"Mum," a male voice calls out.

"Oh. That's Josh now," she says, wiping her eyes again.

"I should really be going anyway," I say, glancing at my watch. "I hope you feel better soon, Sarah."

She nods as we both stand. "Thank you so much, Emerson. It was really nice of you to stay and listen to me."

Sarah walks me back to the kitchen. As we step through the door, a man drops a folded-up newspaper on the island bench with a thud, stopping me in my tracks. When he turns to face us, my mouth goes dry. Incapable of movement or coherent thought, I openly and rudely stare at the stranger in front of me.

He is tall—maybe six foot two or three, with broad shoulders and a strong body that is no stranger to exercise. With dark blond hair pulled back in a short ponytail and scruff that partly covers his handsome face, all I can think is that he's far too good-looking to be real.

"Darling," Sarah says warmly. "How are you?"

Her son waves a set of keys in front of him. "The door wasn't locked, Mum."

She turns to me. "This is my son, Josh. He's a bit of a stickler for home security."

Josh rolls his eyes, but an incredible smile lights up his face, followed by a quizzical expression, as if he's confused by my appearance.

"I was just telling Emerson here what a good son you are and how you look after your favourite mum."

He smiles, looking me in the eye and holding out his hand.

"Well it's good to meet you, Emerson."

I take a tentative step forward and shake his hand. "Nice to meet you too, Josh." I'm proud that my voice sounds even and normal.

When he releases my hand, I realise he'd been holding it for too long—or maybe it was me holding onto him. Either way, it was weird, and my cheeks heat. It occurs to me that perhaps I have some flour or food dye on my face because he is fascinated by me for some reason.

"Emerson delivered the cupcakes for my afternoon tea and was kind enough to stay and keep me company," Sarah says. "I'm afraid she arrived when I was having a pity party."

"Well I hope there are a few cupcakes to spare," Josh says. "I'm starving."

"You keep your greedy mitts off them." Her tone is firm but light. "They're for my guests."

She turns her attention to me and asks, "Do you like art, Emerson?"

Of all the questions in the world, she managed to ask one of the things guaranteed to make me fiercely uncomfortable. "I . . . um . . . well, I used to, but it's not something I kept up."

"My Josh teaches a wonderful art therapy class on Wednesday and Thursday evenings at the gallery just down the street from your work. You must know the one."

My whole body flinches, and I desperately hope it's not too obvious. "Oh wow," I say, awkwardly. "That sounds . . . wonderful."

"He's an amazing artist," she continues. "He's won awards and had work exhibited in some of the major galleries around the country."

"Congratulations," I say to Josh, who shrugs but gives me

another of his megawatt smiles. He's a gorgeous, working artist who looks after his grieving mother. I need to get far away from him before my already inappropriate thoughts do any real damage.

"Stop in at the gallery sometime. Wednesday and Thursday evenings from seven," he says, piercing me with his eyes. "My classes are laidback and friendly, and I like to think my students enjoy them."

"Okay. Sure. Good luck," I say before turning to his mother. "Bye, Mrs Holland. I mean, Sarah."

"Thanks again for the chat, Emerson," she replies, smiling warmly and appearing so much more relaxed.

My heart flips as Josh's eyes fix on me. "It was really nice to meet you," he says. "I'll walk you out."

As we make our way to the front door, I'm painfully aware that he's behind me. It feels as if one of my legs is longer than the other. Like a true gentlemen, Josh moves ahead of me and opens the door. "Hey, Emerson," he says, and I'm fixed to the spot by his emerald gaze. "Thank you."

"What for?"

"For being here for Mum when you didn't have to be."

"It was no trouble." I smile, giving him a small wave as I walk away.

On the slightly overgrown path leading to the front gate, I notice a small and perfectly smooth pebble, which seems completely out of place. Tentatively, I bend down, pick it up and run my thumb over its surface. Almost immediately, I'm slammed with a barrage of childhood memories that I had, until this moment, successfully blocked. Half-walking and half-jogging, I stumble across the road and into a mercifully deserted park where I slump into a swing. No matter how hard I've tried to block out my past, the memories are coming in too fast and with too much clarity. Squeezing my eyes shut and gripping the chains on the swing, I concede defeat as the dam wall breaks and memories of my first eighteen years of life come flooding in.

CHAPTER

2

~ Past ~
Ten Years Old

DESPITE THE FACT I was only ten years old, no one cared where I was or what I was doing, so long as I helped make dinner. We lived on the outskirts of a large country town, but I spent little time at home, primarily to avoid my stepbrother, Trent. Despite being in the same year, I tried to stay out of his way at school, too. My stepfather was always at the pub, so at least I didn't have to see much of him, and my mother either ignored me completely or lectured me on the ways I'd ruined her life and would no doubt ruin my own, too.

On one particularly warm summer's day, I was pretending to be an adventurer from outer space, exploring the town as if it were a new and exciting place. I even made a headband antennae, just for effect. My gaze was focused on the dirt road under my feet, hopeful of finding some coins or other dropped treasure.

A shadow loomed, and I snapped my head up to see Trent with his awful friends standing in my path.

"No wonder you've got no friends," Jacob Smith, the nastiest boy at school said, pointing at my head. "You're a freak." He stepped forward and ripped off my antennae, taking a few strands of my long hair with it.

"Cut it out." Mereki, one of boys by his side, grabbed Jacob's arm in a move that completely surprised me. "Leave her alone."

Jacob brushed him off. "Check this out," he said, holding up my antennae, laughing.

Trent sneered. "Emerson the insect." All the boys laughed, except Mereki. The pained expression on his face was strangely comforting.

"You know what we do to insects?" My attention snapped back to Jacob. I was pinned to the spot with his narrowed eyes and menacing tone.

I shook my head.

He dropped my headband and crushed it under his foot. "We pull their wings off, then we squash them."

I jumped backwards as both he and Trent lunged at me. Then I turned and ran, not even glancing over my shoulder to check if they were following me. Their cruelty continued to play over and over in my head as my feet stamped a rhythm on the hard dirt road.

I didn't stop to take note of what direction I was going. I'd lived in that town my whole life, so I couldn't get too lost. I didn't care. I just wanted to be far away.

When I could no longer keep running, I stopped and rested my hands on my knees while I drew in some deep breaths, looking around me for any sign of my tormentors.

The coast was clear, but they'd gotten what they wanted. They'd ruined something that belonged to me.

I stood up straight and tried to find my bearings. Nothing looked familiar, but I could hear music, and the park across the road was a hive of activity. I figured it was the markets I'd heard about. I checked for any sign of the mean boys one last time before dashing across the street.

I ducked under the wooden railing and crossed the green stretch of grass to the first row of stalls. The first was selling handmade soap. When the scent hit my nostrils, I crossed to the stall opposite, wanting to get away from the old-lady smell.

The woman at the stall opposite was selling honeycomb. When she offered me a piece, I gratefully accepted, then shoved it in my mouth. It was delicious. I thanked her and moved on. Maybe I'd go back and buy some later.

I approached the other stalls and came up with something nice to say to each seller.

"These are very interesting," I said to a man selling sculptures of some kind. "You must be very clever to make them."

The man with the thin, grey hair and matching beard laughed so hard that he had to bend over to catch his breath. "Do you know what they are, sweetie?" he asked, wiping tears from his eyes.

I shook my head.

"They are special toys for adults."

I shrugged, still in the dark but happy with his explanation. "Okay. Bye." I waved and moved on to the next stall.

In the next row, I was stopped in my tracks by a woman selling paintings. They were propped up on small stands on the table. One drew my attention, and I leaned forward to study the patterns.

"Do you like it?"

I tore my eyes away from the painting to see a woman with black frizzy hair and kind brown eyes that matched her beautiful skin that was so much darker than mine.

My mother, stepfather, and stepbrother were all pale-skinned with blonde hair. I wasn't like them either. I was somewhere in between with my light brown hair and olive skin.

Nodding, I returned my attention to the painting, completely mesmerised by every stroke, every dot, and every colour. It was made up of hundreds, if not thousands, of multi-coloured dots of different sizes.

"What is it about?" I asked, scrunching up my nose and squinting.

"It's a secret," she whispered, putting her finger up against her lips.

"Why?" I whispered back.

She leaned forward, and so did I. "Our art tells stories about when the world was created many years ago."

"But how can you tell a story without words?"

"We use symbols, and each symbol means something. We use different symbol combinations to create a scene."

"Why are they hidden behind all the dots?" I asked.

She smiled. "We need permission to paint these stories, and they must belong to our family lineage." She waved her hand over the table. "Our art has only been done on canvas and shared outside our communities in the last fifty years. The dots are used to hide the sacred secrets beneath."

I stood back, taking a long moment to ponder her words. "So I can't paint them because I'm not like you?"

Her smile gave way to a look of sadness before she stepped around the table and drew me into a hug. I didn't know why she hugged me, but I liked it. She pulled back and held me at arm's length, looking me right in the eye. "No one is just like me, and no one is just like you."

Somehow, I knew her words were significant. I repeated them over and over in my head before locking them away in my mind. "Well, I think your art is very beautiful," I announced with reverence. "I think I'd like to be an artist, too."

She picked up my favourite canvas and held it out to me. "A gift from one artist to another."

"But I'm not an artist yet."

"Yes, you are," she insisted, holding her arms out wide. "You just didn't know it until today."

Smiling so hard that my cheeks hurt, I felt the weight of a much bigger gift than I could possibly fathom. "Thank you." I was completely thrilled.

As I walked away, an unusually tall woman caught my eye. Her arms were covered in interesting markings and I stopped to take a better look. Her long, dark brown dreadlocks hung loosely around her shoulders and when she turned to face me, I was struck by her icy blue eyes.

She called me over with a wave and a smile. "What's your name?" she asked as I approached.

"Emerson."

"I'm Jenny," she said, glancing at my canvas.

"I think you've got the coolest hair I've ever seen," I said.

"Why thank you," she replied. "I think you've got the prettiest eyes I've ever seen. They're the same colour as your hair."

I beamed with pride.

She pointed to my canvas and asked, "What have you got there?"

I showed her my painting.

"It's very beautiful," she said. "Would you like to see my art?"

I nodded, and she ushered me over to a stall where a man was painting something on a woman's shoulder blade. He glanced up when we approached. "Found yourself a beautiful, blank canvas?" he asked, chuckling.

"Ignore Evan," the woman said. "We are body artists. We'll paint our own designs or something else of your choosing anywhere on your body."

My eyes widened with awe. "Can you paint something on me?"

"Do you have any money?"

I opened my palm, showing her my entire net worth of three dollars sixty-five.

She scrunched up her nose. "I can't really do anything for that"—she glanced around—"but I'll do a few simple designs while it's quiet."

Barely containing my excitement, I sat on a plastic chair.

Jenny handed me a black folder. "Flip through this and show me the things that speak to you."

"Stories without words," I said, smiling.

"Exactly. Art is independent of language."

Nothing stood out for me until I stopped at a page covered in a variety of feathers. Some were so detailed, they were more like photos. Others were simply an outline. "Close your eyes and tell me what you saw on the page."

I stopped myself from saying 'feathers' because I didn't think that was the point. I thought back to what the kind woman who gave me her painting had said. Closing my eyes, I placed my hand on the page and imagined the feathers flying in the breeze, floating over the markets, over the town, and up into the blue skies, blurred white by the wispy clouds above.

I was no longer looking at the feathers dancing in time to the music playing in my head. I was now up there with them, looking down on the quiet streets of the town. I could see my house, an insignificant blemish, meaningless from my vantage point.

I saw the river, skirting the town and flowing on to its ultimate destination. When I saw Trent and his mates, I flew higher until they were tiny and I was untouchable. "They make me feel light and hopeful," I said, opening my eyes. "They give me wings."

Jenny smiled broadly. "Most people just say 'feathers.'"

I nodded, pointing to the kind woman at the art stall. "She told me I'm an artist," I said proudly. "It's the first time someone has told me I'm anything other than a nuisance, and then she hugged me."

"Then she's a feather in your wings." Jenny picked up her paintbrush and opened a few pots of paint. "For a minute or a lifetime, some people try to clip your wings, while others help you learn to fly."

I flinched at the ticklish sensation of paint gliding over the skin of my upper arm. After rinsing, she dipped the brush into a pot of much darker coloured paint before making one smooth line. "Your first feather," Jenny said, rinsing the brush again.

I twisted my neck and stretched my arm so I could see her work. It was beautiful. A fluffy white feather with a dark stem to give it strength. "Thank you."

"What next?"

I tilted my chin up. "One day, I'd like to see the ocean."

She nodded and proceeded to paint a perfect shell on my other arm.

Perhaps because she was enjoying my rapture or perhaps because she didn't have any other customers, she let me choose another design.

"I want to feel like a warrior. A warrior finding her wings."

For the next fifteen minutes, Jenny painted various patterns on my arms. I asked her to incorporate dots and stars into the arm bands. Then, without offering any explanation, she painted matching designs on my hands.

"Why did you paint eyes on my hands?" I asked, confused.

"It's the Eye of Horus—an ancient Egyptian symbol of protection and power. Each different part of the design is linked to one of the senses. The right side of the eye is smell, the pupil is for sight, and the eyebrow is for thought." She pointed to the left side of the eye. "Hearing." Her finger hovered over my skin, following the curved tail. "This is for taste." Finally, she pointed to the teardrop, then gently tapped me on the nose. "Touch." We smiled at each other as if we'd just shared a great secret. "You're going to start seeing things with more than just your eyes from now on."

My smile dropped as I tried to process everything she'd said. Holding my hands up in front of me, I stared at the beautiful designs with awe, wonder, gratitude, and excitement.

Jenny continued. "Use what you find with your hands and what you see with your mind to make your own art."

Giddy, I jumped out of the chair. "I'm going to start today."

"Did you hear that, Evan?" she called out. "My little blank

canvas is going to be a famous artist one day."

Evan laughed, but I didn't feel like he was laughing at me.

Handing Jenny my money, I couldn't resist hugging her and hoped I wasn't smudging the paint. "Thank you for showing me your art," I said. "I really love it."

"You're welcome, Emerson. Don't let anyone clip your wings, but don't go stealing anyone else's either. Okay?"

At that moment, I felt invincible. With wings, I could fly away from my mother's indifference, my stepbrother's fists, Jacob's taunts, and anyone who told me I'd never amount to anything.

As I walked away from the stall, ideas began to develop and take shape. I could make my own art. I could make something just for me. With a thousand different thoughts rushing through my head, I climbed through the fence and made my way down the gentle slope to the river, relieved by the relatively cool temperature. The hot sun beat down on my bare arms and a droplet of sweat ran down the side of my face. I needed shade and supplies, so my search began. Birds sang a happy tune as I wandered along the riverbank. Perhaps they were cheering me on in their own way. It certainly sounded like it as their song seemed to increase in volume the more pebbles I managed to collect.

When I reached a spot where the riverbank was flat and shaded by large, overhanging trees, I stopped. A large area of soft grass covered half the area, and if I wasn't so intent on starting my art, I would've laid on my back and stared at the clouds all afternoon. Instead I walked over to a clearing at the foot of a large tree, set farthest back from the river. There were some weeds I could easily pull out and some patchy grass, but it could be my first dirt canvas. When I propped the beautiful painting I'd been given against the trunk of the tree, I spied a smooth, white pebble already lodged in the ground next to an exposed root. Excitement bubbled in my tummy, and a peace unlike anything I'd ever felt before, settled around me. *Had I finally found somewhere I belonged?*

Sinking to my knees, I emptied my pockets onto the ground and began sorting my collection. Occasionally I lifted my face to the sun filtering through the branches before returning to my art.

I'll come here everyday after school. It was terrifically exciting to have a secret place that was all my own.

Knowing I was late, I stopped a few houses short of ours to buy some time and plot my next move. I didn't want to go in there and face my stepbrother. Trent was only a few months older than me, but he'd recently had a growth spurt and was now taller than Mum. If I didn't go inside, I'd have to find someone else to take me in for the night, but it would do no good. I'd still have to face him the next day.

Taking a deep breath and clutching my canvas protectively, I edged forward. I dreaded what I was about to face, but as I gingerly opened the screen door, I reminded myself that I was strong.

I took a few cautious steps down the hallway and made a beeline for my room. Placing my backpack and new artwork just inside the door, I headed to the kitchen to make a start on dinner.

There wasn't much food in the house, so I set a pot of water on the stove to boil and grabbed a bag of pasta from the cupboard. As menial as the task was, I was enjoying the peace and quiet—right up until Trent walked in.

"Can't you tell the time?" he boomed from the doorway.

The bag of pasta exploded in my hands as I jumped,

sending pieces sprinkling down like rain. "I . . . um . . . I lost track."

Trent stalked forward, waving my canvas at me. "You stole this, didn't you?" He spat the accusation at me. "You're a thief."

For the first time ever, I didn't want to stand there and simply take his crap. Perhaps it was because I had found a sanctuary by the river, or maybe my new passion for art had something to do with it.

I looked at the painted art on my arm, and a rush of courage hit me. I felt like a warrior with wings. "Leave me alone," I said through gritted teeth. "I didn't steal anything!"

"What the hell is this muck?" he asked, roughly grabbing my arm. "You look like a freak."

Fury overrode fear. How dare he criticise something he could never understand? I snatched my arm free, balled up my fist, and punched his stomach as hard as I could.

Trent's reaction was swift and cruel; he whacked me so hard across the face that I saw stars, and then he coldly strutted out of the room, laughing.

I couldn't help but wonder what he was going to do with my canvas. The answer came later that evening when I returned to my room. I found it laying on my bed, completely destroyed. A hole the size of Trent's fist had been punched through the middle of my beautiful painting.

I saw red—and then I saw every other colour streaming through my mind in a vivid collage of ideas and hopes. Trent probably thought he'd won, but all he'd done was light a fire in my belly that would serve me well for years to come.

CHAPTER

3

THEN, A FEW weeks later, everything changed. When I
arrived at my place, a boy was fishing. He had his back
to me and didn't turn around. I wished he wasn't there. It
wasn't like I owned this section of riverbank, but it felt like I
did. This was *my* place, and I didn't want anything or anyone
to ruin it for me. After taking a deep, calming breath, I made
my way over to the pebble art and sat down, intent on losing
myself in the work. I hoped he might simply leave.

"What are you doing?"

Startled, I looked up into beautiful, dark brown eyes
gazing down at me. I immediately recognised him as Mereki,
the boy who'd stood up for me when Jacob stole my
antennae.

"Are you talking to me?" I asked, in barely more than a
whisper. We were all alone, but I couldn't help associating
him with the bullies.

He looked around, cocked his head, and smiled. "Who
else would I be talking to?"

"Nobody, I guess."

"Well, I'm not nobody." He grinned. "I'm Mereki, but you can call me Ki if you like."

I gave him a half-hearted smile. "I'm Emerson." I scrunched up my nose. "I don't have a nickname."

"I know who you are." He sat down in the dirt in front of me. "So what are you doing?" he asked, studying the pebble design I'd made in the dirt.

I put my finger up against my lips, just as the lady at the market had done weeks ago. "It's a secret."

He appeared interested but perhaps a little puzzled as he jumped up and walked away. I felt a pang of sadness and confusion. He seemed so nice, and I couldn't understand why he'd left. Pushing away my disappointment, I refocused on my artwork.

So far, I'd made a good start despite having no idea what I wanted it to be. A full circle was taking shape, but I'd decided I wouldn't think too much about the overall picture and would simply enjoy it. Not knowing how it would finish up felt like an exciting adventure.

Ten minutes later, Ki returned. "I thought you might need more supplies," he said, upending a bag of pebbles on the ground beside me.

"What?" I asked.

He pointed to the small pile near my design. "You're nearly out."

His kindness reminded me of the lady who gave me her art. "Thank you. That was really nice."

"So what is it?" he asked.

"I'm telling a story without words," I replied, hoping he wouldn't laugh at me.

"With pebbles?"

I shrugged. "Sure, why not?"

Not only did Ki accept my explanation without question, he spent the next half hour collecting more pebbles and helping me sort them. After unloading his third haul onto the ground beside me, he knelt down and pushed two random pebbles into the dirt.

"Yell out if you need more," he instructed. "I've got some fish to catch."

I glanced up from time to time over the next couple of hours, but he remained at his post, standing at the water's edge. I really hoped he'd catch a lot of fish.

Just as I was thinking of leaving, Ki called out to me. "I'm heading back now."

I desperately wanted to walk with him but didn't have the courage to ask. Instead, I waved him off with a smile. "Bye, Ki!"

When I returned the next day, I was thrilled to find him fishing in exactly the same spot. I gave him a small wave, sat down, and quietly continued with my design.

Within minutes, his shadow loomed over me, and a bag of coloured river stones was deposited on the ground beside me. I smiled up at him, wider than ever before. "Thank you."

Ki bent down, sifted through the pile, picked out a smooth, grey pebble and rubbed his thumb along its surface. "Can I help?" he asked.

I shrugged, not entirely sure if I cared or not. It was meant to be just for me, but something about sharing it with someone felt good. "If you want to."

Very carefully, he pushed the pebble into the ground and then ran his finger along the circle. I watched as his finger rose and fell. I was completely mesmerised by his action and found myself doing the same thing. I liked how the different textures felt against my skin. The jagged ones grazed and the rough, dirty ones left a mark, whilst I skimmed easily over the smooth, flawless ones.

"I really like this," Ki said.

"I'm glad," I replied. "I'm just playing with pebbles now, but one day I'm going to be a professional artist." I scrunched up my nose. "Do you think that's silly?"

He shook his head. "I think we can do whatever we want."

"And what do you want to do?" I asked, gaining confidence by the second.

"I want to be an engineer so I can design and build the best skyscrapers anyone has ever seen."

"Have you ever been to a big city?" I asked, thrilled and impressed by his response.

He shook his head. "No, but one day I will." He sat back on his hands and looked to the sky. "I've seen documentaries on TV about how they make the tallest buildings in the world." When he looked back at me, his wide eyes shone. "It's incredible."

His passion for buildings mirrored my feelings about my art. "I would like to see a tall building one day, too, I think."

"When you're a famous artist and I'm an engineer, maybe we'll stand together at the top of the tallest building in the world after you've exhibited at a gallery." His smile was so wide, I thought his face might split in two. "Do we have a deal?"

I laughed. "We definitely do!"

Some days, Ki randomly added to my artwork. Some days he didn't. Over the coming months, I stopped thinking of it as *my* story and started seeing *our* story, never having the slightest clue of the impact it was going to have on the rest of my life.

On the last day of spring, when Ki had finished fishing, he hovered over me. "I'm going to head back now." He rocked from toe to heel a few times before asking, "Are you ready to go?"

I slung my bag over my shoulder then stood. "Yes. I should probably get going."

For the first time, we made the trek back along the river into town together. I had no idea why he waited for me that time, but I was glad.

"Where do you live?" I asked.

"On Murchison St, opposite the park," he replied. "You're outside town, aren't you?"

I nodded. "It's not too far on the bus."

After walking in silence for a while, I decided to ask him something I'd been wondering about since the first time I saw him fishing alone. "How come you don't hang out with Trent, Jacob and the others anymore?"

He stared straight ahead, and for a minute, I didn't think he'd heard me. "I don't like the way they treat people," he said finally, shrugging.

"You don't have to stand up for me at school, you know," I said, fixing my gaze on the road ahead. "I can handle them."

"I know, but Mum says we should treat people the way we'd want to be treated."

My heart exploded with joy, and I felt like hugging him because I knew he was someone special and he was my friend.

"Ki," I said, waiting until he faced me.

"What?" He met my gaze.

"I'm really glad you found me."

The corner of his mouth curled into a smile. "I didn't know you were lost."

"Neither did I."

CHAPTER

4

~ Past ~
Seventeen Years Old

KI RESTED HIS tall frame against the locker next to mine. "Are we still going to the river?" he asked.

"You bet," I replied, stuffing my sketchpad and pencil case into my backpack.

"Good. I need a smoke, and you need another fishing lesson."

I snorted. "You shouldn't smoke, and I'm a lost cause."

"That might be true, but I'm a stubborn bugger and I'll never give up on you."

I absolutely hated fishing but had a great time pretending to have no idea what I was doing just to annoy him.

We were interrupted by a familiar, high-pitched, female voice. "Hey, Emerson."

I rolled my eyes at Ki before turning to face the girl who

liked to refer to me as her best friend. I had no idea why because I could barely tolerate her. She was often rude to my real best friend, and that was a deal breaker for me.

"Hey, Chelsea," I said unenthusiastically.

"I'm having some friends over tonight." She flicked her hair over her shoulder. "Jacob is hoping you'll be there." She took a step closer and whispered, "I think he's going to ask you out." Then she turned to Ki. "Sorry. You're not invited." I wanted to slap the smug expression right off her face. Being the object of Jacob Smith's interest made Chelsea excited for me, as if I'd won the lottery and was going to split the money with her. And given that Jacob's family owned Smith's, a chain of jewellery stores, and he was being groomed to take over, perhaps there was a fortune to be found with him. I didn't care. The fact he'd turned from cruel tormentor to relentless suitor over the past few years was confusing and irritating. He disgusted me in every way. All I wanted to do was hang out with Mereki and work on my art.

"Ki and I have other plans." I scrunched up my nose and tried not to smile. "I'm so sorry." I couldn't be sure if she'd caught my sarcasm.

Chelsea appeared completely oblivious. "Well if you change your mind, we'd love to see *you* there."

She barely even looked at Ki, whereas I could stare at him all day long. I linked my arm through his and ushered him away, lifting my hand to wave without looking back.

As we walked towards the school gate, he put his arm around my shoulders, and I leaned against him. Before long, he picked up a pebble, slipping it in his pocket as I'd seen him do a million times before, then he kicked the dirt as if showing it who was the boss. "We're going to get out of this town in a few months and become somebodies, you know."

"We're already somebodies." I smiled at the only person

in my world who truly cared for me. "We're best friends."

"You have dreams, Emerson," he said, running his hands through his hair. "You can't settle for anything less than you deserve."

His intensity was confusing. "I'm not."

"You are destined for so much more than this."

I grabbed his arm. "Has something happened?" I asked, a sick feeling swirling in my gut. "I don't understand where this is coming from."

"It's nothing, Emerson." He smiled, but it didn't reach his beautiful, expressive eyes. "Forget it."

We left the main road and turned onto the well-worn dirt track that led us along the river.

Ki swatted at his face and arms. "The sand flies are shocking today."

"Stop whining, you big baby," I replied, swatting at my own face.

When we reached our clearing, I pushed a couple of pebbles into the ground. It was now an elaborate design stretching out in all directions from where I'd started all those years ago. It had taken on a life of its own during the past seven years. It had bonded us to each other and to this place.

Sitting down on the soft grass, I watched Ki bait his hooks while I unpacked my sketchpad and pencils from my bag. Years ago, my pebble art had sparked a love affair with expressing myself visually. Drawing, however, had become my focus and I worked tirelessly on improving my skills, pouring over technical textbooks when I wasn't by the river practicing what I'd learnt. Art was obviously my favourite subject at school, and my teacher did her best to accommodate my constant requests for extra tuition.

"Come on," Ki said, waving me over. "First, we fish, then

you work your magic. Deal?"

He was ridiculously cute when he was determined, and I found myself staring at his muscular physique for too long because of it.

"Are you going to quit checking me out and get over here anytime soon?"

Embarrassed that he'd caught me, my cheeks heated as I stood up. "I'm not checking you out," I lied.

When I reached him, I struggled to make eye contact while butterflies somersaulted in my belly.

"You were totally checking me out," he said, gently pushing a loose strand of hair behind my ears.

I snapped my eyes up and found him staring at my mouth. The somersaulting butterflies turned into full-blown acrobats in that split second when our relationship teetered over the edge of the cliff.

Placing his hands on my shoulders, I stared at his mouth and imagined what his lips were going to feel like on mine. Instead of kissing me though, he spun me around so my back was to him. "Do you remember anything from your last lesson?" he asked in a voice that sounded strained as he handed me the rod.

When he looped his arms around me to take control of my fishing technique, I turned my head and looked up at him, batting my eyelashes. "I seem to have forgotten everything you told me." I expected him to roll his eyes when I winked, but he stared at my lips and whispered, "Have I ever told you the story about the girl who made the river flow again?"

Shaking my head, I turned back to the river, disappointed that he didn't kiss me but eager to hear another of his stories. I could listen to his voice forever.

Ki held my arms and guided my movement. I kept my

eyes closed, enjoying being pulled into him as he drew the rod back and forth. I couldn't imagine being more content than I was at that moment.

I leaned into him. "What was her name?"

"Miann. Her name was Miann."

"I've never heard that name before."

"She was unique," he said. "You see, Miann was renowned for her beauty, but she was also kind and loving." He leaned and whispered in my ear, "She was a lot like you."

My smile widened.

"There had been a drought for many years, and the river was barely more than a trickle. The weakest members of the community, along with much of the livestock, perished as food supplies became dangerously scarce."

Staring at the fast-flowing river in front of us, I wondered what life was like for Mereki's ancestors who lived by this river peacefully before European settlement.

Ki continued. "The elders believed that because some of the villagers had not shown sufficient respect for the gods and goddesses, the punishment was for all. Miann couldn't bear to watch any more of her kinsmen suffer, so she went to the riverbed and prayed to Iselele, the goddess of water."

I chuckled. "You're making this up."

Ki pinched me in the side. "I'm not. You take that back."

I squirmed in his arms, but he didn't let go. "Okay, okay. I believe you. Miann prayed to the goddess Iselele. Does she answer her prayers?"

"She told Miann that if she wanted the river to flow again, she must make a sacrifice."

"Oooooh," I said, laughing.

"Do you want me to tickle you?"

"No," I said, stifling another laugh. "What did she have to sacrifice?"

"Her own happiness."

My smile faded. "That's very harsh," I said. "How does she do that?"

"She had to give up the man she loved to prove her devotion to her people. Believing in the greater good, she turned her back on the love of her life, and as a result, he died of a broken heart."

"That's the most depressing story you've ever told me. Whatever became of Miann?"

"She was so devastated by her lover's death, she spent her days inconsolably weeping by the river. Her tears were so plentiful, they gushed into the riverbed. And that's the story of how the girl made the river flow again."

"That was a truly horrible story."

He laughed. "Not every story can have a happy ending."

I huffed. "Don't tell me any more sad stories, please."

"Life isn't always hearts and flowers, Kalimna."

I snapped my head around. "Who's Kalimna?"

He kissed me on the cheek. "It means 'beautiful.'"

"Oh," I said, allowing the pang of jealousy to ebb away.

"Now it's your turn to tell a story," he demanded. "Tell me how we found each other here. How many years ago was it?"

"Seven," I whispered. I'd told him this story so many times, but today was different. Our relationship was changing, and I knew I wanted him to be more than just my friend.

He nodded. "How old were we?"

"Ten," I replied, enjoying having his arms protectively

around me.

When I turned to face him, the electricity in the air was so palpable that the small hairs on the back of my neck stood on end. *Was he going to kiss me now?* I *wanted* him to kiss me. Finally, his mouth was on mine, and I was lost. I dropped the rod to the ground by our feet, then quickly wrapped my arms around his neck while his tongue sought entry to my mouth. As the kiss deepened, he groaned. My brain activity ceased, and the only thing I was aware of was just how right this felt.

My Mereki.

My soulmate.

When he eventually broke our first kiss, he didn't say anything. He bent over, picked up the rod, and resumed our lesson.

"Draw back, throw forward." He guided my actions, and we both watched the line fly out and drop silently into the river. "I think you've got it."

Unlike in previous lessons, he stayed behind me, continually brushing his lips over my neck. I always dreaded the tug on the end of the line, but now I had another reason for not wanting this to end. Would the spell be broken when we left the river? Would he regret crossing the line? Was I overthinking the status of our relationship?

"Stop thinking," he whispered. Ki walked over to his rod and reeled in the line.

I watched as he re-casted his line and dug it into the sand.

He caught several fish after I bowed out. I sat in my usual spot on the soft grass while watching the world around me, unable to focus on my drawings.

When Ki and I had kissed, something inside me awoke. Standing up, I walked over to the pebble art and skirted its perimeter, noticing the subtle shapes that had developed over time. I studied the different sections, then took a step back to see it in its entirety.

Glancing briefly at Ki, a sense of calm strength washed over me. I was whole, I was happy, and I was strong.

To date, my art had predominantly been landscapes, but I had something else in mind. I wanted to capture the way I felt right at that moment. Everything was hopeful and bright, and I wanted to capture our story on paper.

Sitting down, I opened my sketchpad and started to draw. I felt possessed by something otherworldly, as if I couldn't have stopped even if I'd wanted to. From time to time, my attention returned to the pebbles, noting the light and shade and the way the jagged pieces from the road blended seamlessly with the smooth stones found in the riverbed. I was inspired by the powerful way all the tiny pieces, collected over time, had come together to create something breathtaking.

When I was finally done, I could see myself in the drawing so clearly that tears streamed from my eyes.

"Wow, Emerson," Ki marvelled, crouching down in front of me. "That's incredible."

"Thank you."

"Can I see it the right way?" he asked.

I handed him the sketchpad. He stood up, alternating glances between the pebbles and the drawing in his hand. From the look on his face, you'd think I'd invented the wheel. Eventually, he said, "This is perfection." His eyes never left mine, and my heart skipped a beat, maybe two. When he handed it back to me, he said, "It's you."

"It's you, too," I said in a whisper. I stood up and moved to his side. "When I started pushing pebbles into the ground, I was lost and lonely. It gave me purpose, and then it gave me you."

He put his arm around my shoulders, and I leaned into him. "If you ever feel lost and lonely again, always remember that you're made of the strong stuff." He pointed to my drawing. "And this will always be your road map back to the light."

I nodded, allowing more happy tears to escape. He was my compass and, with him by my side, I would never be lost again.

CHAPTER

5

FOR WEEKS AFTER that, we spent a great deal of time lip locked. I really loved kissing him, and the way he groaned into my mouth, I was confident he liked kissing me, too.

"Here comes the rain," Ki said, holding his palm out. "We'd better make a run for it."

I'd known the chances of it raining were high that day, so I'd left my sketch pad at home. Just as Ki helped me to my feet, the heavens opened.

"Too late," he said, smiling at me, both of us soaking wet.

Placing my hands above my head, I stared up at the dark clouds and smiled as the rain splashed down on my face.

"You're so beautiful," Ki said, raising his voice to be heard over the pouring rain.

I dropped my gaze to meet his, and my hands cupped his face. "So are you."

We stumbled away from the clearing to seek protection under one of the trees. The rain continued to pour down, but the only thing I was aware of was his soft lips on mine and his strong arms encircling my body, claiming me. I never wanted this moment to end. So caught up in the moment, I tugged at his shorts. He did the same to mine, and we became a frenzy of fumbling hands and legs. After what felt like an eternity, Ki lifted me up, pushed me against the trunk of the tree and started thrusting into me.

I gave my virginity to the only person I'd ever wanted to take it.

The tree was rough against my back, and I was uncomfortable. It hurt. I always knew my first time wasn't likely to be the incredible experience I'd read about in romance novels, but this was so bad that I couldn't help laughing.

Ki stilled, shifting himself a little. The rain had made everything slippery. "Are you laughing?"

Nodding, I laughed harder as he slid out of me and helped me down. My whole body shivered violently from being in soaking-wet clothes, which just made the whole situation even funnier. Without saying a word, he removed the condom.

"Did that just happen?" I asked, still chuckling.

"You mean did I just ruin our first time?" he asked. He turned away from me with a solemn expression, and I was swamped with guilt. I thought it had been absolutely perfect.

I pulled my shorts up and pushed my slick hair out of my face. "Ki," I said, tapping him on the shoulder. He turned, still looking desolate. "I'm sorry. I didn't mean to hurt your feelings. I am happy, I promise."

He looked incredibly confused. "You're happy I ruined your first time?"

"You didn't ruin anything," I said, stepping closer to him and kissing him lightly on the lips. "I wanted you to be my first, and it had to be here. It was perfect, just like us." Then

I kissed him hard so he knew I meant it. When we parted, I looked him in the eye. "You had a condom."

He nodded. "I've wanted that for so damn long, Emerson."

A pang of jealousy hit me and I winced. "Was I your first, too?"

"Hey," he said, grabbing my chin and forcing my eyes up to his. "Only you, Kalimna. It will only ever be you."

His words meant everything. Knowing we were on the same page, I smiled up at him, loving the goofy grin on his face. Despite feeling warm on the inside, the wet clothes that clung to my body were making me shiver.

"Come on," he said, grabbing my hand. "Let's go."

We ambled along the dirt road, dodging potholes and puddles. The rain had completely cleared, and the sun was peeking through the clouds. "I wish I didn't have to go home," I said, snuggling into his side.

He kissed the top of my head. "Do we need to talk about what happened earlier?"

"I think so," I replied honestly. "Do you regret it?"

"Emerson." He pushed a stray strand of my long hair behind my ear. "The only thing I regret is that it wasn't a better experience for you."

"And I already told you it was perfect."

Our slow wander came to an abrupt end when Ki nudged my shoulder. "Race you back," he teased.

Laughing, I ran after him. When I finally caught up, I was lifted into his arms, my legs automatically wrapping around his body as our lips crashed together in a searing kiss. After only a few moments, Ki stilled, and I felt his whole body tense up. When I turned my head to see why, I dropped my feet to the ground. Trent, Jacob, Isaac and Troy stood in our path.

"Well look at what we have here," Trent sneered.

"Get behind me," Ki whispered, his arm moving across me protectively.

"She's out of your league, mate." Jacob pointed at me without breaking Ki's gaze. "Take a look at her."

"We're not mates," Ki said, taking a step closer to Jacob, and I held my breath. "We haven't been mates for a long time. Remember?" He loomed over Jacob. "Emerson and I are none of your business."

"Emerson is my stepsister and that makes her my business."

The vein in his forehead pulsed, and his fists were clenching and unclenching. I grabbed Ki's arm, knowing he was going to lose his mind at any moment. There were four of them and only two of us. I didn't like our odds, and I didn't want Ki getting hurt.

"Just keep your paws off her, you dirty dog. She's mine." Jacob looked Ki up and down. "Stick to your own kind."

I was taken aback by the look of utter disgust on Jacob's face. How dare he speak to anyone like that, let alone my best friend and the greatest person I knew? Enraged, I stormed forward and around Ki and got up in Trent's face first. "I am none of your business, so don't bother with the stepbrother bullshit. My mother might've married your father, but we're not a family." Then I turned to Jacob. "And what is your problem?" I pushed him hard in the chest with both my hands before Ki grabbed my wrist and pulled me back to him. "We're not even friends, so you have no business caring who I'm with."

Jacob took a step forward. Trent, Isaac and Troy flanked him like bodyguards. "I thought you were just being a little cock-tease, but it seems you were saving yourself for him." He raised his eyebrows. "This lowlife you've been playing with since you were a kid."

"Don't ever speak about him like that again," I said, seething. "You'll never be half the man he is, and I wouldn't touch you if you were the last person on earth. I would never be with someone who treats people the way you do."

Jacob's eyes flared with rage. "You think you're better than everyone, Emerson, but you're not. Just because you're hot doesn't mean you can talk to me like that. Ever."

"Everything alright here?"

Snapping my gaze towards the stern voice, I stiffened. We were all so caught up in the heated exchange, we hadn't heard a car pull up next to us.

"Yes, Officer," Jacob said.

Trent piped up. "We were just messing around."

The police officer pointed at Trent, Jacob, Isaac and Troy. "You've already had warnings. We've got our eyes on you."

They all nodded like naughty school boys.

"Move along then," the Officer said, shooing them away like flies.

Before they left, Jacob turned to Ki and whispered, "You've crossed too many lines, Mereki, and one day it'll catch up with you."

With that malevolent threat lingering in the air, they stalked away, shaking their heads.

"You two okay?" the police officer asked when they'd gone.

"Thank you. We're fine," Ki said, irritation still evident in his voice.

When we were alone, I grabbed Ki's hand, relieved that

the situation had been defused without a fight.

"I'm sorry, Ki," I said as we walked slowly the rest of the way back to town. "They're such arseholes, and I'm really worried they're going to hurt you."

"Don't worry about me," he replied. "They're just words." His fists clenched by his side. "I will kill either one of them if they touch you."

"They won't," I said, taking his hand. "I promise I'll stay as far away from them as I can."

Ki didn't appear even remotely reassured, and the tension only eased when we reached my bus stop and I pulled him in for a kiss. When we broke apart, he cupped my face with his hands and looked into my eyes with an intensity that made my knees buckle.

"I'm so happy we're together," he whispered, his mouth still close to mine.

"Me too." I rested my forehead on his and wondered if it was possible to feel any happier than I did right then. "I want to be . . ." I hesitated briefly before finishing my sentence. "I want to be worthy of you."

He took a step back. His eyebrows knitted together, and worry lines creased his forehead. "What do you mean by that?"

I looked down, digging a small hole as I ground my toe into the grass. "You know." I swallowed hard. "I don't want you to ever leave me."

He grabbed my hands and jerked me forward. "I'll never leave you."

I nodded, fighting back tears and unable to form words.

"You're the most beautiful girl to ever walk this earth. You're kind, resilient, loving, and good, even though you don't receive those things from enough people in your life."

He leaned in and kissed my cheek. "You're my shining light whenever the world is dark." He placed his hand over my heart. "Never let your light die because it's going to brighten more than just my world."

"But you're my world. There is nothing and no one else."

His lips touched mine, and I knew their tenderness would stay with me forever.

When the bus arrived, I climbed aboard and found a window seat so I could wave to Ki. I wanted to stay with him but didn't want to push it with Mum, who'd become increasingly erratic.

"I love you, Emerson," he called.

Before I had a chance to say the words back, the bus pulled away. I'd spent the last seven years caring for this boy, and there wasn't the slightest shadow of doubt that I was now completely and utterly in love with him.

CHAPTER

6

DESPITE THE PRESSURES the final year of high school brings, I was walking on air. Mereki was my constant inspiration, and I knew my drawing skills were improving everyday. Down by the river, life was full of passion. We might've only been seventeen, but we were lovers, and we felt invincible because of it.

After spending the morning doing chores, the rest of the Saturday was mine.

Mereki was waiting when I got off the bus. "Hey, Kalimna," he said.

I smiled broadly and handed him my bag. "Hey, handsome," I replied.

When I reached for his hand, he shied away—and it crushed me. "Everyone knows we're together, Ki," I muttered, following his gaze to a group of guys up ahead. I recognised them from school, but they hadn't noticed us. "I don't understand why you're always trying to pretend like we're just friends in public."

"I just think it's better this way."

"Why?" I asked, trying to hide my hurt.

He stopped and faced me. "Jacob and Trent are always looking for a fight, and as much as I'd love to ram my fist into their ugly mugs, I don't want a record when we're getting out of this town soon."

I kicked my foot in the dirt like a petulant child. "There will always be people who enjoy causing trouble."

"I guess you're right," he said but sounded so resigned, I wondered about the flack he received that I didn't know about. "I'm so proud of you and want to scream our love from the rooftops, but I don't want to be reckless either. I just want to finish school, then get us the hell out of here."

"Come on," I said, jogging ahead a few steps. "Let's get down to the river."

As we made our way to the clearing, I looked up at the dark sky. "I think it's going to rain."

"Probably," he replied, glancing upward. "You wanna turn back?"

I shook my head. "It might hold out."

"How are things at home?" he asked. "Did Trent give you any grief today?"

I shrugged. "No more than usual."

He nodded. "I can't wait until this year is over."

I sighed. "I know. Me too, but there'll be arseholes everywhere, so you need to stop worrying about it."

"I'll never stop trying to protect you from every single one," he said in a tone I didn't like.

"I don't need your protection." I picked up the pace, eager to get to our place by the river. "I can fight my own battles."

Ki groaned but didn't push me on this. We'd had the

conversation so many times.

When we arrived, I sat down next to my pebble art and pulled out my sketchpad.

"It's so amazing," Ki said, squatting next to me and staring at the design. "How many pieces do you think there are?"

"Two," I said, smiling. "Yours and mine." I wrapped my arms around his neck. "We just fit together, you and I."

He shook his head, laughing. "That's a bit cheesy, Emerson."

I smacked him on the chest and tried to pull back, but his strong arms held me in place. "I'm kidding." He kissed me so passionately my knees went weak.

After making out for what seemed like forever, Ki left me with my sketchpad while he baited his hooks.

Every chance I got, I worked on what I now considered to be my self-portrait. It had become a complex layering of light and shade that reflected every aspect of my life.

I deserved this. I'd never intentionally hurt anyone. I worked hard at school and at home. There was no reason I shouldn't be given this amount of happiness because it was pure and good.

"Stay with me tonight," Ki said, as we neared my bus stop a few hours later.

"I'll have to go home to get some things," I replied, already working out what clothes I'd pack in my head.

"Makes sense as we're going to the art gallery tomorrow, and the less time you spend with Trent the better."

"I can handle Trent," I said, pushing my shoulders back and meeting his gaze. "I've taken care of myself all my life, and as much as I appreciate and love that you want to protect me, I don't need you to treat me like some helpless little girl."

He appeared pained. "I know you're not helpless, Kalimna, but I'm worried—and I want you in my bed."

I looked up at him through my lashes and knew I wanted that, too—so much. "I'll go home and get my things, then I'll be back."

Mum was sitting on the benches in front of the small supermarket with a few of her friends, just as she always did in the early evenings. She looked straight at me but didn't say a word. I could feel her eyes on me as I passed, but there was no acknowledgment. She acted as if I was a stranger and realistically, to her, I was. However, that day she followed me home, and I was aware of her close behind me as I unlocked the front door.

While I was packing a few things from my dresser into a bag, my whole body tensed. I glanced towards my bedroom door and my stomach fell. Mum and Trent were blocking my exit.

"Where are you going?" Trent asked, arms tightly folded.

"I'm staying in town tonight," I replied, pushing a pair of jeans into my bag. "Not that it's any business of yours," I mumbled under my breath. These days, I stayed overnight at Mereki's house often, but I'd never had to justify myself before. They were rarely home when I was, and I had no reason to think they cared about my whereabouts any more than I cared about theirs.

"Who with?" Mum asked, then shoved a cigarette in her mouth. Trent whipped a Zippo lighter from his pocket and lit it for her.

"Yeah," Trent sneered. "Who with, Emerson?"

"Um . . . a friend." I clenched my teeth and hoped for the

best.

"You're staying with Mereki, aren't you, you little slut?" Trent laughed, but there was a malicious edge to his voice.

"I'm not a slut," I defended. "He's my boyfriend, and I'm seventeen years old."

"You should be shacking up with Jacob Smith," Mum suggested with her hand on her hip, the cigarette hanging from her red-stained lips. "He's more your type." Then she blew smoke directly into my face.

And follow in your footsteps? I don't think so.

I slung my bag over my shoulder and took a few steps towards them. "This is none of your business," I said, pinning them both with a harsh look. "And for the record, Jacob Smith has never been and will never be my type."

Mum snickered. "You'll learn soon enough that all men leave. Doesn't matter how pretty you are or how often you spread your legs." Pain flashed across her bloodshot eyes. "Cash in with the rich boy while you can."

"You're wrong," I whispered, surprised by how calm I felt. I could've told her Mereki and I were in love and that we were planning the rest of our lives, away from her and this town. I could've told her that we were soulmates and nothing would come between us. I could've said so many things, but I bit my tongue. She was bitter and twisted and I'd be wasting my breath. Silently, I thanked the stars for aligning, the river goddess or whoever led me down to the river all those years ago because what Mereki and I had was forever.

Trent pushed his shoulders back. "Your father ditched you before you were born, then mine, the worthless prick, cut and run, too." His dark eyes were filled with hatred. "What makes you think any man will stick around for you?"

I threw my arms in the air. "Oh my God. This again?

You're so filled with hate, you can't see beyond it." I narrowed my eyes and took another step forward. "I feel sorry for you, Trent. You're going to spend the rest of your days blaming him for your small life."

Pushing my mother aside, he grabbed me by the upper arm, slammed me into the wall, then slapped me hard across my cheek. His mouth was only an inch from mine. "You've always been a spiteful little bitch," he whispered.

Taking a step back, he raised his fist, but there was no way I was going to let him hit me. Channelling all my resentment, anger, and frustration, I slammed my knee into his groin. Completely blindsided, he crumpled to the floor, writhing in agony.

"Enough, Trent," I said with conviction. "Enough."

I picked up my bags and turned to my mother. "I'm staying in town with Mereki. I'm not asking. I'm telling."

As I pushed past them, Trent whipped his hand out and gripped me around the ankle. "You'll pay for this."

I yanked my leg away and walked out the door without so much as a backward glance.

CHAPTER

7

Ki OPENED THE door, pulled me in close and I felt the tension seep from my shoulders.

"Nice to see you, too," I said, smiling as my lips touched his.

"What happened?" he asked, touching my cheek that must've still been red.

"Mum and Trent were being themselves." I shrugged. "But I gave better than I got."

Ki took a step back and ran his hands through his hair. "Antagonising Trent is playing with fire, Emerson."

"I handled it."

He shook his head. "Come on," he said, grabbing my hand and pulling me inside the house.

"Are your parents home?" I asked.

"Nope. Mum is on the road for the next few days, and Dad is on night shift. We're alone tonight."

I was overjoyed. As much as I loved his parents and how

they treated me like I was part of their family, the idea of having a whole night to spend together alone was exciting.

"Mum left a pasta bake for dinner," Ki said, pulling me towards the kitchen. "Are you hungry?"

My stomach growled in response when the delicious smell of bacon and cheese filled my nostrils. "I love your Mum."

Once settled in front of the TV, I flicked channels until I found a *Megastructures* documentary. It was Ki's favourite show, and I loved sharing that with him.

"Are you looking forward to the art show tomorrow?" he asked as the closing credits came up.

"Of course I am," I replied. "It's my dream to be part of it one day. Imagine if my art travelled around the country."

"When, not if," he corrected with a kiss on my forehead.

After we'd cleaned up, we turned on a movie but didn't see much of it. Making out on the couch was far more entertaining. It was almost midnight when we climbed into bed and lay on our sides facing each other.

"This feels so right," Ki whispered. He stroked my cheek and pushed the loose hair behind my ear. "I can't wait until we can have our own place together."

Leaning forward, I placed my lips on his. The kiss deepened, and he groaned when I allowed his tongue entry to my mouth. Our pyjamas were discarded urgently, but we made love as if we had all the time in the world. As far as we were concerned, we did.

Once it was over, we lay facing each other, and I whispered the words I knew to be true. "You'll never leave me."

"Never ever."

The art gallery in our town managed to secure a few travelling exhibitions every year, but this one was the most prestigious they'd ever had. It originated in the city, and it was a huge coup that the curator had managed to secure a slot on its itinerary.

"I love seeing you so happy," Ki said, grinning broadly as we walked through the front door. Art was not his thing at all, but he was supporting my passion in the same way I fished and watched engineering documentaries.

Elated, I darted from one display to the next. It was overwhelming and inspiring seeing so much beautiful art in so many different forms.

"What on earth is this about?" he asked, pointing at the first in a series of installations.

"These are the winners of a state-wide competition," I said. "Light is the theme, and there were no rules or restrictions other than the overall size."

He cocked his head to the side, perhaps trying to make sense of the odd structure of lightbulbs, knotted ropes, and coat hangers. "I think it looks like some kind of torture device."

I chuckled. "Art is art. It's completely subjective. Who the hell knows what the artist is trying to convey here? Perhaps he doesn't even know himself. But someone might see something that speaks to them."

Ki shrugged, but I knew he was intrigued enough to move onto the next installation. It was a series of glass blocks stacked unevenly. Some towers were only three blocks high while others were at least ten blocks above our heads. Each block was lit from within, and the colour changed at seemingly random intervals.

"It's beautiful," I said after we'd stood in silence for

several minutes. "It's hypnotic."

"What makes you happy, Emerson?" Ki asked.

I turned my head and found his gaze still fixed on the art. "Why?"

"When I look at this installation, I think about happiness."

I looked again at the colourful blocks and wondered what he was seeing that I was not. I cocked my head to the side and tried to look at it from a different angle.

"You're responsible for your own life and your own happiness, right?"

I nodded.

"So let's say the blocks each represent different people or things in your life."

I nodded again, starting to see where he was going with this.

"If you stack your life tower with things that make you happy, your life will be filled with colour and light, but if you ignore your passions or fail to invest in the right things or the right people, your life will be flat and dull. You'll live in the shadows."

Taking hold of his hand, I squeezed. "You're the best person I know, Mereki, and you make me so incredibly happy." I glanced at the towers of light. "As long as we're together, I'll smile forever."

We moved across the room to a group of glass cabinets displaying some very expensive-looking jewellery. The first one housed a ring with an enormous pink diamond surrounded by smaller ones. The necklace next to it was breathtaking, too, and I could only imagine its worth.

"I'd love to buy you something like this one day," Ki said.

I shrugged. "I don't need expensive trinkets, Ki."

"I know you don't *need* them," he replied, meeting my gaze. "Nobody needs them, but they would look so beautiful on you, and I'd like to think one day I could be the one to put them there." He kissed my cheek. "I'm just going to pop out for a smoke. Will you be alright for a few minutes?"

"Of course."

I don't know why I continued staring at the jewellery. It was, of course, very beautiful, but I meant what I'd said. I couldn't imagine ever wearing anything like that.

"Like what you see?"

I snapped my head around at the sound of Jacob's voice.

"Hello, Emerson." He moved too close to me.

"Leave me alone, Jacob," I replied, shuffling a few inches away.

He waved his hand over the cabinet. "I can show you jewellery like this in our store anytime you like." His smug expression made my skin crawl.

"No thanks."

His smile faltered. "A girl as pretty as you deserves pretty things." He turned to face me and picked up my hands. "If you were mine . . ."

I cut him off. "I'll never be yours," I said, ripping my hands from his and taking a step back.

His eyes narrowed. "Your loss."

Mereki moved in next to me and put a protective arm around my shoulders. "Get outta here, Smith."

"I'll see you later, Emerson," Jacob said, winking, before slithering away like the snake he was.

"Are you okay?" Ki asked, clenching his fists.

"I'm fine, babe." I took his hand and led him to the other side of the room. "I want to show you this painting over here."

We spent another hour in the gallery before heading down to the river. I was so inspired by the art show that I managed to finish my school project weeks before it was due.

CHAPTER

8

M Y FINAL EXAM was held on my eighteenth birthday—
November fifteenth. Ki finished a few days before me,
and it had been torture studying when freedom was so close.

"Happy birthday, baby," Ki said when I walked out of the
school hall. He pulled me in for a hug and kissed the top of
my head. "How did you do?"

"Nailed it," I replied, kissing him properly. "We
survived."

"We did, and our life is only just beginning."

I reached for his hand and kissed his palm.

As we approached our clearing by the river, thousands of
happy childhood memories flooded my mind. Ki wrapped an
arm around me and covered my eyes with his other hand.

"What's going on?" I asked.

He didn't say anything, but nudged my back to keep me
moving. After a few short steps, he stopped me.

"Open your eyes," he said, dropping his hand.

My hands whipped up to cover my mouth. "Oh my God." When I met his eyes, they were so full of love, I thought I might die. He'd laid out the words 'Happy Birthday' in the ground using pebbles and a few sticks.

"I didn't have enough time to do the whole thing with pebbles," he said, chuckling.

"I love it."

"I actually thought about proposing, you know."

"Really?" I felt a small pang of disappointment that he hadn't, but I shook it off.

"I had a speech planned and everything."

"Tell me," I said. "I'd like to hear it."

"I plan to use it one day though."

"I don't care." I looked up at him through my eyelashes and knew he couldn't refuse. "Please."

He shook his head. "Okay, fine." Taking a deep breath, he began. "My Emerson. My best friend and the love of my life. You will always be the most important person to me, and I want to be your husband more than I want anything in this world."

A few happy tears slipped down my cheeks, and my smile was splitting my face in two.

"I was going to write 'Marry me' or 'Will you marry me?' with pebbles but went with 'Happy Birthday' instead."

I swooned even though the proposal wasn't actually happening.

"I promise to always love you in this life and the next."

"In this life and the next." I repeated his words, staring up into the eyes of the most wonderful person to ever grace this planet. I wanted to be his wife more than I wanted anything.

"Without breaking eye contact, I was going to slip a ring

on your wedding finger, but you wouldn't have looked at it because you don't care about expensive trinkets."

I smiled. "I'd have said yes."

A grin split his face. "Happy birthday, baby," he said and then lifted my hand to his lips and kissed my wedding finger where his ring would one day sit. "In this world and the next."

I looked up, questioning him with my eyes.

"That's what I will have engraved on your ring. I love you in this world and the next."

"You're killing me, Ki. When did you become such a romantic?"

"I guess you bring it out in me." He chuckled, then grabbed something from his back pocket. "Here is something I actually did buy you for your birthday."

He handed me a flyer for the monthly market held in town. "You bought me the markets?" I asked, laughing.

"No," he said, rolling his eyes. "I rented a stall so you can sell your art there this Saturday."

My jaw dropped. "Are you serious?"

"Deadly."

"You think it's good enough to sell?"

He cupped my face with his palms. "Your drawings are amazing, and you're going to be a famous artist one day, Emerson."

I laughed but quietly revelled in his unwavering belief in me.

"Well, as long as you come with me, thank you. I'm excited to give it a shot."

"Of course I'll be there."

We spent the rest of the afternoon and evening soaking

up the beauty of our special place. I was going to miss it, but I knew that I'd always be happy as long as Mereki was by my side.

"I wonder how many hours I've spent fishing here," he said out of the blue.

I looked up and found him staring out towards the river. "Thousands, I guess." I didn't even bother trying to calculate. "Same amount as I spent pushing stones into the ground or sketching."

He turned and looked at me, and I was struck by how mature he now looked compared to when we were young kids. His black hair had grown out a bit, but it was still shorter than it had been when we met. We'd both been scrawny kids, but he'd grown into the striking man in front of me with muscular arms and broad shoulders who completely owned my heart.

"I'm going to miss this place," he said.

"We can come back whenever we want."

He walked over, sat behind me, and wrapped me in his arms. We were quiet for a few moments, staring at the slow-moving water. "I'm happy wherever you are, but this place just feels safe, and it makes me feel that anything is possible."

I leaned back into him. "Life around us can change as much as it wants. As long as we have each other, we're invincible. Nothing can touch what we have right here." I glanced up at the setting sun, drawn to its fading light. "We take the safety of this place wherever we go."

Mereki whispered in my ear, "I want to hold on to this feeling forever."

"As long as you hold onto me forever, too."

CHAPTER
9

MY STALL WAS set up with the drawings I was trying to sell. "They're absolutely incredible," Mereki said. "You're so talented."

Pride swelled in my heart. "Thank you," I said, kissing him briefly on the lips. "For everything."

"You're welcome. I want everyone to know how talented my beautiful girlfriend is." He glanced at the table. "You haven't put your self-portrait out for sale. Why?"

I shook my head. "I don't want to part with it. It's too personal."

"You're a bit crazy. You get that, right?"

I chuckled. "Nothing wrong with a little crazy." I winked at him as two women stopped in front of my table.

"Hello," I said, cheerily.

They both nodded at me, then went back to perusing my art. It was a truly sickening feeling having strangers scrutinise my work, and I was relieved I didn't put my most personal piece on display. Without saying anything, they moved on.

"Don't worry about it," Ki said, putting his arm around my shoulders. "There'll be others with better taste."

"I think you might be a touch biased."

"You might be right about that. I don't have a clue about art, but I like yours, and isn't that what you told me art is all about? Liking what you see?"

"Yes, but I'm going to need more than just my boyfriend to like what they see if I'm going to sell anything."

After having countless people reject my work and move on, the doubt that had been creeping in started to crush me. There had been a few compliments from the kinder patrons, but no sales. The two stallholders on either side of me started packing up because they'd sold out of their candles and honey. I could see the stage being erected for the live music that would be starting up soon, and the beer tent had lines of thirsty people getting ready for the evening entertainment to kick off.

"Shall we start packing up?" I asked Ki.

My heart sank when Jacob approached my table. Of all the people in this town, Jacob was the one I least wanted to see. At least Trent wasn't with him. That was a small mercy.

"Roaring trade, I see?" he asked, snickering.

"Get lost, Jacob," Ki demanded.

Jacob held up his hands as if under arrest. "Hey. I'm just here checking out Emerson's art, and I have to say, it's pretty pathetic." With a chuckle, he turned and sauntered away.

His words cut deep even though I cared little for his opinion. This was my dream, and I'd faced a day of rejection.

"Hello." An older lady who looked like the stereotypical grandma in the American movies I'd watched appeared at my table. She had light grey hair pulled back into a low bun, and she smiled at Mereki and me with nothing but warmth.

"Hello," I said, putting on my happy face.

"Are these yours?" she asked, leaning forward to get a closer look.

"Yes, ma'am."

"Can you tell me a bit about them?"

Pushing back my shoulders, I took a deep breath. "I draw the way I feel about the things I see," I said with as much confidence as I could muster. It was the best way I could think of to describe my art. I picked up one of my drawings. "This one was inspired by the river, but I hope I've conveyed the peace it brings me watching my boyfriend fishing there."

She pushed her glasses farther up her nose and brought the drawing close to her eyes. Judging by the way she studied it, I figured she must be an expert. Her approval would mean so much, and I knew what I wanted to do. With Jacob's cutting words rattling around in my head, I reached down for my bag, pulled the sketchpad out, turned to my self-portrait and held it in my shaking hands.

"Change of heart?" Ki asked, surprise evident in his voice.

I shrugged, unable to look him in the eye as I offered it to the woman. "This is something I've been working on for a while."

The second her hand touched it, I wanted to rip it back from her.

"It's okay." She covered my hand with hers and gently pried it from me. "I'll be careful. I promise."

With an enormous lump in my throat, I shifted awkwardly from one foot to the other. It was too personal, and I'd never intended for anyone other than Mereki to see it.

Eventually, she looked up at me, and I was surprised to see her eyes were a little blurry. "Is this you?"

I nodded. "I actually didn't realise what I was drawing

KATE
STERRITT

until I'd finished."

Her gaze returned to it. "You've captured something special here. I feel like I know so much more about you just by looking at this drawing." She studied it again. "Quite remarkable! There's obviously a great deal of hope and strength in this piece."

"I have my boyfriend here to thank for that."

She held her hand out and shook my hand, then Mereki's. "I'm Madeleine Gibson. I buy art from up and coming Australian artists and offer it for sale from my gallery in Melbourne."

Mereki and I glanced at each other with wide eyes. "I'm Emerson, and this is my Mereki. It's really great to meet you, Madeleine."

She smiled. "I know someone who'd love this. I'd like to buy it if you're willing to sell. I'll give you five hundred dollars."

I leaned into Mereki, unsure if my legs were going to hold my weight. That was more money than I could wrap my head around, and it was such an incredible honour, but I didn't know how I felt about parting with something so personal.

"Can you give me a minute to think about it?" I asked.

"Of course," she replied. "I'll pop back in a while. Take your time."

After a few moments of staring blankly at the place she'd stood with a thousand thoughts flying around in my head, I turned to face Ki. His wide smile lit up his entire face, and pride shone in his eyes.

"When we were ten years old, you told me it was your dream to be a working artist." He placed his hands on either side of my face. "And your dream was just validated by an expert."

I sighed. "It feels like I'm selling a part of me that I'll never be able to get back."

"I think you need to let it go and light up someone else's world." He kissed me lightly on the lips, then studied my face for a few moments. "What are you thinking?"

"That I wish Jacob had stuck around to see me sell my first piece of art." I scrunched up my nose. "That's a terrible thing to say, isn't it?"

He shook his head. "Jacob is nothing. Forget about him."

"I love you," I said. "I'm gonna do it."

"I love you, too." He kissed me again chastely, then wrapped his arms around me. "Congratulations, baby. Your dreams are coming true already."

From the moment I'd started sketching the pebble art, it felt life-changing somehow, as if a force greater than I could understand was at work, guiding my heart and my hand. With her generous offer, Madeleine was offering me more than money. She had gifted me absolute confidence in my chosen path. For the first time in my life, I had no doubt in my ability to live out my wildest dreams. In that moment, I felt as light as a feather, floating high above all the negativity I'd had to endure, and I knew I had no real choice but to sell the drawing. I had to set it free, as it was going to open up the world to me.

When Madeleine returned, she looked at me expectantly. "Did I give you enough time?"

I nodded. "I've decided to sell you my drawing."

Her eyes lit up. "That is wonderful news." She opened her slim, brown leather wallet and removed five crisp one-hundred-dollar notes and handed them to me.

My eyes darted to the left of Madeleine, where Jacob was now standing with Trent, both holding a beer in their hands.

Their eyes were as wide as saucers and fixated on the cash.

I didn't say anything to them, but I felt a sense of deep gratification that they'd both witnessed this moment.

"I hope to see you again one day," Madeleine said. "Do you have plans to come to the city?"

"Ki and I are hoping to do a little travel after we graduate, then we plan to move to Melbourne." I glanced up proudly at Ki. "He's going to study engineering, and I've applied to the National Art School."

"That's wonderful. I'm quite certain you have a very bright future." She handed me a crisp, white business card. "Please come to see me at the gallery when you get to the city. I'd be happy to help you any way I can." She pointed to the card. "The address is on there." I took a quick glance, then placed it carefully in my pocket, completely thrilled.

"Definitely," I said, excited that I now had a contact in the art world.

Jacob and Trent had disappeared by the time we said goodbye to Madeleine. If it weren't for the fact I had all those crisp notes and her card in my pocket, I might've thought I'd imagined the whole thing. It was as if she'd just appeared out of nowhere and disappeared in a puff of smoke. I shook my head, not knowing quite what to do with myself. The one-hundred-and-eighty-degree turn today had taken had shaken me to my core.

Then I felt his arms around me.

"I told you, baby."

"Yes, you're very smart." I hugged him and wanted to savour the moment, successfully pushing away the feeling that things were too good to be true.

Part of me regretted giving up my most personal piece because it was a tangible reminder of how all the struggles in my life had made me who I was—strong and loved. However, a bigger part of me was proud and happy. I'd sold my very first artwork. I'd made a fantastic contact and I had Mereki by my side. I would focus on these things.

It didn't take long to pack up the stall, and soon we were walking hand in hand towards the music. It was a warm, late spring evening, and I sighed, smelling summer in the air. This was going to be a summer to remember.

"New York then Paris?" I asked, patting my pocket and trying to look serious. "We've got five hundred bucks now."

"Paris then New York," he replied, winking.

Mereki and I regularly talked about travelling overseas. One day, we'd spend time in these cities we'd only seen in movies and books. Paris was high on the list for art, but I'd always insist we go to New York first because I knew how much Mereki would love it there with the iconic skyscrapers. We were going to see the world and broaden our horizons one day, and we were going to do it together.

"How do you want to celebrate?" he asked, taking my bag and throwing it over his shoulder. "Do you want to stay here and listen to the live music?"

I shook my head. "I just want to be alone with you down by the river, watching the sunset."

"Now who's the romantic?" he asked, squeezing me closer to him.

"I can't wait to get out of this town, but I'll miss our place by the river, so I want to make the most of it." I stopped walking and slung my hands around his neck, getting lost in his dark eyes. "It's the place that brought me to you."

CHAPTER
10

WHEN MEREKI AND I arrived at the river, we sat on the grass and I snuggled into him.

"Let's make a pact to come back here on this day at sunset every five years, no matter what," he said, staring at the burning orange ball descending towards the horizon. "November nineteenth. I would say every year, but I think that's unrealistic, and I don't want to come back here that often. Do you?"

"Wouldn't you want to visit your mum and dad?"

He shrugged. "They can visit us in the city."

I remained quiet for a few moments, deliberating. Three little words. They could have meant nothing, but in that moment, to me, they meant everything. "I don't like how you said 'no matter what,' as if there might ever be a reason we wouldn't be together."

"Is that what you thought I meant?" he asked, shaking his head. "Of course we'll be together. I just meant that who knows what we'll be doing or where we'll be in five years.

We'll be twenty-three years old and probably finished with our studies by then. Hopefully I'll be kicking arse at a big engineering firm, and you'll be working on a major exhibition."

I laughed at the beautiful picture he'd painted. "Well when you put it like that . . ."

"I just think we should always remember what this place means to us and come back to where it all began. We'll tell the river about all the exciting things we've done since we left."

I pushed up onto my knees and threw my arms around his neck. "That's a wonderful idea. Let's do it." I kissed him hard on the lips before pulling back to meet his gaze. "So, four days after my twenty-third birthday, we'll both be right here watching the sunset, no matter what."

Nothing and no one would ever come between us.

It was late when we finally left the river and started the trek home. As we neared the small row of shops a few streets from his house, Ki's whole body suddenly tensed. His grip around my shoulders tightened, and my heart rate picked up. "What's wrong?"

"I'm not sure, but I thought I saw someone up ahead in front of the milk bar."

The moon and a few flickering streetlights made for reasonable visibility, but I couldn't see anyone. We kept going, but when a stray dog barked, I clutched my chest. "Holy shit."

"Must've just been dogs," Ki said, exhaling. His tight grip around me eased as we picked up the pace, eager to get home. "Get outta here," he growled, flicking his arm as one of the dogs scampered closer.

"I think I just lost a few years off my life," I said, rubbing at my chest.

"Relax, Kalimna." He kissed the top of my head. "Let's just keep moving."

Before we'd taken another step, a strong hand gripped my arm, and my bag was ripped from my shoulder. My heart leapt to my throat. I was yanked away from Ki. I stumbled, struggling against the grip as I was dragged down the small alleyway between the milk bar and the barber shop. There were men, but I wasn't given the opportunity to see them clearly because I was slammed up against a brick wall facing the wrong direction. All I could see were shadows. Were there three of them? Four? I could hear Mereki shouting, but I couldn't make out the words over the blood rushing through my ears.

A hand, large and rough, covered my mouth. As I dragged air in through my nose, I could smell cheap booze. I wanted to scream, but my throat was dry, and in a moment of sheer terror, I wondered if I would die like this.

"Fuck! Let her fucking go!" Mereki screamed.

Fear consumed me. I wanted to see him, but what I wanted more was for him to get away from here. I didn't want him to get hurt trying to save me, but I knew there was absolutely no chance he would leave. I wrestled violently, but it was a wasted effort. Whoever had me was too strong, and I was just wasting energy trying to escape.

"I've got the cash," said one of the men.

They could have it. *Just don't let Mereki be hurt.*

With a hand no longer over my mouth, I screamed. "Get away, Ki. Please get away." I wanted nothing else. "Please let him go. Do whatever you want with me, but don't hurt him."

His life was worth more than anything else to me.

I received a sharp shove to the middle of my back and my knees hit the rough gravel, then I toppled forward. My wrists were held behind me, so I couldn't brace my fall. My face slammed into the ground.

"It's okay, Kalimna." His voice was desperate, and his words were followed by a thump, then a groan. I strained my head to the side and managed to catch a glimpse of him in my peripheral vision. In the moonlight, I could see his nose was bleeding, and one of his eyes was closed. I couldn't take my eyes off him.

"Shut up, you little bitch." I was slapped across the back of the head by a man I could feel kneeling between my legs, pushing them apart. Oh my God. He was going to rape me in front of Ki. This couldn't be happening.

"Please don't hurt Ki." I desperately tried to turn my head again, but now one of his hands was pressing down on the back of my head. The other was pushing up my skirt and yanking at my underwear.

"Don't touch her," Ki roared. "Please don't touch her."

The man behind me was eerily silent. By contrast, my heart hammered, willing Mereki to be quiet. They would hurt him again.

My attacker managed to rip my underwear off, and I closed my eyes, willing my mind to fly away. I thought about the drawing I sold earlier today—the roadmap back to the light. How could I have sold it? Shapes swirled around in my mind. They were usually so clear, but now they were a fuzzy mess, chaotically morphing into a blurry and unrecognizable horror show.

An unearthly roar snapped me back into my horrific reality, and then I was crushed by at least twice as much weight as before.

"I'll save you, Kalimna." Ki's voice was so close to my ear; his words breathed hope into my body. "I love you."

Then he was gone, and my heart was filled with a fear unlike anything I'd ever experienced. It felt like life was being drained from me with every second that passed.

"Ki!" My scream died in my throat as a blow to my head sent me plummeting into darkness.

I floated above my lifeless body, watching in horror as a pool of blood surrounded me, paralysed by confusion and fear. I might've been screaming, but maybe I wasn't doing anything at all. Someone was definitely screaming, but there was no one else here. So this was what it was like to be dead? Where was I? My vision blurred and shimmered, so I closed my eyes, welcoming oblivion.

Pain.

The only thing I could feel. Something wasn't right. I was totally disoriented before even trying to open my eyes. Foreign smells invaded my nostrils, and my brain tried to place the scent of pine, lemon, and bleach. I was lying in a bed—the sheets weren't soft, and they felt cold against my skin, and then I heard beeping. Random beeps coming from somewhere, but my foggy brain couldn't make sense of it. I needed to open my eyes, but I was afraid. My eyelids felt like shields from whatever I was about to face. I hoped that they'd remain closed. Then no one could see me. I could hide.

"Emerson."

I didn't recognise the voice, so I defiantly squeezed my eyes shut tighter.

"Emerson." The female voice repeated. "Can you open your eyes?"

She sounded friendly.

Then my mind flooded with fear. At the edge of my consciousness was an inkling of something so intensely painful that I shoved it away. Absolutely not going there.

Disinfectant. That was what I was smelling. The crisp sheets. The beeping.

Oh my God. I was in a hospital. Why was I in a hospital? My eyes snapped open and were met with a stern, yet friendly-looking woman with a uniform and a name badge.

"How are you feeling, sweetheart?" Nurse Marina asked.

"How did I get here?" I asked groggily, wincing as I propped my body weight onto my elbows.

"Just relax, sweetie." She placed a hand on my shoulder and gently eased me back. "You need to rest. The morphine drip should keep you comfortable."

My eyes drifted tentatively over my body. "What happened to me, and where's my boyfriend?"

"You were attacked and took a blow to the back of your head." She placed a hand on my arm. "The police would like to question you as soon as possible."

"The police?" I asked, my heart catapulting out of my chest.

"They just want to learn what happened so they can find whoever did this."

Before she could answer my question about Ki, I surrendered to the darkness, unwilling to face reality.

When I opened my eyes again, I was floating above my hospital bed, and all I could do was watch myself asleep.

The door opened and to my relief, Marina, the friendly

nurse, was now accompanied by Mereki. I was overcome with joy and tried desperately to call out to him but couldn't use my voice.

"Wake up!" I screamed at my sleeping form. "Wake up, Emerson. Mereki is here to look after you now."

While Marina busied herself tucking in my sheets and checking my chart, Ki stood next to my bed, intently gazing at me with his beautiful, loving eyes. It gave me great peace to know that when I woke, he'd be there to hold my hand and tell me everything was going to be okay. We could talk to the police together and find a way to move on with our lives. I just needed to wake up.

PART

two

CHAPTER

11

~ Present ~

"HEY, HONEY. I'M home," I say, slamming the front door so hard it shudders.

Mereki doesn't turn to acknowledge me. I've learned to simply be grateful he's still here at all, when each time I come home, I wonder if today's the day he'll be gone for good. I've learned to accept the heartbreaking anticipation and take joy from the gift of another day, but that doesn't mean it hurts any less when he ignores me so blatantly. I'll find a way to turn this all around.

"I'm going to take a shower," I say, breaking the crushing silence. Making my way to the bedroom, I strip off my flour-covered clothing and hit the shower. I need to wash my hair most days. It's an occupational hazard of making cakes for a living.

Clean and refreshed, I collect my strewn clothes and place them in the laundry basket. It's then I notice the pebble on the floor. I left the park a mess, but thankfully, Carrie didn't notice I'd been crying when I got back to work. One little pebble, responsible for such mental anguish. It must've fallen out of my pocket, and I quickly pick it up, smoothing my thumb across the surface.

When I return to the lounge room, Mereki appears completely exhausted but still devastatingly handsome and still very much mine. He doesn't look at me, but I plonk myself down beside him anyway.

"Do you remember the day we met?" I ask, gripping the pebble in my closed fist. Gaining his attention is becoming an almost impossible task lately.

He nods but doesn't smile or even look at me. I've loved this man for more than half my life, and I hate what has become of us. This isn't what I wanted.

"I think back to those days by the river when we were kids."

Nothing.

He is blocking me out, and it's suffocating.

Before I can say anything else, he pushes himself up and walks out the door. No backward glance or simple goodbye—he just leaves, and my always-hopeful heart takes yet another blow.

Rather than focusing on where he's gone or when he'll return, I spend the evening reading. At least I can allow my mind to take me away from my increasingly bleak reality.

When I finally go to bed, he's still not home. I am sadly accustomed to going to sleep alone but know I'll stir from sleep at some stage, and he'll be there because we love each other on a level that transcends all.

Ki has already left when I wake up the next morning. He works so hard, and I'm sure he's going to quickly climb the corporate ladder. I know there is travel coming up that he's excited about it. His job is going to take him places—places far away from me.

Reaching over to my bedside table, I pick up the framed picture of us. Mereki's mother took the photo at their home on my eleventh birthday. Realising that my own mother probably wouldn't even remember my birthday, she'd invited me to dinner and made me a cake. I was about to blow out the candles and make my wish when Ki put his arm around my shoulders. We both had the biggest grins on our faces. It was a perfect moment, and I'm so grateful it was captured.

Absently, I run my finger over the photo, tracing Ki's strong profile, still taken aback by how much he already cared for me, even then.

Eventually, I drag myself out of bed, throw my hair in a bun, and pull myself together for work. My morning train ride to the city is around twenty-five minutes, and I typically spend the time reading. Today, I pull the smooth, white pebble from my bag and stare at it. I have become completely fixated on it, and I pull out a scrap piece of paper, place the pebble down, and trace around it with my pencil. As if on instinct, I start to shade it in. By the time the train arrives at my stop, I've covered the paper in shapes of varying sizes, some shaded dark and others left as just outlines. I am focused and my heart is racing.

On my walk from the station to work, I collect several more pebbles that catch my eye and place them in my bag. Somehow, they make it feel lighter.

My morning is a blur of baking, icing, and decorating. I love the creative side of this job, and Carrie allows me free rein on the cupcakes we sell in the shopfront. The custom orders are usually quite specific, but I do love it when the client consults us for design and colour inspiration. This morning, I spent hours cutting one hundred twenty various-sized butterflies from pink fondant, folding them into shape, and leaving them to dry in pre-prepared foil. The result when they set is a beautiful flurry of winged beauties looking ready to take flight.

Instead of heading to the park on my lunchbreak, I go for a walk. I try telling myself I don't have a destination in mind, but when I stop in front of the art gallery, I know exactly what I'm doing there. Ever since I heard about Josh's art therapy classes, I can't stop thinking about them. Why now? I gave up art years ago and thought I'd found peace with it. Now that I think about it, all I've done is become an expert in avoidance.

Gallery on the Park has a well-maintained frontage. The brickwork around the large picture window is painted a deep crimson. Several easels are set up on the other side of the glass, and I find myself moving closer to get a better look. The one that makes me gasp is a sketch of a man's face. Half is perfectly drawn with such fine detail, it's almost like a photograph, but the other half is mostly shaded and drifts off to the edge, distorting him completely. Before I have a chance to look closer and read the artist's name, the door at the back of the gallery space opens. I don't want to be caught here, but I don't know why. I dash away, which is irrational but instinctual—and I don't ever fight instincts anymore.

I finish work at five but offer to stay behind to clean the ovens. Who does that? Perhaps I'm just killing time, but they do need a clean, and we're always too busy during the day to get it done. Glancing at the clock on the wall, I can see it's not long until Josh's class will be starting. Carrie always tells me I can take any cakes that don't sell, but I rarely do. Tonight, I pack them into a small box and lock up.

Sarah Holland is a potentially fantastic client and Josh is her son, so I tell myself that I'm doing this to help Carrie's business. It sounds so legitimate in my head—as if I have no other motive.

I am an excellent liar.

I walk down the street whistling a tune that I have stuck in my head. I don't know what the song is called, but it's catchy. It allows me to feign a carefree attitude. My stomach, however, twists into knots when I see Josh holding a crate under one arm, hovering on the footpath at the gallery door. I'm too close to risk turning around, but I slow my pace and do my best to relax.

Glancing in my direction when I'm only a few feet away, he smiles. "Emerson," he says, pulling a key out of his pocket. "Are you coming to my class?"

Balancing the cupcake box in one hand, I push my other hand against my stomach, willing the knots to loosen a bit. "Oh no," I say, furrowing my brow and shaking my head. "I just thought you and your students might like these." I push the box towards him. "They were leftovers and were just going to be thrown out."

Balancing the cake box in one hand, Josh lowers his crate of art supplies to the ground.

His eyes light up as he lifts the lid. "Thank you so much."

I nervously shift from one foot to the other. "Well, I hope you enjoy them."

He gestures to the door with an upward nod. "Are you sure you don't want to check out my class tonight? You're welcome to just pop in to see if you like it."

Part of me wants to scream yes, drawn to the art supplies and the happy childhood memories, but I don't. I shake my head. "I'd better get home. Maybe another time."

With a disappointed expression, he shrugs. "Well, thanks again for the cupcakes."

I begin walking away, leaving Josh right where I found him, except now he's weighed down by cupcakes and a confused look.

Cursing myself for being so inept, I pick up the pace, determined to avoid the gallery from this point forward. He probably thinks I'm a lunatic and I'll never see him again. Then he calls my name.

Stopping dead in my tracks, I slowly turn around.

"Do you want to grab a coffee sometime?" he asks.

Delight tingles through me. It's been a long time since I've felt something like that, and those tingles are reserved for Ki.

Of course, I can't accept, so I politely say no. The light disappears from his eyes as he's rejected for the second time by me this evening. With nothing left to say, I continue my lonely trip home.

CHAPTER

12

"Hey, honey. I'm home." I've said the same thing every day, but this time it's only a whisper. I'm saying it more to myself than him.

I walk briskly through the small apartment, flicking lights on as I go. When I reach the doorway to the bedroom, Mereki is standing out on the balcony.

His back is to me, but just seeing him there fills me with warmth. He is, always has been, and always will be my everything.

Sliding open the glass door, I step outside and stand beside him at the railing. "You're here." I choke back a sob, relieved to see him, as always.

There are things I need to say—some of which I haven't said out loud in years. I haven't allowed myself to even think them. "It feels like you don't want to be here with me anymore, and I don't know what I'm doing wrong. Even when you're here, I miss you." A loud sigh escapes from deep in my chest. When I get no reaction, I ask, "Did you hear me, Mereki?"

He doesn't say anything, but I can see sadness in his eyes. He doesn't know what to say to make this gulf of misery between us disappear.

I don't push. Growing up together, communication was always our thing. We could tell what the other was thinking without having to say the words. But things are different now.

I blow out a long breath of frustration, lean my body against the railing, and tip myself forward, focusing on the view below. A few stray cats are fighting by the rubbish bins, and I wish they'd stop. I took one of them to the vet last week, and the bill was almost a whole week's salary. Ronnie, our downstairs neighbour, lights up a cigarette on the balcony below, and I wave my hand in front of my face when the smoke rises to meet me. I've always hated the smell of cigarette smoke.

I don't know how much time passes, but when a shiver brought on by the cool night air snaps me back to reality, I notice that Mereki has gone back inside.

I feel bereft, confused, and sad. He is slipping away from me, and I don't know how to halt this runaway train before we crash and burn. I can't live without him, and I know that if he truly leaves me, I'll die of a broken heart.

Swatting at a few rogue tears that slip down my cheeks, I return to the bedroom and strip off my clothes. I have a quick shower, brush my teeth, and change into my very conservative cotton pyjamas before slipping into bed. I'm not only alone. I'm lonely. I want my best friend back. I want my lover back.

As always, sleep doesn't come easy. Sobs wrack my body until, mercifully, exhaustion overtakes me and eventually drags me under.

At some point in the night, I wake up and can feel his

warm body so close to mine. I want to reach out and touch him, but I don't. I stare at the ceiling and think back to our first kiss as sleep reclaims me. We were already so desperately in love.

The next time I wake, the bed is empty. He's left me again.

CHAPTER

13

WHEN I ARRIVE at work Friday morning, an envelope with my name on it is under the door. Inside is an exquisitely detailed drawing of one of the cupcakes I'd left, signed by Josh Holland. I know he's saying thank you in his own beautiful way.

The following Thursday, I stay until six-thirty. I then box up the unsold cupcakes, including my favourite one with the fondant butterfly perched on top, and leave them in front of the gallery.

I don't trust the way Josh makes me feel, so I get there early to avoid running into him. He is a risk, and I never take risks with my body, my heart, or my soul. Those things belong to Mereki, and nothing will ever change that.

I do, however, want another of Josh's drawings, and sure enough, there is another envelope waiting for me under the door the next morning. This time it's of a delicate butterfly, exploding with colour.

Over the coming months, I leave a box of cupcakes at the gallery door most Thursday evenings. Whenever I do, I know there will be an envelope with my name on it under the cake shop door the next day. Inside will be a beautiful drawing. The drawings are of something different and seemingly random every time, but they tug at something deep inside me. I wonder whether they are somehow connected to each other or if each one was inspired by something he saw that day. It reminds me of when I discovered how much I loved creating art because I could tell a story even when I had no words. I place them carefully in between pages of a sketchpad I bought myself but haven't yet drawn in.

When I get home, I relocate them to a shoebox in my cupboard that sits next to the large glass jar I have for my new pebble collection. Both bring me a sense of purpose and a glimmer of hope. And both are taunting reminders of my past.

Despite not seeing Josh all winter, I feel an ever-growing connection to him through his drawings. On some level, a new friendship has started. Josh has no idea that his weekly drawings have become my lifeline, desperately trying to set me free from my depressing and lacklustre existence.

And I need setting free. Every day, Mereki spends less and less time with me, and the loneliness I've fought so hard against tethers me like a rope around my throat until I'm utterly consumed by it.

I've never needed wings like I need them now.

CHAPTER

14

THE JAR OF pebbles in my cupboard is now full. I must decide whether to find a new jar or put into action what I have been subconsciously planning for months now. Finding the pebble outside Sarah Holland's house after meeting Josh set the wheels in motion. It brought back some really fond memories for me, and I hope it holds the key to working through my flailing relationship with Ki.

The drawing I receive from Josh this morning spurs me on, and the idea that's gaining strength makes my heart beat a little faster. The drawing, by contrast to most I've received from him, is abstract. He has captured a sense of movement in the flowing lines. It makes me think of the river back home where Ki and I spent so much time together, and it feels like a sign.

As usual, Ki doesn't come home until after I've gone to sleep on Friday night and is already up when I wake. Knowing he'll be in the lounge room, I throw on jeans and a short-sleeved, pale yellow shirt—something I haven't worn in a long time. Yellow is a happy colour, and I'm embracing the new season.

"There's someplace I'd like to take you," I say when I enter the lounge and find him sitting on the couch, staring straight ahead at the blank TV screen. His eyes drift from the TV to me, eyebrows quizzically arching, but he drags his butt off the couch, and we leave the apartment together. He has never been able to say no to me, even when he's angry, and I try not to take advantage of it too often.

Ki just stares out the window, so we drive in silence. I spend the time thinking about those early days of our friendship by the river. Back then, the world seemed so full of hope and opportunity. Those were the happiest days of my life.

Perhaps if I'd talked more freely about those days instead of shutting down when our world fell apart, things could be different now. I was meant to be pursuing my dreams when I came to the city, not letting them die.

I'm not sure exactly where I'm going, but I know a river runs through a suburb not far from where we live. Given that we both grew up spending so much time by the water, it's sad how we've avoided it.

I park on a quiet street at the end of a cul-de-sac. Clutching the pebble jar to my chest, I get out and wait for Ki to join me. He glances at the jar and frowns.

"Trust me," I say, setting off towards the pathway. "This is going to be perfect."

Unable to restrain my excitement, I break into a jog, leaving Ki behind. Just as I hoped, the path leads to a beautiful park along the riverbank, and I almost cry with joy remembering the day I found our place all those years ago.

I wait for Ki to catch up, and we make our way to a more secluded section of the park further along the river. It doesn't take long before I'm presented with the perfect place. I climb over a large log with ease, even holding the pebble jar. We've had quite a bit of rain lately, so the river is high and the current is fast. Memories continue to flood my mind as I make my way towards the water and wait for Ki to catch up. I drop to my knees and upend the jar, scattering pebbles onto the ground. When the pebble that started this collection catches my eye, I stoop and pick it up, reverently smoothing my thumb across its cold, marble-like surface. *This is a fantastic idea.*

Wondering what's taking Mereki so long, I stand and jog back the way I'd come.

Then I see him—standing stock still on the other side of the log. His hands are in his pockets, and his shoulders are slumped.

"What's wrong?" I ask, more pissed off than anything. "We can start fresh, Ki. Our story isn't over." My voice is shaky. "It can't be over. We can start a new story."

He shakes his head, and suppressed rage rumbles in my gut. I've been holding on to so much pain and anguish for far too long.

"Why won't you do this for me?" It comes out as a growl, and I'm surprised by the sound of my own voice. "You told me if I ever feel lost and lonely again, I should remember that I'm made of the strong stuff." I hold up the smooth pebble. "And I have a road map back to the light." I throw my hands up in the air. "I'm trying to make another goddamned road map, you bastard, and I never thought I'd need to because you're still with me, and you've always been my light."

His deafening silence is beyond irritating. Without thinking, I throw the pebble right in his face. He deftly swerves his head, and my perfect pebble disappears behind him without making contact. I don't know why he's being so stubborn. He must know that I need this.

When he turns and walks away, I'm left to deal with my own messed-up emotions.

"I hate you, Mereki," I scream out the lie, and he continues to walk as if I hadn't spoken.

Scrambling over the log, I drop to my hands and knees, desperately clawing through the dirt and grass looking for the stupid, perfect pebble. When my fingers make contact with it, another wave of fresh tears erupts. I bury my face in my hands and sit back on my heels.

I am all alone on a deserted riverbank in some stupid suburb, sobbing like a baby. I may be clutching a pebble, but I've hit rock bottom.

Is this not enough for him? Am I not enough?

Eventually, I drag myself to my feet, broken and desperately disappointed that the excited feeling I arrived with is shattered. As I walk back to the car, carrying my empty pebble jar, I try to work out whether or not I want to scream at him again and relieve more of my pent-up rage. The stricken look on his face makes my decision for me.

"I'm so sorry," I say when I take my place in the driver's seat. "I don't know what came over me." I pause, reliving the horrible, cruel words I said to the love of my life. "You know I didn't mean it. You know I love you more than anyone has ever loved another person. Right?"

The air in the car is thick with hurt, unsaid truths, and almost an entire lifetime of desperate love. No combination of words is enough, so we sit in silence, brooding in misery and confusion.

Eventually, I pull myself together, and we drive back to our apartment building in silence. As soon as I pull into the designated spot, Ki disappears out the door.

I rest my head on the steering wheel. *What is happening to us?*

Running from this is pointless, but so is standing still hoping something is going to change. I can't keep torturing myself, wondering why Mereki is breaking his promise to stay no matter what. I can't go inside yet. I'll either say more things I'll regret or suffer further from his crushing silence, so instead, I drive around until I feel ready to go home.

CHAPTER

15

IT'S THE CRACK of dawn on Sunday morning, and Mereki is leaving for a two-month work project in Sydney. He's going to miss my twenty-third birthday, and I can't bring myself to raise the subject of our five-year pact to return to the river.

"Wait," I say, halting his approach to the front door. "I need to say something."

He turns to face me with a stony expression.

"This can't go on," I say, directing my gaze at the floor rather than him. This is hard, but I have to get the words out before he leaves. I owe this to myself at the very least. "I love you, and I know you still love me, but I can't keep hoping things are going to get better because they're not." Glancing up, I think his eyes have softened slightly, but his tight jaw and clenched teeth speak volumes. "We need this break." I can barely stand to say those traitorous words, but the truth often hurts far more than the lies we tell ourselves.

Striding purposefully past him, I open the door and lean against it. "Things will either be better when you return, or we're done."

As he passes me, he nods and holds up his hand in a small wave. I want to curl into a ball on the floor. He wasn't supposed to agree to that. How could he agree to the possibility of us being over?

Defiantly shaking my head, I slam the door shut, then whisper, "I'll never say goodbye to you."

Yesterday was the wake-up call I needed. Pushing some pebbles into the ground wasn't going to magically solve anything between Mereki and me, but it reminded me of the passion I once felt burning inside. I miss that feeling so much. How could I have expected him to stick around with a drifting shell of a person? I know he loves me, but he didn't sign up for this.

Instead of moping around the apartment, I drive myself to some markets south of the city. A flyer had been pushed under the door at work one day last week, and it had caught my eye. I find a park easily and kick myself for not having come here before. It's a lively cacophony of sights, sounds, and smells.

My mouth waters when irresistible wafts of freshly-baked bread hit my nostrils. As if I have no control over my legs, I'm walking towards the stall responsible for my body's reaction. The large selection of loaves, rolls, and pastries make my mouth water. Classic French baguettes stand tall in a row of baskets along the front of the stall, and a rotund man with a big smile, rosy cheeks and a black beret perched on his head holds his arms out wide.

"Bonjour, mademoiselle. Ca va?"

"Bonjour," I reply, my cheeks heating. I was always hopeless with languages and desperately wish I could reply with more than just a meek hello.

"Emerson?"

I look up and find Josh standing next to me holding a big bunch of flowers. "Oh. Hey, Josh." I shift on my feet. It feels strange seeing him in person after months of communicating via cupcakes and art.

"How are you?" he asks, swapping the enormous bouquet from one arm to the other.

"I'm good. Fine. I was just going to buy some bread."

"I see that." He glances at the stall, then back to me. "It smells amazing."

Unsure whether this is the end of our conversation, I turn my attention to the friendly vendor. "I'd like a light rye sourdough loaf, please."

"Great choice," Josh says. "I'll take one of those, too, please."

We both thank the vendor after paying and take our loaves wrapped in paper a few steps away from the stall.

"Are you here alone?" Josh asks, looking around me.

I nod, trying and most likely failing, to hide my sadness.

"I know the last time I asked, you shot me down, but I'm willing to risk one more rejection. Can I buy you a coffee?" Without waiting for my response, he continues, gesturing with a wave of his arm towards the other end of the market. "There's a new stall selling beans. I'm pretty sure they're making takeaway coffees, too. I was just on my way there when I saw you." His easy-going personality makes me feel so comfortable.

"I would love a coffee," I reply, not allowing myself to second-guess my decision. "You like markets?" I ask as we jostle our way through the crowds, passing a variety of stalls.

"Some," he replies. "What about you?"

"I love these markets so far."

Once Josh has ordered our coffees, he turns back to me, and it's the first time I've seen a glimmer of nervousness mar his features and I find it charming. "So. How have you been?" he asks.

"I'm okay, thanks." I swish my yellow sundress and smile in a way I fear is flirtatious. "I'm enjoying this warmer weather."

His eyes appear to drink me in, and my whole body reacts. It feels as if I'm being awakened from a long sleep and I want him to touch me. It's a shocking thought, and I know the smile disappears from my face. *What is wrong with me?* This man is playing havoc with my body, and I instinctively take a step back.

If he notices, he doesn't say anything. "Shall we walk and talk?" he asks, and I quickly agree. It is far less confronting having a conversation on the move than face-to-face, where the only thing I'll be looking at is him.

"I love your drawings, Josh," I say after a beat.

"I love your cupcakes," he says, winking at me.

"Will you tell me more about your classes? What does art therapy actually mean?"

"It can mean whatever you want it to mean."

I study his features to try to work out if he's being serious or not. That makes no sense at all.

"Some of my students know why they're there and what they need, and others discover along the way." He smiles warmly. "I like to think I'm helping them help themselves."

I school my features because what he says impacts me, and I don't want him to know how much. "That sounds really fascinating."

"I have a new group starting on Wednesday if you'd like to stop by and check it out. If you hate it, you don't have to come back on Thursday."

I take a sip of my coffee to avoid answering straight away. "Is it the same class both nights?"

He shakes his head. "Each class follows on from the next, and I encourage my students to attend both sessions each week. I find we can achieve more if there isn't a whole week in between."

"What's involved in art therapy exactly?" I ask, genuinely interested.

"Why don't you let me show you on Wednesday evening," he says with a wry smile.

I meet his gaze but not his humour. I'm still torn. "It's a definite maybe."

For the next hour, we stroll around the remaining stalls, picking up the occasional thing we fancy. I can't help buying half the chocolate stall, and he purchases a large selection of nuts. I smile more than I have in quite a long time and don't want it to end. Inevitably, we run out of stalls, and I know we will be parting ways soon when we find ourselves back at the bread stand.

"Well thanks for keeping me company, Josh," I say, as lightheartedly as I can.

He steps forward and kisses me on the cheek, then whispers in my ear, "The pleasure was all mine. Come to my class on Wednesday."

My breath hitches, and a small gasp escapes my lips. My whole body is on fire, and I raise my hand to where he kissed me in a bid to cool down the flush that is no doubt flaming across my cheeks.

Gracelessly, I stumble back a few steps and mutter a

stuttered goodbye.

When I'm far enough away to be able to breathe again, I can't resist a glance over my shoulder. Josh is still standing there holding the enormous bouquet of flowers, watching me leave.

CHAPTER

16

ON WEDNESDAY EVENING, with a box of leftover cupcakes and a belly full of nerves, I show up a little late for Josh's class. Glancing around the room, I count five students of varying ages sitting on stools in a circle. Each one has their own easel and a table covered with art supplies and a small stack of magazines. It's a far more informal setup than I was expecting, and the atmosphere is welcoming and airy.

"Good evening, Emerson." Josh's deep voice draws my gaze to the front of the room, and I'm completely disarmed by his warm smile. As he closes the distance between us, my heart beats faster. "Welcome," he says when he's only a few feet away. "I was hoping to see you here tonight."

I hand him the cupcakes. "I didn't want to show up empty-handed."

"Thank you." He takes the box, and I try not to flinch when his fingers brush over mine. "We were just about to start."

Choosing one of the available places, I drop my bag under the table and take a seat. An older man with greying hair sits to my left, and a girl about my age with jet black hair sits to my right.

Josh claps his hands. "Okay. Let's get started with some introductions." He pushes off the table he was leaning against and takes a step forward. "I'll go first." He opens his arms wide. "I'm Josh Holland, and I'm so happy to welcome you to my class. I hope it will be, at the very least, an enjoyable life experience." All the other students are nodding, gazing at him as if he's some kind of god.

"Let's see. What can I tell you about myself?" He glances at the ceiling briefly. "I'm thirty-one. I love windsurfing and my dog, Leroy, a chocolate Labrador."

I swoon at the mention of his dog. I've always wanted my own dog.

"I graduated from the National Art School eight years ago, then followed that up with a teaching degree," he says. "I'm a working artist and run a variety of workshops. Art therapy is my specialty, and I'm very passionate about it." He clasps his hands together. "That's a little about me." With his eyebrows raised, he glances around the room. "I'd love it if you'd introduce yourselves and, if you're comfortable, let us know what you hope to get out of this class."

The lady closest to Josh pipes up. "I'm Zoey Smith," she says. "I'm forty-four years young, and I'm doing something for myself for the first time since I got married in my early twenties and started popping out kids." She looks tired but has a fierce edge to her voice. "I have no idea who I am anymore, and I'm hoping this class might help me with that."

"Thanks, Zoey," Josh says, warmly.

"Eric Daniels," an older man says. "I'm fifty-five years old, and I'm a paediatric surgeon." He wrings his hands on his lap.

"So you need an outlet from the stress?" Josh guesses.

He shakes his head. "My wife passed away recently."

"I'm so sorry," Josh says.

"Art was her passion, and I only realized that after she died." His eyes glaze, and my chest aches. "I'm not exactly sure what I'm doing here, but I guess I'm trying to pay tribute to her? Does that make sense?"

"Absolutely. I'm glad you're here."

I know it's my turn, so I take a deep breath and meet Josh's gaze. "I'm Emerson. I'm twenty-two." I sigh, unsure how comfortable I am divulging anything about my life. "When I was a kid, I wanted to be a famous artist, but somewhere along the way, I lost that desire." I know exactly when it happened, but I'm definitely not sharing that.

"You're here to find that desire again?" Josh asks, a sparkle evident in his eyes.

I sit up a little straighter. "I am."

Josh doesn't react verbally to my words. He maintains eye contact and, for a moment, I feel completely vulnerable. It's an unpleasant sensation, and I rip my gaze away to look to the girl next to me, hoping she'll take over.

Perhaps sensing my discomfort, she smiles at me, then faces the class. "I'm Brooke, and I'm twenty-three. Oh God, I'm getting old." A few of us chuckle while the older students roll their eyes and groan. "I'm an actress." She announces, then pushes herself off her stool to take a bow. "You probably recognise me from my role in the TV show, *Cousins*."

I've never actually seen the show, but a few of the others appear relieved. The familiarity must've been bugging them.

"So why did you enrol in my class, Brooke?" Josh asks.

"I'm auditioning for a role as the muse for a depressed

artist, so this is research."

"Well that's a first," Josh says, chuckling. "Welcome, Brooke." He nods to the next student. She's an attractive older woman.

"I'm Kaye Wager," she says. Her frameless glasses slip down her nose, and she props them up before continuing. "I was an interior designer for forty years but have been thinking about a new career."

"Go on," Josh says.

"I'd like to run art workshops in aged-care facilities."

"I think that's a wonderful idea," Zoey says. "My mother was recently moved into a retirement home, and it can be so depressing."

"Exactly," Kaye says, enthusiastically. "I want to bring some colour and creativity to their lives."

"That's fantastic. Thanks, Kaye," Josh says.

The man on the other side of Brooke pipes up. "I'm Tenn, short for Tennyson. Thirty-year-old divorcee." The way he says 'divorcee' through clenched teeth makes me think it's recent and raw. "I'm a computer programmer—a career my ex-wife found unacceptable and dreary." His shoulders drop as he takes a deep breath. "I guess I'm looking to expand my horizons and maybe become less dreary. No offense, Josh, but I'm literally doing every course I can find."

Josh laughs. "No offense taken. Thanks for sharing with us, Tenn. I don't think you seem dreary at all."

Tenn shrugs. "Thanks, man."

"Okay," Josh says, pushing his hair behind his ears. "Creative expression is a known healer. By expressing yourself through the medium of art, you may well find many areas of your life benefit. You all have your own reasons for being here, and perhaps there'll be reasons you're not yet aware of. That's what is so exciting about this class."

Part of me wants to get up and run. As excited as I am by the thought of doing art again, I don't need this therapy mumbo-jumbo messing with my mind.

"We'll start off with a simple exercise." Josh moves to his table and shuffles some paper. "It's just an ice breaker, but it's also fundamental to what we're doing here," he says, looking straight at me.

I want to glance around the room, but I can't stop staring at Josh. His green eyes burn brightly with passion. I know that look; it's the look of someone who loves what they do with their entire soul.

"Love and hate." Josh passes two blank pieces of white paper to each student. "You have two minutes to express these emotions using the black ink and brushes provided." He smiles as he hands me mine. "Use some of the time to think about the people or things that bring out these intense emotions in you. Try to channel that through the paintbrush, and let's see what you come up with." He moves around the room ensuring everyone's paper is correctly attached to the easel before returning to the front of the room. "Your time starts now."

I pick up my paintbrush and dip it in the small pot of black ink.

Love.

I know all about loving someone with all my heart, so this should be easy.

You can do this, Emerson.

The brush moves slowly across the page in soft waves. I dip the brush several more times to complete the circles that beg to be painted.

Hate.

I have experienced this emotion in spades, but I'm far more hesitant to paint it. Focusing on this emotion takes me to places I try my hardest to avoid.

Jagged lines rip across the page, and hate is done.

Josh asks us to bring our results to the front. We all place our completed pages in rows of love and hate on the large table, then take a step back.

"Who wants to tell me what's interesting about this exercise?" he asks.

Brooke speaks up. "They're all pretty much the same."

Josh nods, and I go back to staring at the six very similar expressions of the strong emotions. "Love can take so many forms, but it's typically expressed visually in very similar ways. Same with hate."

"How cool was that?" Brooke asks, as we return to our seats. "I was sure they were going to be different."

"Me too," I reply.

"The next exercise involves thinking about who you are as an individual," says Josh. "What makes you, you?" He sits on a round stool, resting his foot on the low rung. He's wearing a loose, grey T-shirt over ripped jeans, but the way he carries himself tells me he's athletic and fit. I can't help wondering what he does to stay in shape.

When our eyes meet, I'm irritated that he's smiling right at me. Does he think I was ogling him? Ugh.

"I'd like you to go through the magazines on your tables and tear out anything that appeals to you or causes any type of reaction. It doesn't matter what it is. There's no right or wrong."

I pick up the first magazine and start flicking through the pages.

Who am I? I repeat the question over and over in my mind.

My heart rate races when I reach the end of the first one and haven't ripped out a single page. Trying not to panic, I reach for another magazine. Why should I be worried that I can't relate to anything in a glossy magazine? Maybe it's a good thing.

No one else seems to be having this problem. Pages are being ripped with abandon, and each one feels like a stab into my flailing identity.

Josh crouches down and whispers in my ear, "It's okay, Emerson." He rests his hand on mine, perhaps aware that I'm close to bolting.

"I don't know who I am anymore," I whisper.

"I'm going to help you find out. Okay?"

I nod, managing to fight back the tears and take a few deep breaths. "Thank you."

I can't look at him as he stands, but the light squeeze he gives my shoulder lets me know he heard me. The physical contact sets my entire body ablaze, conjuring up both the strong emotions I painted earlier.

Something fundamental inside me has begun to shift. I love Mereki with all my heart, but my life is passing me by while he slips further and further away. He always wanted me to be strong and fight for my dreams, never settling for anything less than greatness. With that thought in mind, I find myself pushing the door of the gallery open the following evening with an open mind and a hopeful heart.

"Welcome back, everyone," Josh says in a voice that makes my heart race. "Tonight's class is all about self-expression. What you do here is so intensely personal, and it's a completely safe space. We are ever-changing creatures, and it's important to listen to your inner voice. There is no one who will be more honest with you if you allow yourself to listen."

I don't like the sound of this. My inner voice is not to be trifled with.

Josh continues, "If you had to describe yourself, could you do it? What words would you use?"

Zoey's hand shoots up. "Punching bag, janitor, taxi driver." She pauses briefly. "I've felt like a punching bag for my family in various ways for almost two decades, and I'm so tired. But I let that happen and I don't blame them."

"This exercise is going to be perfect for you, Zoey," Josh says, waving at the rest of us to gather around.

We all congregate behind Zoey. Josh sets up a blank canvas on her easel. He dips a paintbrush in the black ink and hands it to Zoey who glances around with a nervous expression. "Consider how you feel about what you just told me, and then mark the canvas to express it."

Zoe nods and stares at the blank canvas for a few moments before, out of nowhere, her hand darts out and smacks the paintbrush against it. She sits back, drops the brush in the ink pot, and looks up at Josh. I can't take my eyes off the dark ink blotch that's exploded over the light background. It is strangely beautiful.

"What did you leave on the canvas?" Josh asks.

"My frustration," Zoey replies.

"There's more to you than this." Again, he picks up the paintbrush and hands it to her. "Turn your frustration into something else entirely. Use colour, too, if you wish."

He turns to the rest of us. "If anyone else wants to try this, I think it's a very interesting exercise, but there's no pressure."

We all return to our stools, and I glance around at my fellow students who are eagerly reaching for their paintbrushes.

I feel Josh before I see him. His powerful presence both intimidates and excites me.

"What words would you use to describe yourself, Emerson?"

"I'd rather not use words," I say.

"Okay. That's good. Just mark the canvas with whatever you feel. Or leave it blank if you want to." He squeezes my shoulder and walks away.

Closing my eyes, I allow my mind to see beyond the limited vision of my eyes, and what I see is startling.

Without thinking too much about what it means, I pick up my brush and paint a heart split down the middle.

Brooke leans across to see what I've done. "You have a broken heart?"

I fix my gaze on the two mirrored shapes. "I do, but I know how to fix it."

"Go ahead and fix it then," Josh says, approaching my workspace.

He moves to the front of the room and turns on some classical music. I don't recognise it, but it is inspiring and non-intrusive.

My first marks are pale and hesitant. I am being a coward. I close my eyes and refocus on the canvas in my mind. When I open them, I make more confident strokes, revelling in the way the brush glides across the paper. Perhaps it's muscle memory mixed in with a healthy dose of nostalgia, but it comes so naturally, and I can't help wondering how I managed to turn my back on my passion for so long without completely fading away. At regular intervals, I close my eyes and float like a feather above it all like I did that day at the markets all those years ago.

By the time Josh announces our time is up, I'm staring at the very thing I've needed but haven't been able to find. I shake my head, swallowing the lump in my throat. My skin starts to crawl, and a sharp pain shoots through my hand. When I glance down, I'm shocked to see that I've broken the paintbrush I'm holding. Rather than draw further attention to myself, I close my hand around the splintered wood and compose myself as best I can. The walls are closing in on me, and I feel lightheaded.

"Everything okay?" Josh's voice startles me.

"Yep," I reply.

"Will you tell me about this?" he asks, gesturing towards my canvas.

"I need to learn to fly again," I whisper.

"You didn't paint a broken heart, did you, Emerson?" I stare into his emerald eyes and know he gets it. "You painted wings."

I nod slowly, gritting my teeth. "I forgot how to fly."

"Something tells me it's coming back to you."

The air between us crackles with electricity, and my breath hitches, unable to deal with what's happening.

A bell breaks us from our heated moment, and both our gazes snap to the opening door. I gasp when someone I haven't seen in a long time appears. I feel cold all over as memories from the day I met her flood me. My breathing is laboured, and I have to hold on to my stool when I start to sway.

Josh makes a beeline for her and they hug, warmly. I don't want to look at them for fear of recognition, but I can't help the quick glances. My past is catching up to me.

"Everyone," Josh says, after several minutes. "I'd like to introduce you to a very good friend of mine and the owner of this gallery, Madeleine Gibson. She's just returned from a two-month trip to Europe."

He then goes around the class, introducing us. I sit there frozen, but when he introduces me, I nod my head, allowing my long hair to shield my face.

"Thank you so much, Josh," she says, warmly. "Lovely to meet you all."

When she disappears behind a door at the back of the room, I exhale. With any luck, she won't come back out before I leave.

"That's all we have time for this evening," Josh says. "Please bring in an object of your choosing next week. It can be any three-dimensional object—probably best if it isn't anything too large."

"Will we be drawing it?" Tennyson asks.

Josh cocks his head to the side. "You'll just have to wait and find out."

CHAPTER

17

DURING MY LUNCHBREAK, I return to the gallery, filled with both trepidation and determination. No one is in the gallery when I arrive, but my presence is alerted by a bell. I need to speak to Madeleine, just not in front of Josh.

Within a few moments, Madeleine appears through the door at the back. I have no idea if she'll recognise me, so I stand my ground, studying one of the paintings on the wall as I wait for her to approach me.

"Can I help you?" she asks. "Are you looking for something or just browsing?"

I push my hair behind my ears and turn to face her. She smiles, but when her eyes widen and she rocks from toe to heel, I know she recognises me. "Emerson?"

I nod. "Long time no see," I say, feeling both happy and desperately sad.

"Oh my goodness. I can't believe it's really you. I thought you'd have shown up years ago."

"I'm sorry. I . . ." My determination has left me, and I'm

now stuttering words while I wade through my frazzled thoughts.

"Come to my office." She places her hand on my back and ushers me to the back of the gallery and through the door.

Her office is a chaotic mess of canvases, paint pots, half-finished sketches, and paperwork piled high on every surface. A large, glass desk takes centre stage, and the chair behind it is more like a throne.

"When did you arrive in Melbourne?" she asks once we're seated.

"Oh. Well." This is so awkward. "Five years ago."

"What?" Her eyes widen with the disbelief I was anticipating. "Why has it taken you so long to look me up?"

I chew my bottom lip until I'm about to draw blood. "I didn't exactly look you up," I reply honestly. "I'm still in shock that I've ended up taking an art class at all, let alone one in your gallery."

"You were the girl last night who didn't look at me when we were introduced."

I nod. "I was shocked to see you and panicked. I'm sorry. That was rude."

"Why on earth would you panic, sweetheart? I don't understand." She shifts forward in her seat, props her elbow on the armrest, and leans forward. "Why didn't you call me when you moved to the city? I could've helped you."

"Why do you think I needed help?" I ask, defensively.

She takes a deep breath and sighs. "You've lived here for five years, and you're taking an art therapy class. I could be jumping to conclusions, but something tells me you could've used a friendly face."

I don't know what to say to that. It's true that I haven't

thrived in the city, but she was a big part of my most painful memory, and I never planned on seeing her again.

"The girl you met five years ago is long gone. I'm not the naïve teenager with stars in her eyes, and I'd really appreciate you keeping our connection between us. I don't want Josh or anyone else in the class knowing about the silly dreams of my past life."

"Why are you doing Josh's class if you've turned your back on your passion and your incredible talent?"

"His class is just an itch I felt like scratching. I certainly didn't seek it out."

"I think Josh would love to know who you are. Actually, he—"

I cut her off. "Please, Madeleine. I know it seems strange to you, but I don't talk about my past with anyone, and I'd appreciate you respecting that."

She stands and moves over to a stained-oak sideboard. Picking up a jug of water, she pours two glasses. "If you're not pursuing your dreams, what do you do?" She raises an eyebrow, and I feel as if she's looking straight into my soul. It's disarming, and I squirm uncomfortably in my seat.

"I recently started working at Carrie's Cupcakes just up the street."

"Oh. How long have you been there?"

"Not long."

She looks pensive. "So you happened to take a job up the street from my gallery, but you've never been in here. I've been away for the past two months, otherwise I might've run into you sooner."

I shake my head.

"I feel like maybe you wanted this to happen, Emerson."

"What do you mean? I lost your card. I had no idea it was your gallery."

She holds up her hands defensively. "Look, I meant it when I said I would help you in any way I could. At the time, I meant with contacts and maybe some mentoring, but I think now you need someone to listen."

"Did you sell my drawing?" I ask. Ironically, I hope she was never able to find a buyer.

"I bought it as a gift for a friend." Her eyes softened. "I did consider keeping it, figuring it was a good investment. I believed you'd be a famous artist one day and that I'd have one of your originals."

"You gave it away?"

She nods. "I gave it to Josh."

"Josh the art teacher?" I ask, shocked.

"The one and only," she replies. "That's who I bought it for. I mentored him through his studies, and I believe we have a special bond. When his father passed away, God rest his soul, Josh practically lived in my gallery, and I ended up giving him a job. When I came back from the trip where I'd met you, it was his job to unpack the artwork I had accumulated on my travels."

I take a long sip of water, trying hard to process what she's saying.

"When he came across your drawing, he stopped and stared at it for so long. Then, for the first time since his father died, he smiled, and I knew it had made the impact I hoped it would."

I suck in a deep breath.

"I'll never forget his words." She fixes me with her gaze. "He said it made him feel hopeful."

"I can't believe it. I honestly just can't believe it."

"What happened to you, Emerson?" Her eyes are soft, and her words are whispered. "You were so full of life and passion when I met you five years ago. I've thought of you so many times over the years and wondered if you'd ever call."

I pause, unable to tell her because I don't tell anyone. "Life happened." I stand and give her a strained smile. "Please don't tell Josh about me or the drawing."

"I'll respect your wishes, but Josh is a good man—a phenomenal artist and tutor. Open your mind and your heart again. You never know what might happen in the big city."

I reach for my bag. "It was good to see you again, Madeleine."

"Emerson?" She calls out as I'm about to open the door, and I turn back to face her. "Whatever happened to the boy you were with then? What was his name? Malaki? I guess he isn't a boy any longer, but I remember the way he looked at you like you were the centre of his universe."

"Mereki," I correct her, swallowing the enormous lump in my throat. I place my hand over my heart. "He's here with me." I walk out the door and allow the tears to stream down my face as I move through the gallery. I step onto the street swiping at my face, taking some deep breaths as I stare up at the night sky. Mereki had told me I'd drawn a guide to my own happiness, but I never thought I'd need it again with him by my side. Now another man possesses my roadmap, and he has no clue what it means to me. That drawing was created with love and sold with hope, but my life was ruined because of it.

Crossing the road, I glance up and see two magpies attacking each other. The screeching is like fingernails running down a blackboard, and I cup my ears in an attempt to block it out. With the sound muffled, I can't help but watch their violent behaviour. It's a welcome escape from my own torment. *Since when did I will others to suffer for my own selfish escapism?*

In the next shocking moment, one of the black and white birds crashes to the concrete right in front of me, battered and bloody. The victor's screeches fade away into the distance while the victim stares directly at me before giving up its fight for life. Revolted, I retch and only just manage to make it to the slip of grass a few feet away before gracelessly emptying the contents of my stomach.

CHAPTER

18

SINCE THE LAST class, I've made a point not to think about Josh, Madeleine, or my past.

When Wednesday rolls around and I make the decision to go back to class, Josh appears to be genuinely happy to see me. I hand him my enrolment form and payment details to confirm my commitment to his class, then take my seat next to Brooke. Just after seven, when everyone is seated, he walks to the front of the class and leans against the long table, crossing his legs at his ankles.

"For those of you who don't know, as part of this course, I offer an optional full-day class at my place down on the Mornington Peninsula, and it's this coming Saturday." He glances around the room at the six of us in attendance this evening. "I know it's a long weekend, so you might have other plans, but will any of you be making the trip?"

"I'm in," Zoey says, raising her hand.

Everyone else confirms their attendance, leaving me to stare at my fingernails.

"Do you have plans this Saturday?" Josh asks, directing his eyes on me.

"I'll have to check my calendar," I say, refusing to commit.

His smile dips, but he recovers quickly. "Okay. Did everyone remember to bring in an object?"

"Oh, man," Eric throws his hands in the air. "I forgot."

"It's no problem." Josh reassures him. He retrieves a box from the open shelves and holds it out for Eric. "Choose anything from here."

Eric studies the contents, then pulls out a piece of rope, knotted in two places. "Thanks."

Josh places the box on the front table before addressing us. "First exercise for this evening is drawing from memory." He picks up a calico bag. "You each have one of these, and I'd like you to place your item inside." I place my object, a piece of driftwood, into the bag and pull the drawstring tight. "Right. Now, using any of the supplies available, draw, paint, sketch or sculpt your object."

"What's the point of this, Josh?" Brooke asks.

"Honestly? There is no point other than switching your mind off. You might find it relaxing."

I reach for the pencils and start sketching my object from memory. Last Sunday morning, I'd returned to the river on my own and picked up a piece of driftwood, struck by its tortured form. There was a kind of beauty in its jagged lines and gaping holes.

With confidence I haven't felt in far too long, I put pencil to paper. Closing my eyes, I remember one of the times in my life when darkness was no match for the shining light of Mereki and me together in our place by the river. My mind takes me back to when I was maybe fourteen or fifteen and in a horribly dark mood. As usual, my mother was taking out all her frustration and humiliation on me.

"You wait and see, Emerson, you silly girl," she said, then took a long drag on her cigarette. Her gaunt cheeks hollowed into deep canyons as she inhaled the smoke.

Fixated on the ash teetering on the end of her cigarette, I wondered when it was going to drop to the threadbare carpet. I also imagined the path of the smoke as it entered her lungs and stole an unknown fraction of her life expectancy. Did I care? When the ash dropped, it refocused my attention on her words, and I was unable to miss the end of today's lecture.

"You're wasting your time with your silly drawings and ridiculous dreams of getting out of this shithole," she said, sneering.

Grabbing my bag, I bolted out the door and headed into town. I knew of only one place I wanted to be and one person I wanted to be with.

Mereki was sitting on a swing chair on his family's front verandah, scribbling in his notebook.

"What are you writing?" I asked, standing at the bottom of the steps.

His eyes snapped to mine, and a broad smile lit up his handsome face. "Emerson." He said my name reverently, making my heart flutter around in my chest. This boy cared about me, and I believed he always would. "What are you doing here? I thought you had to study."

Shaking my head, I started walking backwards. "Come to the river with me?"

My best friend in the whole world jumped up and trotted down the steps to me. "Like you have to ask."

When we arrived at our special place, we sat side by side on the riverbank. A few birds squawked angrily in the overhanging trees, but it was otherwise completely serene.

Mereki nudged me. "Have I ever told you the story about Aberforth, the boy who turned into a fish to save his town?"

Shaking my head, I let it fall on his shoulder. "Tell me everything there is to know." Closing my eyes, I felt a deep sense of peace and gratitude for this boy who seemed to know exactly what I needed.

"He was cursed by the river god, Riopelle."

"How do you come up with this stuff?" I ask, unable to resist interrupting his story.

"I don't come up with it," he replied. "I simply listen to the river and it tells me stories. I write them down in my notebook to remember all the details."

"That is totally crazy, but I kinda love it." I linked my arm through his. "Tell me the rest of the story please."

Before long, I feel the movement of the river. Its power pulses through me, guiding my hand until it completely consumes me. The driftwood bobs and dips in my current, grazing my submerged rocks. I watch its progress as both a spectator and participant, never wanting it to stop. The water feels cold and unforgiving. It apologises to no one for its relentless force. The driftwood is just out of my reach, but I'm not scared. I don't need it. I'm not treading water. I *am* the water.

"Wow, Emerson." Brooke's voice sounds right beside me. I jump. "That is phenomenal," she continues. "Where did you learn to draw like that?"

My body tingles with awareness that Josh is near, and when I look at him, he is standing so close, completely fixated on my drawing. Realising I haven't followed Josh's instructions, I make the snap decision to rip off the page, scrunch it into a ball and drop it to the floor.

"What did you do that for?" Brooke cries. "It was so beautiful."

I shrug, but my hands shake. Josh leans down and

retrieves my discarded drawing.

"Okay. Next exercise," he says in a loud voice to the entire class. "Take your object out of your bag and hold it in your non-dominant hand." I sit there frozen, unwilling to participate. "This is going to sound a bit strange, but I want you to pretend you're an ant exploring your object. In any way you see fit, show your journey over your object on paper. Perhaps it will be one long line or maybe a series of small markings. It really doesn't matter, but you'll have your eyes closed and one hand on your object while you work."

When everyone closes their eyes and starts their journeys, Josh waves me over as he heads for the door. I stand up quietly and follow him outside.

"Talk to me," he says, gesturing to the ball of paper in his hand.

I chew on my bottom lip, staring straight ahead. "I didn't mean to draw that," I whisper. "I'm sorry."

"There was a lot of pain in that drawing, but what also came through was strength and resolve," he says, softly. His voice is full of encouragement and warmth. "You're able to express a wide range of emotions through your drawings, Emerson. I see talent in your work that I've rarely seen before. One minute you're drawing detailed feathers for your wings showing light and hope, and the next, the light goes out and a darkness creeps in."

"I think you're overthinking this," I say, deflecting.

"Do you ever feel like you're drowning?" he asks.

I shake my head, unsure if I'm lying or not. "I was thinking about a sad story a friend told me a long time ago. That's all."

He places his hand on the small of my back and holds the door open for me. "You're a beautiful artist, Emerson."

"Thank you," I whisper, smiling as I turn back. "That means a lot."

"That's all we have time for this evening," Josh says. "Thanks for coming." His gaze zeroes in on me. "And, for those of you coming on Saturday, I'll see you at the Cat and Mouse Café next to the Tourist Information Centre." I drop my eyes to the flyer he left on each of our tables with the address. "It's not far from my place, and we'll convoy from there around nine-thirty."

I take my time packing up my things and am the last to leave.

"Come on Saturday," Josh says, opening the door for me. "I think it'll do you good."

I nod. "It's a definite maybe."

CHAPTER
19

TEARS STREAM DOWN my face. I know I should be getting in the car now, but I can't bring myself to leave the house. I'm safe here, and I don't have to pretend to be okay. Out there, I'm completely vulnerable, especially with Josh.

I want to call Mereki. I want to tell him to come back to me. I want him to hold me in his arms and tell me that the last five years have just been a rough patch to end all rough patches and that we are going to be okay. Is that too much to ask?

I pick up my phone and drop it again like it's on fire. I can't call him. He won't answer. The bastard won't pick up the fucking phone. Anger rises in my belly, and I scoop up the phone again, tossing it across the room. To my irritation, it doesn't make contact with anything hard and just slides across the carpet and bumps limply into the couch.

Returning to the bedroom, I catch sight of myself in the full-length mirrored doors of the built-in wardrobe and sigh. I am a mess. Puffy, red eyes, a blotchy face, slumped shoulders. I am dishevelled in my melancholy. Perhaps I can call Josh and tell him I can't make it today. Then what? I mope around the house all weekend, missing Mereki? I'm so pathetic. It's all I ever seem to do. It's a good thing he keeps going away for short work stints, I tell myself.

"I can't do this," I say out loud to my reflection in the mirror. I hate the sound of those defeatist words, and I hate the person I see staring back at me. I barely recognise her anymore from the strong, resilient survivor I was as a child. I'm now just a breathing shell of a person shuffling my way through a miserable existence. "Something has to change." I narrow my eyes. "You." I point at myself in the mirror. "Need to sort out your shit, and you need to sort it out quickly."

I'm dancing on dangerous territory here, and I have no idea how I feel about it. One thing I do know is that nothing changes if you keep doing the same thing over and over expecting a different result. That's the definition of insanity, and I know I'm walking a fine line.

With that pep talk spurring me on, I pick up my bag, leaving my home and my comfort zone in my wake.

It takes me an hour and fifteen minutes to arrive at the Cat and Mouse. Despite leaving later than I planned, the traffic was light, and I arrive just after nine. I might even be the first of the group to arrive, so I take the opportunity to get a coffee and use the facilities. Holding my takeaway coffee cup, I wander out onto the back deck.

"It's beautiful here, isn't it?" Josh asks.

I hadn't even realised he had joined me; I was so entranced by the forest surrounding me. I meet his gaze and smile, nodding, before taking another sip of coffee. "How long have you lived here?"

"Ten years give or take," he replies. "The land has been in our family forever, and my father would bring us here for camping weekends when we were kids."

"And you like it here more than the city."

He nods, then sips his coffee and says nothing further. I peek up at him over my coffee cup and stare at his profile. He appears lost in thought, and it gives me a moment to appreciate his strong jawline. There is something incredibly calm about him. He appears so self-assured and at peace with his life. I could be making wild assumptions. I, of all people, know how to put on a happy face, but I can't shake the feeling that this man is content in his own skin.

He meets my gaze and holds it for a few seconds until I'm forced to look away. He peeled back a layer of my defences with just one intense look, and I feel exposed despite the multitude remaining. "We better head back out the front in case others have arrived," he says, a warm smile lighting his hypnotic eyes.

I nod, turning on my heel and heading back through the cafe, tossing my half-empty coffee in the trash, and out onto the gravel verge to where my car is parked.

Zoey, Brooke, Tennyson, Kaye, and Eric are all assembled out front standing by two cars. They must have shared, and I'm struck by how much of a loner I am. I would never have thought to arrange carpooling. I've become accustomed to doing everything on my own.

"Emerson," Brooke says, waving her whole arm excitedly. "You made it."

"I did." I smile. "I'm looking forward to it."

"Okay," Josh says, waving his arm over his head in a beckoning gesture. "I'm in the white Landcruiser, so just follow me. It's only ten or fifteen minutes away, but the entrance is not easily spotted."

Returning to our respective cars, I fall in behind Josh, and we follow him along a winding road weaving through a forest. We pass the occasional driveway but not many, and it's a far cry from the hustle and bustle of the city. After no more than fifteen minutes, Josh turns into a gravel driveway, and we follow. There is no gate, but we bump over a cattle grid to gain entry. He was right. There are no clear identifiers marking the property other than a small, black mailbox and, with no house visible from the road, it would be easy to miss the driveway altogether. It is so very private, and it feels like it's a privilege to be here. We weave through tall trees before ascending a small incline.

Josh's Landcruiser disappears over the crest ahead of me, and I hit the accelerator a little harder to keep up. When I reach the top, the view that greets me is awe-inspiring.

CHAPTER

20

I PARK MY car alongside Josh's and stare through the front windscreen. "Wow," I say to myself, my mouth agape.

Josh stands in front of his car, leaning against the bumper. I watch, riveted as his shoulders rise and fall with his deep breaths. He lives here, but I can tell he never takes this beauty for granted. A dog I presume must be Leroy—the one he mentioned when he introduced himself at the first class— bounds up the hill to Josh, and my heart melts when he squats down to pat his head with obvious affection.

I get out of the car and am immediately accosted by the big, brown dog, wagging his entire body, clearly thrilled by the company.

"Sorry," Josh says when I'm nearly bowled over by so much gorgeous exuberance. "Hey, Leroy." He picks up a stick and throws it down the hill. "Fetch." Leroy flies down the hill.

"It's absolutely fine," I say. "I love dogs."

Neither of us says another word as we stare at each other

for a beat before I break eye contact to glance at the surroundings. To our left, a wooden, cabin-style home has been built into the side of the hill, completely hidden from the road and with an uninterrupted view of the lush, green fields surrounding the water. Black cows drink at the water's edge. There are a few other buildings I can see, which I presume are barns or maybe machinery sheds. I may have been brought up in the country, but I've never spent any time on a farm. I haven't the first clue about farm animals or anything farm-related at all.

"This is amazing," Brooke exclaims, appearing in front of us, holding out her arms wide and spinning in a circle.

Zoey, Eric, Kaye, and Tennyson have similar reactions. No wonder Josh loves it here so much.

"Do you live out here all alone?" Brooke asks, and we all turn to face Josh. I hate that I want him to say yes.

He shakes his head, and my heart drops. "Leroy keeps me company." He reaches down and pats his dog, who has returned with the stick, proud as punch. The relief I feel at his answer is unsettling.

"Is this where all your inspiration comes from?" Kaye stares into the distance.

"Sometimes," he replies. "Sometimes not. But my hope is that all of you find some today. In my experience, a change of scenery and surrounding yourself with like-minded people certainly can't hurt creativity."

"Can't argue with that," Tennyson says.

"The day is ultimately yours, so find somewhere you're comfortable." He waves his hand towards the house. "All the supplies are on the back deck, but you're welcome to take them anywhere you like on the property."

We follow Josh towards the large deck that spans the

entire length of the house. Everyone else chooses supplies, then they return to the grassy hill. Josh and I are left alone and I'm glad. I shouldn't be, but I am. There are several easels set up, and I notice a stunning painting that appears to be half-finished. Glancing back, I can see the others have either found a spot on the hill or are still walking around enjoying the scenery.

"Looks like it's just you and me," Josh says, smiling.

"Looks like it," I reply, awkwardly.

"What made you decide to come today?" Josh asks as I take a seat in front of one of the other easels. "I was a little surprised to see you."

I shrug. "I had nothing else to do." It sounds lame and rude, but it's the truth.

Josh chuckles, clearly unoffended. "Well I'm glad. Perhaps this is going to be what you need to start creating again."

"Maybe."

"I obviously don't know you very well, but I just get the feeling you're looking for an exit strategy at all times."

Wow. I guess we're not going to talk about the weather then. I chew on the inside of my cheek, rattled by his brutal honesty.

"Hey." He takes my arm gently and stops me, pushing me gently to face him. "I don't mean to offend you. I'm just trying to work you out, I guess."

"There's nothing to work out." I pull back so his hand drops from my arm. "It takes me a while to warm up to people." I scoop my hair over one shoulder and twirl it around my fingers.

"When I met you last summer, you froze when Mum asked if you liked art. I'll never forget that look on your face, and now more than ever I want to know why it seemed to pain you when it's obviously something you love."

I look at him incredulously, unable to believe he's broaching such an intensely personal topic, ripping me open within five minutes of our conversation. I open and close my mouth a few times before managing to come up with something to shut this down. "Art is something I did when I was a kid. It's something I left behind for reasons I don't really want to get into with you or anyone. So, if we can just leave it at that, I'd appreciate it."

"Okay," Josh says, but sounds anything but content with my response. "But I'm not giving up on you, Emerson."

My body tenses. Mereki used to say the same thing to me.

Pulling a paintbrush from behind his ear, Josh waves it between us. "Remember what this is?"

"A paintbrush," I deadpan.

"It's a lifeline." He picks up my hand and closes my fingers around it. "Drawing, painting, creating art—it's your lifeline, and you need to embrace it."

I stare down at his large hand wrapped around mine, wrapped around the paintbrush. It's a powerful connection, and I can't decide if I should cry with joy or scream out in pain.

"Close your eyes," he urges.

"Excuse me?" I ask, taken aback.

"Just do it. Please."

Feeling defeated, I close my eyes, exhaling as I wait for further instructions. There is nothing but silence for at least a minute, maybe more.

"Tell me what you can smell."

Strange, but I'm willing to humour him. I inhale deeply

and smile. "Paint."

More silence, and then I'm aware of movement as I hear the creak of wood. I think he's sitting down on his stool. My ears prick to the sound of swishing water and the tap of wood on glass. *He's rinsing his paintbrush.*

The next few minutes are a symphony of melodic sounds.

"Brushstrokes," I whisper, and my heart rate slows. I saw what he was working on earlier, and now I'm imagining him adding to the rural landscape.

"What colour do you think I'm using?"

Without hesitating, I answer, "Green."

"Why?" he asks, his voice stern and demanding.

"The grasslands are crimson. You've only done the base layer and need to add the green."

"Open your eyes."

I open them, and he's holding up his brush coated in dark green paint. "Why are you pushing me on this?" I ask. "I'm attending your classes, and I turned up today. What more do you want from me?"

Josh drops his paintbrush back in the water jar, then runs his hands through his hair. "The short answer is I don't know." He stands and takes a step toward me. "I know it might seem crazy, but I feel like I've met you before, or maybe you remind me of someone." He pauses, obviously struggling to verbalise what he's thinking. "I want to help you but don't know how because you're hiding so much of yourself." He smiles. "It's very frustrating."

His intuition is both unsettling and comforting. He seems to genuinely care, and I realise I trust him. Perhaps it's because of all the drawings he left for me, or perhaps it's the way my body reacts to him that I trust him. But I can't see any benefit in telling him about what I went through five years ago.

I pick up one of the paintbrushes and dip it in the blue paint. Without meeting Josh's gaze, I say, "Maybe it's best if we just focus on the art for now."

For the rest of the day, Josh gives each of us equal attention just like he does in every class. With every passing minute and every quiet brushstroke, I feel more alive than I have in a long time. The colour of the lake darkens with the sky.

The storm clouds roll in, and I wrap my arms around myself, feeling the chill in the air as the temperature quickly drops.

"What a shame," Josh says. "Time to go, ladies and gents. I reckon it'll be pouring within the hour, so best you get back on the road as soon as possible. My bet is it'll be dry as a bone past the Cat and Mouse. I've seen it so many times— torrential here and nowhere else."

"This has been a wonderful day," Zoey says, picking up her canvas. "Thank you for having us out here, Josh."

"You're welcome, Zoey."

"Absolutely," Eric says, shaking his hand. "I'll be returning next month, for sure."

For some reason, I'm still standing by Josh's side while the two cars disappear down the driveway. To an outsider, I guess it would look like we're a couple saying goodbye to our guests. I feel way too comfortable with this man and realise that I need to get going, too.

"Thank you," I say quietly when Josh looks down at me. "I'm glad I came."

Josh smiles, but there's a sad tinge to it. It might be wishful thinking, but I wonder if he's disappointed that I'm leaving. If he could see my thoughts, he'd know that I'm disappointed, too. I love it here, but it's not the farm I'm sad to leave—it's him.

"I hope you don't think this is inappropriate or pushy, but you can stay here tonight if you want. I promise my intentions are almost entirely honourable." He glances back towards the house. "I have several spare rooms, and I'm worried about you driving alone in this weather."

We both look up at the sky. It has darkened considerably even in the short time since the others left.

"That's sweet of you, Josh, but I should get home, and I'm comfortable driving in the rain." I smile up at him. "I'm a country girl."

He sighs, nodding. "Take it easy then, okay?" He walks me to my car. "It'll be really slippery when it starts to rain. We haven't had any in a while."

"Will do." I rummage in my bag for my keys, then climb in. "Thanks again for today. I enjoyed the change of scenery. I think I needed it more than I thought."

"You're welcome any time," he says, tapping the roof of my car.

I glance back at the cabin and the lake beyond and hope I do have the opportunity to return. "That's very generous of you."

"It's just nice to see you smile."

It's been so long since I've felt so welcome and wanted. My friendship with Josh is bringing me back to life. As long as I don't cross any lines, I can't see the harm in it.

As I drive away, I glance in the rear-view mirror and see him watching me leave, and I can't help but smile.

Happiness soon fades when the heavens open, and a deluge of rain hits. As I bump across the cattle grid, I lose all vision through the windscreen. The sensible thing to do would be to turn back, but I don't.

I've only been driving for a few minutes when the car jolts, forcing me to slam on the brakes. I fight to keep it under control as I slip and slide across the road, eventually coming to a stop on the gravel shoulder—and that's when I discover that I have a flat tyre.

That's just freaking perfect. Dusk, deserted road, dark forest, torrential rain. Of course I have a flat tyre. That's Sod's Law, right?

"Shit-fuckity-fuck-fuck-shitty-shit-fuck-fuckity-shit!" Thumping the palms of my hands against the steering wheel, I cry out in frustration.

I want to get home, and this is the last thing I need. When I've calmed down somewhat, I weigh up my options. Stay in my car and wait for the rain to stop, and who knows when that will be, or suck it up and change the tyre in the rain. I take a few deep breaths, count myself down, then leap out.

"Ahhhh," I screech, soaking wet. Realising there's no point worrying about getting wet given I can't actually get any wetter, I look up. The road has been carved through the forest, so I'm looking through a gap in the trees to the darkening sky. It's actually quite breathtaking seeing thousands of droplets streaming down to smack me in the face. Leaning back on the car, I stretch my arms out beside me and close my eyes, allowing the rain to machine gun my body as I lean back into the hard metal and remember being caught in the rain with Ki.

"Too late," he said, smiling at me, both of us soaking wet.

Placing my hands above my head, I stared up at the dark clouds and smiled as the rain splashed down on my face.

"You're so beautiful," Ki said, raising his voice to be heard over the pouring rain.

I dropped my gaze to meet his, and my hands cupped his face. "So are you."

We stumbled away from the clearing to seek protection under one of the trees. The rain continued to pour down, but the only thing I was aware of was his soft lips on mine and his strong arms encircling my body, claiming me. I never wanted this moment to end.

CHAPTER

2 1

A LOUD CLAP of thunder snaps me back to the present. Pushing off the car, I open the boot to find the jack and spare. The spare is easy to locate, but the jack isn't anywhere obvious. Where the hell is it?

"Shit-fuckity-fuck-fuck-shitty-shit-fuck-fuckity-shit!"

I haven't had a flat tyre since buying this car second-hand a few years ago, so now I'm wondering if it ever had one. Determined to not let this situation get the better of me, I keep searching and eventually find it in a side compartment I hadn't even realised existed.

Mereki made me practice changing the tyre on his mum's car, so I know what to do, but there's a big difference between changing a tyre on a flat driveway on a sunny day and this. Thankfully, where I pulled over is almost flat, but it is getting muddier by the second, and it's also getting darker. I need to get this done as soon as possible.

After loosening the nuts with the crossbar, I drop to my knees beside the car and peer under, trying to locate the jack point. I've been told it's typically in the same position in all cars, so I know where to look and sure enough, I find it. Positioning the jack, I manage to raise the car enough to remove the tyre. Once I have the spare in place, I tighten the nuts, release the jack, then give the wheel brace one last turn. Standing up, completely covered in mud and drenched from head to toe, I place my hands on my hips and smile. I feel a sense of accomplishment and give myself a mental pat on the back. I am a strong, independent woman who can take care of herself.

Returning the flat tyre and jack to the boot, I saunter back to the driver's seat. If I'm honest, I'm feeling smug and almost wish someone was around to witness my awesome display of girl power. This lasts for about as long as it takes to turn the key in the ignition and hear the dreaded click of an engine that refuses to turn over.

"What now?" I screech, scanning the dash for any warning lights. My heart sinks when I see the fuel gauge below the empty line.

"Shit-fuckity-fuck-fuck-shitty-shit-fuck-fuckity-shit!" I say, thumping the steering wheel even harder this time.

Getting out of the car, I look up and down the street. I am no damsel in distress ordinarily, but I am at a dead end. Again, I only have two options. Walk for God knows how long back to the Cat and Mouse, which may or may not be open, hoping no axe murderer stops and chops me up. Or I can walk the short distance back to Josh's farm. Axe murderer or Josh.

Grabbing my bag, I jump out then lock the car. I don't know why I locked it when a prospective thief wouldn't get far unless they happened to be carrying petrol with them, but it's a force of habit. Without any further hesitation, I start the short trek. This is so humiliating.

"Emerson?" Josh rushes forward when he opens the door

and finds me standing on his front porch like a drowned rat.

A full-body shake has taken hold, and my hair clings to my face and shoulders. I'm sure what little makeup I was wearing is now a streaky mess down my cheeks. Even without looking in a mirror, I know I must look like a complete and utter disaster.

I shrug. "I changed my mind about staying."

He chuckles, ushering me inside, but I hold my hands up in protest.

"This is stating the obvious, but I'm soaking wet. I don't want to mess up your floors." I try to push the hair away from my face. "Maybe you could bring me a towel or something out here?"

"Emerson. Please come inside. You're gonna catch your death out here unless you get dried off, and I don't give a shit about the floors."

Relenting, I step inside, wrapping my arms around my body. Looking down, I can see a puddle already forming at my feet. "I got a flat tyre and ran out of fuel a little way down the road." I cringe at how pathetic I sound. "Perhaps you wouldn't mind taking me to the closest . . ."

"You can't drive back to the city soaking wet, and the rain is getting harder. I'm going to insist you stay the night, and we'll sort out your car in the morning."

I rub my face, frustrated with the whole situation and by the fact I'm actually happy with the turn of events. I want to be here, and I want to spend more time with Josh.

"This way," he says, walking ahead of me down a hallway off to the left of the entry. He continues right to the end, then opens a door and walks in. I follow him into what I find to be a gorgeous bedroom, but Josh has disappeared through another door I assume to be an en-suite. I rush towards it, not wanting to keep dripping on the carpet. Sure enough, he's pulling some fluffy, white towels down from a rack and placing them on the vanity. "This is the room my mum stays in, so there's some girly stuff in here you're welcome to use, and I was about to put a load of washing on, so just leave your wet clothes outside the door." I rub my hands up and down my goosebump-covered arms. "A warm shower will sort you out. I'll find some dry clothes for you to wear, then come to the kitchen. I make a mean hot chocolate."

"This is so nice of you, Josh. I'm really sorry for all the hassle. I can't believe I didn't fill up on the way, and I feel like a complete—"

Josh cuts me off by placing his fingertips gently on my lips. "Stop, Emerson. You might remember you staying is what I'd hoped for, so please don't apologise for me getting what I want."

I smile against his fingertips, and his eyes drop to where he's touching me. My eyes track his, and I'm momentarily entranced by our connection.

"You should get warmed up," Josh says and takes a step back. It should've been me who pushed him away, but I was enjoying his touch too much. This is bad. Really, really bad.

I nod and give him a small smile that slips away the second Josh turns and disappears through the door. I give myself a quick pep talk. I didn't choose this, and I didn't want to break down with no alternative but to return here. This was not my doing.

While the water heats up in the shower, I squelch awkwardly out of my soaking T-shirt, jeans, and underwear. It is such a relief to feel my body warm up, and I could stand here for hours if I wasn't conscious of being water smart in the country. I also don't want to give myself too much time to think about the fact that I am alone, miles from anywhere, with a man I find devastatingly attractive both in looks and personality. As I towel myself dry, I'm hit with the idea that maybe the universe is trying to push me towards Josh. But why? If it was just about the art, surely the universe would've had the decency to give me a woman tutor rather than someone I would be so physically drawn to.

Josh has laid out one of his white T-shirts and a pair of navy, drawstring track pants. Once I'm dressed, I bundle my wet clothes in the towel and head out to find him. The house is easy to navigate. The bedrooms run along the front facing the driveway whilst the whole back of the house is mostly open plan with the spectacular views across the lake.

"I considered floor-to-ceiling glass all the way along but decided against it for environmental reasons. I wanted it to be as environmentally friendly as possible, and it would be too costly to heat and cool with that much glass. The carbon footprint would be horrible."

"That's very responsible of you," I say, taking the cup of steaming hot chocolate from him and wandering over to the large picture window in the kitchen. "The view is still incredible."

"This house was my father's dream, but he never got to see it built. We'd come out here most weekends and stay in the boathouse, or we'd camp."

"Why didn't he build the house?"

He shakes his head, and sadness descends over his features. "My dad was more of a talker than a doer. We'd talk in detail about every aspect of the house, and I'd always push him to get an architect to draw up some plans. His response was always the same." He takes a sip from his mug before continuing. "One day."

"He put it off too long," I say in a whisper.

"Yep. I should've pushed harder or told Mum about his dream, but I never did."

"You weren't to know he was going to die, Josh. You can't carry around guilt for what you think you should've done when you were so young."

"I built this house for him and tried to make it as close to what he described as I could remember."

We walk around the island bench and into the lounge. French doors lead out onto the deck where we'd been painting earlier, but it's hard to see the view properly, as the glass is fogged up. The rain is still heavy but has eased since I arrived. It is dark outside, and I'm certainly glad I made the decision to walk back here rather than wait it out in my car. I could've been there all night if I'd waited for the rain to stop.

"Do you ever get lonely out here alone?" I ask. Josh looks at me, and I scrunch my whole face up, hoping it didn't sound like I was hinting at anything. Why am I so interested in his relationship status when it's absolutely none of my business?

"I'm not always alone, Emerson. No."

My cheeks heat at the implication he's brought women out here. The idea makes my stomach drop. "Oh. Of course. I don't know why I asked that."

Josh laughs. "Mum and my brothers come and stay on a fairly regular basis."

"Oh, right. So, you don't have a girlfriend?"

"The answer is no."

Oh, I mouth, failing miserably to hide my smile.

Taking another sip from his steaming mug, Josh places it down on the timber dining table and moves closer to me. "I told you already I'm drawn to you in a way I've never experienced before." He takes my mug from me and places it down next to his, then moves right into my personal space.

I can't breathe. "Josh. I . . ."

He places his hands on my cheeks, pushing the loose strands of my hair out of my wide eyes. "Shh, Emerson."

My mind goes completely blank when he says my name, and all I can do is stare at his mouth. It's obviously an unwritten invitation as that mouth is suddenly on mine.

I must be having an out-of-body experience. It can't possibly be my arms wrapping around his neck and pulling him closer while I open my mouth to his greedy tongue. It can't be me groaning as Josh's hands move from my face to the back of my head then down my back before hugging me so close, I can feel him hard against me. This just can't possibly be me—the girl who hasn't been kissed by anyone other than her first and only love. The problem is this feels way too natural and way too good to be wrong. Josh is making me feel as if I'm the most precious thing in the world. I know, because it's the way Ki used to make me feel every day. Now I don't exist.

Is it wrong to want to feel like I matter?

Is it wrong to want to feel important to someone?

Is it wrong to want to feel again?

Maybe it is, but I don't think I can stop. I've crossed the line, and I take full responsibility. Josh has no idea about my circumstances, and I want to keep it that way for this weekend at least. I need to escape and to feel alive again, but can I live with the consequences?

I think Josh senses the chaos decimating my brain cells because he pulls back and holds my face reverently in his hands, again looking me in the eyes. "Is this too fast?" he asks. "I promised myself I wouldn't push, and we can stop right now if this isn't what you want. I don't want you regretting anything you do with me."

I squeeze my eyes shut briefly before meeting his concerned gaze again. "I have no regrets with you, Josh, but thank you for stopping when you did."

"The ball's in your court here, Emerson." His eyes are soft and clear. As far as I can tell, this man has no secrets, no baggage, and his heart is completely open to what is so obviously happening between us. I might just be the worst thing that ever happened to him.

I nod, loving the feel of his large hands on me. I can feel the callouses and wonder whether it's from working outdoors or from pencils and paintbrushes. My brain imagines how it would feel to have them roaming my naked body, perhaps when I'm leaning back against my car in the rain. Oh my God. I need my brain to shut it down before I rip our clothes off and have my wicked way. Who am I, and why am I still having an out-of-body experience?

"The rain's stopped," Josh announces, dropping his hands and walking back to the kitchen with our mugs, snapping me out of my sexy thoughts. "That was quite a storm, huh?"

I follow him, feeling the natural tug I am starting to associate with being in Josh's vicinity.

"You hungry?" he asks, peering into the oven. "I made a tuna bake, and there's plenty. I'm sure I can rustle up a salad to go with it."

I raise two fingers to my lips and press gently on them. I am still reeling from the life-altering kiss minutes ago and now feel a little awkward being domestic with him. "If you have enough, that would be great. Thank you."

"If I knew I was having company, I would've made

something a little more impressive."

"I'm not fussy. It sounds perfect to me."

The timer pings, and Josh retrieves the white baking dish from the oven, removing the foil as he places it on the stovetop, then moves fluidly around the kitchen getting plates and ingredients for a salad.

I draw in a shaky breath as his arm brushes mine. "You like to cook?" I ask. My voice is raspy, and I clear my throat, adding to my awkward state.

Josh seems entirely unaffected and relaxed. I guess he would, given he isn't suffering any kind of dilemma that's threatening to swallow him whole. I, on the other hand, think I might implode at any moment.

"I love to cook." He gives me one of his incredible smiles that make me turn to jelly. "Wine?" he asks, reaching for a bottle of red he must've opened earlier.

God yes! "That would be lovely," I say, trying to hide my sudden desperation for alcohol's calming qualities.

"Do you like cooking?" he asks, pouring the wine.

I shake my head. "I despise it."

He laughs, handing me a glass. "To thunderstorms and flat tyres," he says, smiling as if they are the two greatest events in the history of the world.

I scrunch up my nose but can't help grinning as we chink glasses because it's the sweetest toast ever.

"Mmmm," I groan, sipping the wine. "This is fantastic. What is it?"

"It's a local Pinot."

I nod enthusiastically. "I'll need to make an effort to come back this way for the vineyards. I don't know that much about wine, but this tastes really good."

"Well, I hope you'll come back for more than just the vineyards." This man is so goddamn cute. "There are some fantastic markets around here, too."

We take our plates and wine back to the dining room, then Josh returns to the kitchen to grab the salad bowl. The table is situated next to a large picture window just beyond the French doors. "Look. The clouds have all but gone."

I peer out the window. With the lights on inside, it's hard to see a whole lot, but I can make out the moon and the soft light it casts across the lake. Millions upon millions of stars prick the black sky, and I'm spellbound. "It's quite the turnaround from a few hours ago."

"Happens quite regularly. It's pretty much over soon after it begins."

I gulp my wine, cringing at the irony of his words and whatever is happening between us. "You said there are markets around here?" I ask.

"Yes. There are lots of markets, but there's one I'd really like to take you to that's on tomorrow."

"You love this area, don't you?"

He takes a bite of his dinner and is obviously giving some serious thought to his response. "This is where I feel closest to my father."

Without thinking about it, I reach over and place my hand in his. He laces our fingers together, lifting my hand up to his lips for a gentle kiss. My gaze follows our hands, fixating on his perfect mouth I know I'd really like to feel on mine again. Being here with Josh just feels so incredibly right, even though I know I'm messing everything up with my dishonesty. It is breaking my heart, and my heart has suffered enough. My poor, trusting, naive heart deserves to swell with joy, beat with excitement, and heal with the love it thought it had forever with Ki but might just be finding somewhere else.

Josh locks eyes with me, and I smile, a warm and genuine smile.

"This is delicious," I say in a whisper.

"It's one of my specialties." He drops my hand, but we both know we just shared a moment.

"Tell me about your father," I say, eager to learn more about him. "Are you like him?"

He raises his glass and takes a sip. "Mum says my eldest brother, Hunter, looks like him, but I'm most like him in personality and temperament."

"I really like your mum," I say. "Makes me sad she's still grieving your dad, and it seems she always will."

"They were lucky in a lot of ways. They were so in love, and Dad dying when he did is just . . . well, it's just fucking annoying. Excuse my French."

I shake my head. "Sounds like a perfect way to describe it actually."

"I never saw them fight, and they always held hands." He chuckles. "We used to groan about their kissing in front of us or how they would snuggle on the couch watching television, but now I'd do anything to have him back holding her hand."

Tears prick my eyes hearing his heart breaking for his parents. "You're a wonderful son looking out for her the way you do."

"I can't stand the thought of her alone in that big house. It kills me to think of her wandering around, seeing him in every room. I check in with her as much as possible to stop her wallowing in her grief. I can distract her by keeping her company." He sighs. "But then she unloads on the cupcake girl, and I realise she is still so fragile."

"Cupcake girl?" I remember him calling me that as I said goodbye at his mum's house. For some reason, it warms me from the inside out.

He laughs. "You're the cupcake girl." His eyes widen with delight. "For someone who despises cooking, they were phenomenal."

"Baking is different," I say, placing my knife and fork together on my empty plate. "It's creative. Cooking is practical and boring."

"Maybe you're doing it wrong. I don't find cooking boring."

I hold my hands up defensively. "You cook. I'll bake. And all will be right in the world."

"I'll cook, you bake, and we'll both do our art." He raises his eyebrows. "Deal?"

At the mention of the love of art we share, my heart does a little flip-flop. "We'll see."

"Wait here," he says, standing and picking up both our plates. "I'll be back in a second."

He returns from the kitchen with the wine bottle and fills both our glasses. He ushers me over, and we move towards the most comfortable corner lounge suite in front of an open fireplace. It's incredibly cosy, and I feel strangely right at home—something I've been fighting for my whole life.

We sit next to each other and prop our knees up so we are face-to-face. It's very intimate, and I know in that moment that there's no place I'd rather be and no one I'd rather be with. It's both terrifying and exhilarating as the weight I've been crushed with for years feels lighter and somehow manageable.

"So . . ."

Josh cuts me off. "It's my turn to ask the questions,

cupcake girl."

I shake my head, chuckling at my new nickname. "What do you want to know?" I ask, praying he doesn't ask the wrong, or maybe the right, questions.

"You know something about my parents. Can you tell me a bit about yours?"

Okay, so I can answer this one. "My own mother never really wanted me. We haven't spoken in almost five years." I don't tell him that I left a message on her phone when I found a place to live in the city, but she never called me back. "And my father . . ." I blow out a long breath. "Let's just say I was the result of a good time, not a long time." I shrug. "I never met him, and I have no idea who he is."

"Did you ever ask your mum about him?"

I nod. "I went through a phase of being desperate to find out about him, but my mother claimed she didn't know, and it just made her angry if I asked too many questions."

"I'm sorry, Emerson." Josh places his hand on my knee and squeezes it gently. "I hope you don't mind talking about it."

Staring at his hand on my knee, I reply, "I do my best not to dwell on it."

"There's is a big part of you that's completely shut off, and it makes more sense to me now." I raise my eyes to his. "What you do show is sweet, compassionate, talented, and beautiful, but I want to know what's hidden beneath all that."

"You think I'm ugly and evil below the surface?"

He shakes his head. "Not at all. I think there's something infinitely more beautiful."

"You don't know me well enough to make those kind of judgements."

"I can't really explain it, but I feel like I've known you for a lot longer than I have. What I really want to know is what happened to make you stop drawing and following your dreams."

"There are so many things I'll share with you, but I've already told you that isn't one of them," I say honestly and with conviction I hope he takes seriously.

"It's not healthy to bottle things up, Emerson."

"That's what any good shrink would say, and I get it, but this is my way and my choice."

"Thank you." He takes a sip of his wine, never taking his eyes off me. "You've shared a lot with me tonight."

"What do you mean?" I ask. "I didn't tell you what you wanted to know."

"I didn't know for sure that something happened to you to make you quit your art, and now I do."

My stomach drops. I've never spoken about this before with anyone and, without realising, I've opened that can of worms. "Can we drop this subject please?"

"Of course," he says. "Would you like some more wine?"

I shake my head. "I think I've probably had enough for the evening. I'm really tired." Glancing at my watch, I see it's almost midnight. I'm shocked it's so late, and a yawn follows. "Do you mind if I call it a night?" I'm emotionally and physically exhausted and desperately hope the sleeping arrangement isn't awkward. I can't take things any further with him.

"Absolutely. I'm ready to turn in, too." He holds up his hands obviously as a response to my stricken look. "Don't worry. Separate rooms."

I smile, embarrassed by my rudeness, but relieved at the same time. "Thank you, Josh. For everything."

He smiles and picks up my empty glass, and I follow him

back to the kitchen. Once he's placed the glasses in the sink, we make our way back to the bedrooms and stop outside the one I used earlier.

"This is you," he says, then pulls me into him.

My initial reaction is to tense up, but something about being cocooned in his arms makes me relax in moments. It's undeniable how safe and protected I feel with Josh's hard body pressed against mine and his muscular arms firmly securing me to him. I want to be a strong, independent woman, but it's nice to feel cared for and precious. It's been a long time, and I miss it desperately. Clinging to the back of his shirt, I bury my face into the soft material and inhale. He still smells of soap, probably from a shower he had before I arrived. I remember when he first opened the door, I was struck by his fresh-out-of-the-shower appearance. Damp hair, effortlessly tousled to perfection. I am really freaking attracted to this man both on the superficial, physical level and the deeper, more important level of feeling connected in a unique way. That's something some people search for their whole lives. Is it possible I've found it twice?

"Goodnight, cupcake girl," he whispers, then kisses the top of my head. His lips stay there for what feels like a really long time, but when he pulls away, it's nowhere near long enough. Looking me right in the eye, he says, "Thanks for coming back to me, and I promise I won't push you for anything you're not completely ready for."

I smile. "You can thank my irresponsible car ownership skills." I have relaxed considerably knowing this isn't going to go any further than it has already. I need some space and some sleep to work out why I feel so desperately disappointed that he's leaving me to go to his own room.

Ki . . . I'm so, so sorry. My heart is torn in two.

I'm in a world of trouble.

CHAPTER

22

THE DIGITAL CLOCK on the bedside table tells me it's 6:19 in the morning, but something about the digital screen catches my eye. The one and the nine appear to be disappearing bit by bit. I shuffle closer and rub my eyes, still blurry with sleep. I am now inches away from the display and, to my astonishment, I can see a tiny person inside the clock painting over the numbers. When they're gone, he, or maybe she, starts painting a two and a zero in red paint. What the hell? I'm sure I'm not imagining it, but I'm a little concerned I'm losing my mind. The voice in my head reminds me it isn't completely ludicrous to be concerned by that. I watch for another ten minutes and sure enough, the little person I've discovered on closer inspection is an old lady using her paintbrush and a ladder if needed to ensure the correct time is kept. It is the strangest but coolest thing I've ever seen.

Dragging myself away from my little time-keeping friend, I get up and use the bathroom, then open my bedroom door to go and look for Josh. Outside my bedroom door are my clothes and underwear from yesterday, clean, dry, and folded.

Grateful, impressed and a little embarrassed, I quickly take them and change. As promised, I found various toiletries in the bathroom cabinet, including women's deodorant and a toothbrush, so I'm feeling completely human.

The house is quiet, and I would assume Josh is asleep except for my laundered clothes. In the kitchen, I find a note on the bench telling me to help myself to coffee and anything for breakfast if I'm hungry if he isn't yet back from taking Leroy for a walk by the lake. From the kitchen window, I can see him by the water's edge in the distance. Finding my shoes by the French doors leading onto the deck, I head outside into the fresh morning air.

Even though my need to be near Josh feels almost desperate, I stop at the railing of the deck and close my eyes, breathing in deeply. Opening them, I take in the panoramic vista. After the rain, everything looks and smells so fresh. I love the anonymity of the city, but I never consider myself a city-girl convert. I haven't returned to my hometown since leaving five years ago, but that isn't because I don't still have great love for it. Thanks to Mereki, I had eight wonderful years there, filled with happy memories. In the space of no more than ten minutes, I was robbed of any desire to set foot in that town ever again. I was robbed of so much more than that, but it's best I don't think about that anymore. I'm happy here, and that seems to have a whole lot to do with the man I'm now walking towards.

He is getting farther away, but I can still see him and Leroy quite clearly. Like a moth to the flame attracted to the light despite its danger, I walk towards him.

Josh turns when I'm still a fair distance from him, as if he sensed my presence. His smile lights up his face, and I swoon.

"How did you sleep?" Josh asks, kissing me on the cheek when I reach him.

"Really well. You?"

"I always sleep well out here," he replies, as he tosses something out across the still water.

My eyes widen as I stare in disbelief. Whatever he threw bounces across the surface one, two, three, four, five times before disappearing. "How did you do that?" I ask, spellbound.

"Depending on where you're from, it's known as skipping, skiffing, or skimming stones. The Brits call it ducks and drakes. I've heard it called frog jumps, too. There is something really rewarding and relaxing about it." He crouches down and picks up another white pebble from a pile at his feet. "It's all in the angle. Want me to teach you?"

With all the years I spent by a river playing with pebbles, I can't believe I've never tried this. "Sure. That would be great."

He picks up a selection of pebbles for me. "They are all carefully selected for their flat, smooth surface, but I think you should try with this one." He hands me the one that is slightly bigger than the others. "The light, small ones typically skip more times and go farther, but a medium weight, like this one, usually works best for beginners."

"What now?" I ask, running my thumb over the smooth surface.

He holds his own stone to show me. "Place your index finger against the edge of the stone. Hold the flat sides with your thumb on one side and your middle finger on the other. You want to be able to send the stone spinning in a straight line with the flat end almost parallel to the water." He waits for me to follow his instructions before continuing. "You should make sure to place the stone in the crook of your index finger while placing your thumb on top of the rock to maintain control of it."

"Okay," I say when I'm sure I have it right. "What next?"

"Face the water sideways, with your feet shoulder-width apart." He comes around behind me and places his hands on my shoulders to correct my position. "You're right-handed, so you need to stand with your left or non-dominant side closest to the water's edge, with your shoulder turned toward the water." I feel pressure on my shoulders. "Squat down so that when you throw, your rock will be close to parallel with the surface."

"This is all very scientific," I say, chuckling. "I thought we were just throwing stones."

"Actually, scientists have found that the ideal angle between the stone and the water is twenty degrees."

"Scientists have spent time on this?" I ask, incredulous.

"It's serious business, Emerson."

I look up into his eyes and see the sparkle. I don't know if he's pulling my leg or not about the scientists, but he isn't taking it too seriously.

"Any less than that twenty degrees," he says, "and the friction slows it down. Any more than that, and it cuts the water and sinks."

"Okay, well my legs are starting to ache, so hit me with the throwing instructions now, please."

He laughs. "Sorry. Bend your wrist all the way back and then snap it forward to flick the stone against the surface of the water. Don't think of it as throwing an overhand Frisbee, but as throwing an underhand softball. You can also think of it like cracking a whip sideways. The important thing is that you carefully bend your wrist all the way back to generate some power, and that you then flick it forward quickly and at the right angle, allowing it to spin counter-clockwise. Throw it as fast as you can without losing form. Angle and spin are more important than speed."

I throw my head back and laugh. "I think my head just exploded."

"Give it a go and you might find my instructions aren't just a bunch of hosh posh."

"Hosh posh?" I keep laughing. "What the hell is hosh posh?"

"Shut up, smart arse, and throw the goddamn pebble." He can't help laughing, too, though.

I run his crazy complicated instructions over in my head, then execute them as best as I can. My stone flies out of my hand and ungracefully plops into the lake not too far from us.

I scrunch up my nose, and my shoulders drop in defeat. "Your instructions are faulty," I say, trying not to laugh.

Josh groans. "You didn't follow through."

"You didn't tell me to follow through," I reply like a diva.

"When you bend your wrist back, make sure to whip your throwing arm all the way across your chest, finishing near the shoulder of your opposite arm."

"Was that my only error?"

"It takes practice, Emerson." His jovial tone is now completely gone. "Like art, some people are more naturally gifted than others, but a lot of progress can be made by applying yourself to it." I think about how I completely rejected my art and how much I missed it. "Following through will ensure that you've put all of your power and momentum into the throw and will make the stone travel the farthest and skip the longest."

"Whatever you say, Mr Rock Science Man."

"Mr Rock Science Man?"

I laugh as I reach down and pick up another stone. "Yup."

Twenty-five tosses and several pebble retrieval missions later, and I am yet to see a single bounce. I am beyond frustrated watching every single one of Josh's skip across the surface effortlessly.

"Ready for the best breakfast you've ever had?" Josh asks, obviously sensing the end of my patience.

Sighing, I nod. "Guess so."

Josh whistles to Leroy, who obediently returns to him. On the walk back to the house, Josh reaches for my hand, and I let him hold it. Somehow, I've managed to create a whole alternative life for myself out here with Josh where I'm allowed to feel good about this incredible man holding my hand and offering to make me breakfast.

"When did you learn to skim stones?" I ask, breaking the comfortable silence.

"My dad taught us when we were kids." He glances out over the lake. "He wanted my brothers and me to be outside as much as possible."

"Where are your brothers now?"

"Two live in the city. The eldest, Hunter, is a hotshot lawyer and living the high life."

"How old is he?"

"Hunter's thirty-two, I'm thirty-one, Luca and Max are twenty-eight."

"Four boys and twins. Your mum must've been busy when you were all little."

He laughs. "She has many stories I'm sure she'd love to tell you to embarrass us."

"So Hunter's a hotshot lawyer. What about Luca and Max?"

"Luca's a tech nerd. He develops apps and sells them for ridiculous sums of money."

"I've no idea how all that stuff works."

Josh shakes his head. "Me neither, but Luca is a bit of a wiz."

"Sounds like you get on with them."

"I do. We don't see each other as much as Mum particularly would like, but we'd all drop everything for each other, and we do as much as we can to help Mum cope."

"What about your other brother?"

"Max lives in South Africa as a foreign correspondent," he replies, holding the door open for me.

"All so different," I say as I take my shoes off and leave them by the door where I found them earlier.

"Max risks his life with his job, but I can't imagine him doing anything else. Some of the stories he's managed to get have stressed Mum out so much, but even she knows it's his life, and he has to live it on his terms."

I can hear the reverence he obviously feels for all his brothers, and it warms my heart. "You're closest to Max, and he's the farthest away. That must be hard."

"Are you a psychic or something?"

I chuckle. "No. It's hardly rocket science listening not just to what you said but how you said it. Sometimes it's all in the tone."

Josh stares at me, seemingly deep in thought. "You intrigue me more than anyone ever has, Emerson." He shakes his head, then gestures towards the kitchen.

As Josh starts pulling mixing bowls and fry pans out of cupboards, I find myself marvelling at how this incredibly good-looking, talented, and resourceful man is single.

"How are you single?" My thought tumbles out of my mouth.

"I could ask you the same thing," he says, raising his eyebrows.

I don't answer, wishing I hadn't brought up the subject but realising it's now too late. "Are any of your brothers married or in serious relationships?"

"Max married his high school sweetheart, Cami, and they have twin daughters, Arabella and Maggie."

"Given his job, he was the one I was least expecting."

"South Africa can be a very dangerous place, but they live in a gated community, and their safety is Max's number-one priority. He even said they could move home when Cami fell pregnant over there, but she refused to let him give up his dream." He continues working his magic while we chat. "She loves it over there and has made a lot of friends with the other ex-pats."

"I'd love to go on a safari," I say, remembering a documentary I watched once about Kruger National Park.

"Then you should make it happen," he says, nonchalantly. "You're young and healthy. You should be checking off bucket list items, not just talking about them."

"Do you have a bucket list?" I ask.

"Sure I do. I think most people have things they hope to do or experience in their lives, even if they don't write them down."

I pull out a stool from under the island bench and take a seat. "I'd offer to help you, but you seem to have it under control."

"You just sit there and look pretty."

I chuckle, leaning forward, resting my chin in my palms, and resting my elbows on the bench. "What are you making me?"

"A bacon and egg wrap," he says. "I hope you're not allergic to anything."

I shake my head. "Sounds wonderful."

"Do you have any siblings?" he asks as he places a large tortilla on each plate. "You know so much about me, and I don't even know if you have brothers and sisters."

"I had a stepbrother, Trent."

Josh stands on the opposite side of the bench with a frypan in his hand, about to scoop scrambled eggs onto the tortillas. "Had?"

"He was never a brother to me." I clench my teeth. "We don't keep in touch."

"Hearing this makes me so grateful for the happy childhood."

"I need coffee," I say, climbing down from my stool and walking over to the coffee machine. "Do you want one?"

"Sure. Black, one sugar, please."

His coffee machine takes pods and has a separate milk frother. Carrie has the same set-up in our break room at work, so I can make myself useful here at least.

When I finish, Josh has constructed two delicious-looking and smelling wraps next to each other. I take my place back on the same stool, and Josh sits beside me. I hand him his coffee and take a sip of mine, inhaling the steam. "Mmmm," I say, enjoying the liquid gold.

"You drive me completely insane. Do you know that?" he asks.

I put my mug down and pick up my wrap. "I do? Why?"

He shakes his head and groans. "You're just so incredibly beautiful, and you don't even know it."

My cheeks heat, and I take a small bite of my wrap, not sure how to respond to his compliment. Josh watches me, and his smile broadens.

In a bid to change the subject, I ask, "Are you able to drive me to a petrol station to buy some fuel?"

He nods, waving his hand in the air as if my predicament is nothing. "Do you have time to hang out with me today?" He looks at me as if he's contemplating something but is unsure whether he should say it.

"What is it, Josh?"

"I'm assuming you don't have to go to work tomorrow on the public holiday?"

I suspect I know where he's going with this. "That's right. I have the day off."

"I hoped you'd consider staying another night."

I chew on the inside of my cheek and stare at my empty plate. I am enjoying this extension from my reality, and the idea of returning to my empty house is depressing. I look up at him and smile. "I'd love to."

He stands with a grin from ear to ear and clears our plates. "I'm really bloody happy about that."

CHAPTER

23

AFTER WE'VE CLEARED away breakfast and washed up, we head outside.

His Landcruiser is in the driveway, but Josh disappears into the wooden shed beside the house, so I follow him. What I find inside surprises me. It's like I've just stepped into a mechanic's workshop, complete with a range of cars of varying makes and models. One is raised off the ground whilst another is missing its doors and wheels.

"You like cars," I say, still looking around the extensive setup.

"I do. It's another of my hobbies, I guess." He waves his arm around the shed. "Dad and I used to restore old cars together, then sell them for profit. I still tinker with it."

"I feel like I misjudged you somehow," I say.

"What do you mean?"

"You said I'm an enigma. I'd say you're the one full of surprises."

"You're just not asking the right questions." He winks at

me, then walks to the back where racks of tyres and various spare parts are kept. He finds what he's looking for and returns to where I'm still standing holding a metal can.

"I really chose the right place to break down, didn't I?"

He laughs. "I like to think so."

We stop in at the service station, then return to my car. Maybe forgetting to fill up with fuel on the way here was fate intervening. Who knows?

We return to the house and I grab my spare jacket from the backseat before jumping back into Josh's car for the trip into town.

"I can't believe this has been practically on my doorstep for the past five years, and I've never been here," I say as we weave our way through stunning scenery.

"I love it out here, but I love the contrast of the city, so I'm grateful I get to spend plenty of time there, too," he says. I turn back to face him. "I'm lucky I get to have the best of both worlds."

"Do you think your mum will stay in that big house forever?"

He nods, but even from the side, I can see the sadness flash across his features. His hands grip the steering wheel just a little tighter, and his shoulders bunch up slightly. He worries about his mother so much, and I find it endearing. I'm also struck with a pang of guilt that I don't miss my mother. I never shed a tear when I left her and everyone I'd ever known behind, and I rarely spare her a thought. Does that make me a monster?

"She clings to that house as if her connection to Dad depends on it." He glances at me briefly before returning his focus to the road ahead. "I don't think it's healthy."

"What do you mean?"

He takes a deep breath and then sighs. "She's no longer living."

I pause to process what he's saying. I wonder about her life before she lost her husband. "What did your father do for a job?"

"He was an investment banker for one of the big firms in the city."

"How did your parents meet?"

He smiles. "Childhood sweethearts."

"Sounds like they were really happy together."

"They were." He shakes his head. "It is an absolute tragedy that he was taken away from her when they had their whole retirement planned out. They were best friends."

"He sounds like he was a great man."

"My dad had the best work ethic of anyone I've ever known, but he had his priorities straight." Josh's Adam's apple bobs as he focuses on the road ahead. This is obviously a tough topic for him. "His wife and kids were everything to him, and he never let Mum down. She was an amazing mother and supportive wife, but she knew if things got overwhelming for her at home, she could call him and he'd be there." He glances at me again briefly. "He was a real man."

"Something tells me you're a lot like your dad."

We stop at a red light where he can look at me properly. "All I've ever wanted to be is someone both my parents could be proud of."

I swallow the lump in my throat. Josh and I couldn't have had a more different childhood. "I've only met your mum once, but she spoke so highly of you."

The light turns green, and we cross the intersection before Josh speaks again. "She's my rock, and I just try to be the best son I can possibly be to her."

"Tell me about how you came to teach art therapy."

"I was good at art in high school," he says, glancing briefly at me. "But I never considered it to be a career. As you know, Dad died a few years after I finished school. I sketched him in such detail so I could remember, and it became a type of therapy for me. Every day for months, I'd draw something that reminded me of him. It was something tangible and completely personal. I allowed my grief to bleed out of me onto the paper, and it helped."

"You studied art so you could help others?"

"Initially it was to help myself, but I found teaching so rewarding and decided I could make the grief I experienced mean something."

I reach out and touch his upper arm, needing to make physical contact with this beautiful man. "I think what you're doing is incredible."

"My life was something out of some goddamn fairy tale. Parents together and happy, no financial worries, good friends, and good health." He glances down at my hand on him and smiles, meeting my eyes. "I knew Dad wouldn't want any of us to stop living because he died, so everything I do now is because I will always strive to be even half the man he was." He nods as we pass a sign. "This is it. Clare, one of my best friends, makes candles and sells them here, so I like to come to support her." He says her name with great affection, and I'm intrigued to meet her.

The markets are held in the grounds of the local primary school. Josh parks the car and we climb out. The vendors appear to be in the final stages of setup, and there aren't many people here yet.

"Do you feel like another coffee?" Josh asks. "Looks like

it doesn't open until ten."

"Why not?" I say, smiling. "Do you know somewhere good?"

"Come on," he says, nodding enthusiastically. "There's someone else I'd love you to meet."

We walk down the street to a row of shops, and Josh leads me into The Coffee Press, a bookshop that I quickly discover is also a café when I draw in a deep breath. The smell is heavenly. Ground coffee beans, hot chocolate, and books—an intoxicating combination of indulgence, addiction, and stories begging to be devoured. I glance around the shop, taking in the bookshelves. There is no one style of furniture that I can make out. Every set of shelves, each table and even each chair is different, but somehow the eclectic mix works perfectly. The owner has managed to blend styles, eras, and colours to make a cosy and welcoming ambience that would absolutely encourage patrons to stay.

"Hey, Jane. Is Todd here?" Josh asks the girl behind the coffee machine.

"You just missed him." She cocks her head in the direction of the door. "He's helping Clare set up her stall. Should be back soon though."

"Okay. Thanks. Can I grab a flat white and long black please?"

I smile. "You remembered what coffee I like." He shrugs as if it's nothing. "Thank you."

"You're very welcome."

"I might just browse the bookshelves." I run my finger along the undulating spines on the shelf closest to me.

Continuing my perusal, I stop at the small sports section. A book catches my eye, one I've seen before, a long time ago. I pull it out carefully and hold it reverently in my hands, trying to push down the emotion bubbling out of me at the sight of something so nostalgic.

"You like fishing?" Josh asks, looking over my shoulder.

I glance down at the book's cover that has a man kissing a fish on it. "I gave this book as a gift to my best friend when he turned eleven. I can't believe your friend has it here."

"*Catch and Kiss?* That's an absolute classic." He chuckles. "Todd's father is a keen fisherman, so he always stocks a few fishing books in case he ever visits." He gives me a sad smile. "He never visits."

I clutch the book to my chest and recall the day I gave it to Ki. We'd been friends for more than a year by then, and I wanted to get him something but only had a few dollars made up mostly of five and ten-cent pieces. I'd been to the bookstore and found nothing below ten dollars, but then one day I passed a house having a garage sale in their front yard. I noticed a box labelled 'Books' so I rummaged through, looking for something I thought Ki would like. *Catch and Kiss* jumped out at me because of the man kissing the fish. Gross, I'd thought. I look at Josh and smile but try to school my mouth into a straight line. He'd just told me about his friend's estranged father.

"Josh Holland," a man's voice calls out, but I can't see him. "Get that mighty fine arse over here."

Well, that was a strange greeting, and I can't help the chuckle that escapes my lips. Josh groans.

A tall, lean man who I would guess is the same age as Josh appears from the other side of a bookshelf. He is immaculately attired in slim-fitting jeans, a white collared shirt, a tweed waistcoat, and a bow tie. Opening his arms as he approaches, he lunges forward. Despite Josh having a much bulkier frame than Todd, he is swallowed up by this man's enthusiastic embrace. After a few moments, I start to wonder if he'll ever let him go as he rests his cheek on Josh's shoulder. He obviously has great affection for him, and it seems it's mutual.

"Okay, okay," Josh says. "That's enough now." In good humour, he pushes Todd back and puts his arm around my shoulders, and I lean into him. "This is my friend, Emerson. Emerson, this is my friend, Todd."

"Nice to meet you," I say, shaking his outstretched hand.

"Absolute pleasure to meet you, Emerson. It's about time Joshy here introduced me to a woman. I was going to start thinking I had a shot at him." He laughs with such gusto, and I can't help but join in.

Josh groans, rolling his eyes, but his smile is genuine.

"I was just helping Clare," Todd says, walking back to the coffee machine. He shakes his head. "She always gets so stressed before the market, and I have no idea why. She sells out every time."

"Clare's Todd's twin sister," Josh explains, ushering me forward towards the few tables set up along the back wall.

"You have a beautiful shop, Todd."

Todd's chest puffs up, and his eyes glimmer behind the frameless glasses. "Thank you, my love. You're looking at my three favourite things right here," he says, winking as Jane deposits my flat white down in front of me and the long black in front of Josh.

"Three? I'm thinking books and coffee . . . but what's the third?"

Todd throws Josh a cheeky glance. "Hot men!" He throws his arms up in the air and laughs.

It feels so good to laugh, and I realise suddenly how little I have done so in the past five years. Despite the pang of guilt I experience that I'm here having a great time with two men who aren't Mereki, I don't want to leave. I don't want to return to the city and face my lonely reality. Refusing to allow myself to ruin this beautiful morning, I push all depressing thoughts to the back of my mind and live in the moment. Another thing I haven't done in way too long.

"How do you know each other?" I ask, sipping on my coffee.

Josh looks at Todd, then back at me. "We went to school together, then when I moved out here, they visited regularly and eventually made the move themselves."

"Josh helped both Clare and me get our businesses started two years ago. We joke around a lot together, but he's the best person in the world, and we'd do anything for him to pay back his generosity."

"Oh stop," Josh says with a huff. "Free coffees and candles for my mum. We're square."

Todd looks me in the eye and shakes his head slightly. "This guy is way too modest. A blind man could see the chemistry between the two of you lovebirds, so you hold on to him and don't let go." He pats Josh on the shoulder. "He's one of the really good ones."

I look at Josh, and he stays silent. I bite my bottom lip, knowing I shouldn't feel so good about what Todd said, so I bite down harder.

"If you're done with your coffee, shall we go meet Clare?" Josh asks.

I nod. "Let's go."

"Dinner at the pub tonight?" Todd asks as he picks up our empty cups and saucers.

Josh looks to me and raises his eyebrows. "What do you think? Interested in a pub meal for dinner?"

I shrug. "Sure. Why not?"

"Fabulous," Todd says, putting his arm around my shoulder and escorting me back through his shop, leaving Josh to trail behind us. "See you at seven." He wraps me in a hug and kisses my cheek. "Great to meet you, Emerson."

"Thanks for the coffee," I say, smiling. I'm genuinely happy I'll get to see him again.

Josh and I walk back to the market, and I notice the increase in cars and people. The markets are now in full swing, and I can't wait to check them out.

"Why didn't you tell Todd we're not together?" I ask as we walk past the first stall without hesitation—baby clothes.

"Why didn't you?"

It's my turn to remain silent, knowing he has a point. When Josh stops at a stand selling a range of salts, I keep walking.

"Local honey," a woman calls out, gaining my attention. "Would you like to try some local honey?"

"Yes, please," I say, walking over to her stand. I place the tasting spoon in my mouth. "Mmmm. Honey is one of those things I always try to buy from markets. It tastes so much better than the highly-processed stuff you buy in stores."

"I believe you," he says, but his eyes are on my lips. I turn away. "How many are you going to buy?"

"Two," I say. "It's only me, so I really can't justify more than that." Mereki stopped eating honey when we were twelve years old and he got stung by four bees. He blew up like a balloon and came out in itchy hives. He held a grudge. I smile at the memory.

"We'll take four jars," Josh says, addressing the vendor. He turns to me. "Two for you and two for me."

I go for my wallet, but he holds up his hand in protest. "I'll get this."

I shake my head but don't argue. I'm sure I can square us up at another stall.

Josh carries the bag with the four honey jars, and we keep walking. It's a beautiful, sunny day, and I take my light jacket off to enjoy the warmth on my skin. I raise my face to the sky and close my eyes, breathing in the fresh country air. With Josh walking beside me between rows of passionate people selling their homemade goods, I feel a sense of contentedness. It isn't nostalgia, as I've never actually experienced it before. Even back in my hometown when things were great with Ki, there was always a sense of foreboding following us around. When it had all seemed too good to be true, it was.

"What are you thinking about?" Josh asks, snapping me out of my thoughts.

I open my eyes and face him. "I am having a good day," I answer honestly.

Josh smiles. "Me too."

We stare at each other, and the connection I know we both feel crackles the air between us. For a minute, I wonder if he's going to kiss me again, this time in public in front of the Ugg boot stall with background music provided by twenty wind chimes.

Staring at his mouth, I remember how wonderful it had felt on mine. I draw in a breath when his tongue darts out and wets his bottom lip. Desire shoots through me, and in that moment, I can think of nothing I want more than him. To hell with the consequences and my warped moral compass. Josh takes a step closer, and now I can't breathe. He lifts his hand to my face and gently grazes his knuckles across my cheekbone. My eyes widen as his incredibly sensual mouth gets closer and closer to me.

With mere inches between us and my brain about to have

a complete and cataclysmic meltdown, I hold my breath. This is it. He's going to kiss me. My mind spins. God, I want this more than anything. I—

"Josh! Josh!"

He doesn't pull away, but he doesn't come any closer. Our eyes are locked, and I can see his every desire swirling around in his emerald irises, up close and personal.

"Joshua Holland," the voice calls out, closer now.

Groaning, he kisses the tip of my nose, then turns away, taking a step back. I can't move, but I'm forced to drag air into my oxygen-deprived lungs. My eyes are still locked on him, but I'm now staring at his strong side profile. His dark blond hair is tucked behind his ears, and he runs his free hand through the length of it as he greets whoever it is who stopped our kiss.

"Emerson."

I shake my head and acknowledge him saying my name, possibly not for the first time.

"Sorry," I say, cringing slightly. I look up and am confronted by a female clone of Todd. "You must be Clare." I hold out my hand and shake hers.

"Nice to meet you," she says in a friendly, but nowhere-near-as-warm, tone as her brother's.

Clare reaches for Josh's hand and pulls him away from me. I don't love that, even though I have no claim to him whatsoever. Jealousy knows nothing of right and wrong, and I have to stop myself from marching forward and ripping his hand from hers. What a shitty thing that would be for me to do, but it flashes through my mind before I have a chance to control it.

"Your stand looks fantastic as always," Josh says, praising her undoubtedly wonderful setup. "How are sales going so far?"

Clare beams under his approval. "Strong so far. I've sold out of my Christmas range already."

I step forward to take a closer look at her candles, picking one up every so often to breathe in the scent. "Is this the one in your mum's entry foyer?" I ask, holding up the one that reminds me of the day I was there.

Clare looks to Josh, then back to me. "Oh, you've met Sarah?"

I nod and smile.

Josh glances back and forth between us, then interjects, "Todd suggested dinner at the pub tonight if you're keen?"

She looks up at him with puppy-dog eyes. "Of course. I was going to suggest the same thing."

A crowd of prospective customers has arrived at Clare's stall, and she needs to get back to work.

"We'll leave you to it then," Josh says, placing his hand at the small of my back. It feels intimate. "See you tonight."

"Oh. Okay. See you tonight." Clare appears torn, and I catch the tightening between her brows. She is jealous, and I wonder what their relationship is, or perhaps, was.

As we walk away, I decide not to pry. It is none of my business.

We spend another hour at the markets making a few more purchases. While Josh is preoccupied chatting to an elderly couple he knows, I find a stall selling beautiful, handmade dresses and a select range of underwear. I choose my favourites, relieved I'll have something to wear to dinner tonight with Todd and Clare.

When I meet up with Josh, we grab hot dogs for lunch before heading back to his house mid-afternoon.

He turns the car off in the driveway, but neither of us makes a move to get out. "I'd like to sketch you," he says.

My head snaps to his. "What? Why?"

His eyes soften. "It's just something I've wanted to do for a while now."

And even though nothing he's said is suggestive, even though it's all quite simple, something in my stomach tells me this is very, very wrong.

CHAPTER

24

AFTER DEPOSITING MY purchases in the spare bedroom, I return to the kitchen to find Josh. "Where do you want to do this?" I ask, trying to sound less nervous than I feel.

Picking up his sketch pad, he ushers me towards the French doors leading to the deck. "Let's go to the boat shed."

We make our way down the slope. When we reach the small, wooden building, Josh moves ahead of me to open the door.

Instead of following him inside, I stop to admire the craftsmanship of the structure. Up close, it's beautiful, obviously made with care and attention to detail.

"Are you coming in?" Josh asks.

I nod. "Sorry."

"Don't be." He touches my shoulder as I walk past him into the cabin, and a jolt of electricity pulses through my entire body.

It is bigger on the inside than I'd expected, housing all manner of tools, water sport equipment, and fishing gear.

Clearly, the Hollands are the outdoorsy types.

"Where do you want me?" I ask, glancing around the room looking for somewhere to sit.

He shakes his head and beckons me towards the back door. "This way."

The door leads out onto a jetty, and I follow him without thinking twice. In that moment, I realise I would follow him anywhere. He makes me feel safe, and I haven't felt that in far too long.

"You can swim, right?" he asks, gesturing to the dinghy bobbing in the water. "Not that I plan on throwing you overboard, of course."

"Like a fish," I reply, stepping in, arms out wide to balance, then taking a seat.

Josh climbs in, dropping his backpack to the floor before taking a seat opposite me. He then unties the rope tethering us to the jetty. Locking the oars in place, he starts rowing while I take in the scenery. It's a calm, clear day, but I wish I'd brought a light jacket or cardigan as the breeze on the water whips up around us.

Without saying anything, Josh pulls a blanket from the backpack and hands it to me.

"Thanks," I say, wrapping it around me.

When we reach the middle of the expansive lake, Josh brings the oars back into the boat. We drift for a few moments before he reaches back into his bag and retrieves his sketchpad and pencils.

"Are you comfortable?" he asks.

"Not really," I reply, scrunching up my nose. "No one has ever drawn me before."

"I'm glad I'm your first," he says, a hint of a smile teasing the corner of his mouth.

I roll my eyes. "Just hurry up and draw me already."

"You're a hard taskmaster, cupcake girl."

Shaking my head, I can't help smiling at the nickname.

"Okay. For a few minutes, just pretend I'm not here. Do you think you can do that for me?"

"That's no problem at all."

He clutches his chest. "I feel like I should be offended."

Smiling, I drop my shoulders and the tension in my body eases a little. But when he leans forward and appears to be studying me, I feel vulnerable to his scrutiny. It's as if he's trying to discover all my secrets simply by looking closely enough.

"Why did we come out to the middle of the lake?" I'm whispering, but I'm not really sure why.

He doesn't answer immediately and I find myself leaning forward, weakening against the magnetic pull I've felt since the moment we met.

"I didn't want you to be able to run away," he says eventually, edging forward.

We're so close now I can feel his breath on me. "Fair enough."

Josh grazes his lips across mine but doesn't kiss me. Instead, he whispers directly in my ear. "I'm trying to work you out and didn't want to take any chances." Pushing the loose strands of my hair behind my ears, he must know the breathtaking effect he's having on me. "Plus I thought you'd like it out here," he says, his eyes back on mine. "You get a blissful expression on your face whenever you're looking at the water."

Closing my eyes, I nod, accepting his answer. I'm falling under his spell, and there's not a damn thing I can do about it.

When I hear the familiar sound of lead on paper, I allow my mind to drift away with the cool afternoon breeze. A thousand thoughts jumble together like carriages on a runaway train. For some reason, each one of the many jobs I undertook since moving to Melbourne takes its turn up front before bouncing back to the recesses of my brain. My heart muscles constrict remembering the overwhelming loneliness I experienced by never staying anywhere long enough to make any real connections. I was there simply to do the job, then I'd rush home to Mereki, who was no company at all.

"Hey, Emerson," Josh says, interrupting my thoughts. "Breathe."

Opening my eyes, I suck in a breath and scrunch up my nose. "Sorry. I guess I'm still nervous."

His brows are furrowed with concern. "I won't be much longer. I can finish it up later."

"Okay." I wring my hands in my lap, unsure if I'm disappointed or relieved.

He fixes me with his intense gaze. "I could've drawn you in detail without you being here at all." He cups me under the chin and strokes his thumb across my cheek. "I just wanted the excuse to be this close to you."

His words both slay and heal. "Can I see what you've done so far?"

He turns his sketchpad over and passes it to me. I gasp with rapture, shock, and recognition all at the same time. "It was your drawing I saw displayed in Madeleine's gallery window the first time I ever went there." I recall the beautiful drawing of a man's face, half perfectly detailed while the other half was completely blurred.

"My only self-portrait," he says, nodding. "Madeleine is my greatest supporter and often displays my work."

Returning my gaze to the drawing he's done of me, I'm again struck by the detail he's managed to include in such a short period of time. "Why the blurred lines?"

He shrugs. "No one's life is black and white. We all have grey areas—insecurities, flaws, imperfections, secrets. We're all just human, and there's a kind of beauty in that."

CHAPTER

25

WHEN WE RETURN to the house, I hurry to the privacy of the spare bedroom, needing a little space from the incredibly talented and devastatingly attractive Josh Holland. For the longest time, I lie flat on my back on the bed and stare at the ceiling, mulling his words and that drawing over in my head.

Eventually, I glance at the clock and see it's after six, and Josh had told me we'd be leaving at six-thirty to go to meet Clare and Todd. I remove the dress and underwear from the bag and lay them on the bed. It's the prettiest dress I've ever seen, and I can't wait to try it on, desperately hoping it fits. After a quick shower, I pull it over my head and let it glide over my body. The hem, collar, and sleeves are bordered by tiny green gemstones that catch the light as I move, and I hope it's not too dressy for the pub. Applying lip gloss I had in my bag and putting my hair in a quick braid over my left shoulder, I allow a few strands to hang loosely around my face. It's Ki's favourite hairstyle on me, and I feel a nasty twinge of guilt for hoping Josh likes it, too.

"You ready?" Josh calls from the hallway.

When I open the door, Josh's eyes widen before raking up and down my body with obvious appreciation. When he meets my gaze, his emerald orbs are now a darker shade of green, and the only word that springs into my head is lust. Josh is lusting for me, and the beast that's awoken inside me roars in delight. Since I met him, I've been unable to deny the chemistry between us. I have no doubt he can see my own lustful thoughts dancing in my eyes.

Swallowing hard, I run my sweaty palms over my hips, smoothing the fabric that isn't wrinkled. "It fits," I whisper.

"It most certainly does," he says, stepping forward into my personal space.

My breath hitches as he captures my face in his large palms. "You are breathtaking, Emerson."

I am rendered mute, unable to tear my eyes from his as he runs his thumbs across my cheekbones. I want to step closer and eradicate the small distance keeping our bodies apart, but I don't. I just stand there, enjoying his touch, revelling in his closeness and being tortured by my secret. This man wants me, and something tells me he isn't into one-night stands or no-strings-attached flings. He strikes me as the long-term relationship kind of guy who isn't afraid of commitment. In different circumstances, perhaps I could be his happily-ever-after, but the fact is I am forever spoken for by another man. I don't know what game I'm playing at here, but I know I rolled the dice when I delivered those cupcakes to the gallery, and I've made increasingly strategic moves ever since.

"Thank you," I say eventually, but I sound croaky, and he must know how his touch, his gaze, and his words affect me.

Taking a step back, he lets his hands drop from my face. "Let's go."

I'm a little disappointed that the moment is over, but relief is the dominating emotion.

We drive in the opposite direction to the way we'd travelled to the markets earlier today, but it takes us a similar amount of time to reach the pub. I'm really looking forward to seeing Todd again. Clare gave me a strange vibe, so I'm interested to see if it was because she was stressed or because she is protective of Josh. When we get there, I'll put her mind at ease that we're just friends.

Harrigan's is an authentic Irish pub located in a small township. It's welcoming and warm, just like the company I'm keeping. Casting my gaze around the busy room, I see around ten tables and a few booths along the back wall, all full. Todd and Clare sit opposite each other in one of the booths, and Todd waves enthusiastically when he sees us.

Josh acknowledges them with a wave, then turns to me. "What would you like to drink?"

"The red you gave me last night would be great if they have it. Or something similar. Thank you."

We walk to the bar, and he orders a red for me and a beer for himself, then carries them towards the booth where his friends are waiting. We have to jostle between the many patrons out for a good time at this very popular establishment.

"Damn, girlfriend," Todd says, standing up and hugging me. "I knew you were gorgeous, but you look radiant in that dress."

My cheeks blaze. "Thank you."

"Hi again," Clare says, remaining seated but shifting along, no doubt hoping Josh will sit beside her.

"Hi, Clare," I say, sitting down next to her. "Good to see you again."

Josh confirms they're both okay for drinks before sliding in next to Todd. "So how did the rest of the day go at the markets, Clare?"

"I sold out," she replies, with a wide grin on her face. "Plus, I got several additional orders and requests for my business card."

"That's fantastic," Josh says, beaming. "Next stop: world domination."

Clare smiles. "You know I'd be nowhere without you."

"Who am I?" Todd asks, leaning forward and feigning hurt. "Chopped liver?"

"Oh, Toddy. I'd be nowhere without you either, little brother."

Todd shakes his head. "Two minutes." He looks at me and raises his eyebrows. "I'm two minutes younger."

We all laugh and sip our drinks.

"Are you one of Josh's students?" Clare asks, a wicked glint in her eye.

"Geez, Clare," Todd interjects. "They're not in high school. You make it sound so sordid."

"Emerson and I were friends before she started coming to my classes," Josh says, looking directly at me.

Breaking eye contact, I say, "I was meant to go back to the city last night, but my car got a flat tyre and ran out of petrol before I got far."

I'm sure Clare just winked at Josh.

"I invited her to stay to see a bit more of the area," Josh says. "Can you believe she's never been down here before?"

"That is a tragedy," Todd says dramatically. "I love the

city, but you're missing out if you don't get out of the rat race from time to time."

"I'll keep that in mind," I say.

When Josh and Todd go to the bar to order more drinks and some food to share, I'm left with Clare, and I'm certain I'm about to get the third degree about my intentions with Josh.

Sure enough, the second the guys are out of earshot, she starts her inquisition.

"What's going on with you and Josh?"

"What do you mean?" I ask, knowing exactly what she means.

"Josh has never asked any of his students to stay at his place. Ever."

I shrug. "Well I'm honoured to be the first, and it definitely wasn't planned. Honestly, we're just friends."

"But you both want more, right?" she asks, and I can't read her tone.

"Why are you asking?"

She chuckles, shaking her head. "I'm not jealous if that's what you're thinking." She picks at the label on the cider bottle she's holding. "Josh is a really special person, and I'm protective of him is all."

Glancing towards the bar, Josh and Todd are having what looks like an animated conversation. "Have you and Josh dated?" I ask, returning my gaze to her.

She nods. "It was after Todd and I moved down here, and we were spending a lot of time together setting up my candle business." She glances towards the bar, then back at me. "I thought we were going to fall madly in love, get married, and have a bunch of kids." She chuckles, but there's lingering sadness in her eyes.

"What happened?" I ask, rubbing at my chest

"Josh broke up with me saying he didn't feel the same, but he did me a favour in a way."

"He did?" I ask, my heart rate picking up.

"He's searching for someone or something, and I think, deep down, I always knew I would never have been enough." She takes a sip of her cider and sighs. "No one wants to be the consolation prize."

"I'm sorry," I say, hoping it sounds as sincere as I mean it to be. Clare is lovely and warm and was obviously very open to loving Josh. She's the type of woman he deserves but not the woman he seems to want. I'm apologising not just to Clare, but to Josh, too, because what he seems to want can bring him nothing but pain.

She touches my arm. "Oh, please don't apologise. It was years ago now, and I'm over it. I'm honestly so grateful to have him in my life, and seeing the way he looks at you makes me wonder if he's found who he's been looking for."

My cheeks burn, and my skin prickles with discomfort. Before I can say anything in response, the guys return with more drinks and the subject is changed.

The noise level in the pub gets louder with every passing hour. I've just eaten the best fish and chips of my life and laughed harder than I have possibly ever. Todd is hilarious, and it isn't just what he says. It's his delivery. He could read a shopping list and have me in stitches. It might be the wine talking when I tell him I love him.

"Well of course you do, sweetheart," he says, putting his arm around me. "I'm hot, funny, and unattainable."

Throwing my arms around his neck, I agree with him on all three counts. We say our goodbyes, and I realise my inhibitions have decreased as my blood-alcohol level increases. Josh only had the one beer, as he's driving, and I catch him gazing at me throughout the evening whenever I look his way. I can't deny I like the attention and the way his lips curl upwards as our eyes meet. There is a connection between us, and it scares me as much as it excites me.

We remain silent on the drive home, but the steady beat of my heart is deafening. I want him and am beyond caring about the consequences. I want my mind to be silent so my heart can be open to what I think is about to happen.

CHAPTER

26

WHEN WE ENTER the house, he takes my hand and leads me down the hallway. Without hesitating as we pass the room I stayed in last night, I'm led through the door at the end. There are no curtains or blinds, but the house is in a private location, so there isn't any need. I imagine the view across the surrounding fields will be breathtaking in the daylight. My attention is drawn to the king-size bed, and I wonder if I should continue to stand where I am or move toward it. All thoughts are halted when Josh moves behind me and places his hands on my waist.

"Tell me what you want, Emerson," Josh says, his lips grazing against my shoulder.

"I want you," I reply. "I want you so damn much."

"Can I have you?" he asks, so softly I can barely hear him.

It doesn't matter, though. I don't need to hear the words to understand his plea. I can't push him away despite knowing I may not be emotionally prepared to face the consequences of my actions.

He spins me around and pushes me the few steps until the backs of my legs hit the bed. When his lips connect with the sensitive skin of my neck and down my collarbone, I cry out, "Yes."

I feel his whole body tense then relax in a split second before he crashes his lips to mine. The kiss is hungry, urgent, and loaded with sexual frustration. Without breaking our kiss, Josh's hands find the hem of my dress, and my breath hitches when his fingers tickle my bare skin as he pulls it up and over my head. I am on fire for him, and he groans when I grind myself against his erection.

He stops kissing me, but his lips are still touching mine when he says, "You are so beautiful, Emerson."

I don't want him to talk. I want him to make me forget, so I kiss him harder this time, pulling him closer as I lie back on the bed, forcing him on top of me. Fortunately, he gets the hint, putting his hand behind his neck and tugging his T-shirt over his head. My greedy hands roam over his now-shirtless torso, marvelling at the toned muscles I long suspected were hidden beneath his clothes. He has an understated strength I am wildly attracted to, and I allow my mind to go exactly where I don't want it to go for a split second, and I compare him to Mereki. They are so physically similar and they both feel like home to me. It's equally devastating and wondrous.

With my eyes closed, I could be in the arms of the only man I've ever slept with. I revel in it, pulling Josh closer with my hands, my lips, my legs as they open for him and wrap around his butt. I'm trapping him in my web and making no apologies for my insensitivity.

With my lips ravaging his, I push my hands between us and unbuckle his jeans, pushing them and his boxers down to his knees, then kicking them all the way off with my feet.

I'm possessed with need and behaving like a starved, wild animal. This virile, talented, and kind man has no idea he's the lame zebra, caught in the wilds of my messed-up life, and he's about to become my prey.

Josh makes quick work of my bra and underwear, and in a frenzy of hands and flying clothes, we are finally naked and I can feel his need pressing firmly against my stomach.

"Do you have condoms?" I ask, my voice whispered, but my tone laced in desperation.

Josh nods and reaches to his nightstand, opening the drawer to retrieve the square packet. I'm out of character; this is the most reckless thing I've done in my life. I take it from him like the vixen I never knew I could be—like it isn't my first time handling a condom. The last time Ki and I had sex was so long ago, I wonder if there will be cobwebs down there. Ki always used to take care of everything. Not anymore though, and I'll be damned if I'll let Josh take charge now. This is my decision, my reckless one-night stand, and I need to be someone else. I need to be the lioness for a change.

Feeling a surge of power, I push Josh onto his back. His chuckle dies when I glide down his naked body and take him in my mouth. With the death of his laughter comes the birth of primal groaning. I am drunk with power that I'm the one eliciting this reaction from a man. His obvious pleasure gives me reassurance that he's gaining something from this sordid interlude. I'm taking what I want, but I'm also giving him something in return. I just hope it's enough.

When he grows impossibly harder in my mouth, Josh grabs me under the arms, and I'm pulled back up his body.

"I need to be inside you," he says, his eyes dark with lust.

Nodding, I grab the condom from the pillow where I'd left it, rip the packet open with my teeth and roll it down over him with surprising ease. I glance up at Josh and smile. His eyes are closed, and his breaths are ragged. I'm confident he's close to the edge of the cliff, and I can't wait to push him off.

Without hesitation, I straddle him, raising myself higher on my knees to line him up with where I desperately need him to be. Josh's eyes fly open when I sink down just a little, allowing his tip to enter me. Neither of us breathe as I sink, inch by delicious inch. I stop halfway, allowing myself to adjust to his size before my inner voice growls again, and I slam down the rest of the way.

Josh bolts up into a seated position. "Fuck, Emerson! Emerson! Oh my God, Emerson!" He chants my name in a plea that I never stop and a prayer that he hopes I'll answer.

His arms wrap around my waist holding me to him, and his mouth devours my right breast, sucking and nipping like he knows exactly what will drive me insane and wild with lust. When I start to move, he rewards my other breast with equal fervour. Stars form behind my closed eyes, and the pleasure is becoming unbearable.

We fly higher and higher. The stars I was seeing minutes earlier are now a full galaxy of blinding lights. My body is riding him harder and harder, and he's meeting me blow for blow, working me up with every kiss, every suck and every touch, higher and higher.

I'm convinced I'm going to explode, liquefying into a sea of pleasure. *Can you die from this? Is this normal?*

"I'm gonna come," Josh says on a low groan. "Come with me, baby."

I can't respond with words. I don't even think I can speak anymore. I don't push him off the cliff. I'm just one big ball of sensation and, with one final grind of my hips and one more thrust of his, I hold his hand and leap off into the darkness.

Eventually, the aftershocks subside and we hold each other, unwilling to pull apart after such a powerful experience. I climb off and lie down next to him. My breathing is still uneven, so I close my eyes and focus on drawing in oxygen. I hear him moving about, and the bed raises as he gets up. Moments later, he returns to the bed and climbs in, lying next to me. Opening my eyes, I turn on my side to face him, desperately hoping this isn't going to be awkward.

"That was . . ." He stops, and I wonder if he's having trouble verbalising just how incredible it was.

"I know." Whatever it is he's thinking, we're on the same page.

"I've never . . ." Again, he can't finish his sentence.

"Me neither."

"You were . . ."

"You were, too." I say, smiling, a little incredulous that this is so comfortable and perfectly intimate.

I glance over at the clock—an exact replica of the one in the room I slept in. "What's with the time painter?"

Josh chuckles. "It's an app. Luca sucks me into all these crazy things. The developer made the video of the old woman painting, then it's run to keep perfect time. I can't tell you how much time I've wasted watching her."

"I can imagine."

We're both lying on his bed facing each other, grinning like idiots. What do I do now, though? I really want to take a shower, but do I go back to the spare room and stay there or do I use his en-suite then assume I'm sharing his bed? *Oh my God.*

"Your eyes are so expressive," Josh says, interrupting my internal chaos. "I could see the moment you stopped just relaxing and enjoying the aftermath and started fretting about something." He raises an eyebrow and pushes the hair that's fallen across my face behind my ear. "I'm guessing you're wondering if you should stay in here with me tonight or go back to the spare room." He narrows his eyes, obviously thinking he's super smart.

"Actually," I say, "I was also wondering which shower I should use." I seem to be an open book to this man and am quietly pleased he cares so much to read me.

"Use my shower." He kisses my lips briefly. "Then stay with me here."

"Are you sure?" I ask, rolling my eyes at my own stupid question. Of course he's sure. Why wouldn't he be? We just had the most incredible sex, and he's probably warming up for round two in the shower, then maybe he's into morning sex. He probably thinks this is the start of something between us, and I've given him no reason to think otherwise.

After proving there was more than enough room for two in his shower, Josh falls into a deep sleep seconds after saying goodnight, completely sated. I, on the other hand, am wide awake, alone with my guilt and tormented thoughts.

The day was too perfect.

Josh was too perfect.

I am a monster.

Unable to sleep with my demons ravaging my mind, I eventually give up. Trying to switch off, I've watched my little old lady friend in the clock paint hours' worth of minutes. She has just completed one fifteen, and I feel no closer to sleep than I did when Josh nodded off. I decide to get up and walk around a bit. Maybe I'll go outside and try to quiet my mind.

After pulling my clothes back on, I tiptoe through the

silent house. When I step outside, Leroy comes out of his kennel to join me, and I'm actually grateful for his company.

Despite the late hour, the full moon gives me decent visibility. The lake is eerily beautiful in the soft light. An owl hoots, breaking the silence that I find so incredibly peaceful. The serenity reminds me of the time spent by the river with Mereki back in our home town.

I walk down the path to the water's edge. Mist rises from the lake, and I'm struck by the idea that this could be a scene from a murder thriller movie.

When I stop and stare out across the still water, every single emotion I've managed to push away for the past twenty-four hours comes flying to the surface. I'm overcome with the need to cry, and before I know it, I'm sinking to my knees and sobbing uncontrollably.

I have no idea how long I cry for, but when I have no tears left, I push myself back to standing and wipe my face with the sleeves of my shirt. I feel Josh's presence before he reaches me, but I don't turn to acknowledge him. I don't want him to see my puffy, tear-streaked face.

"What are you doing out here?" Josh asks, closing the distance so he's right in front of me. "I woke up and you were gone."

I drag my gaze away from the tranquillity of the lake and into the hurricane raging in his eyes. Instead of looking away, I fall into the eye of the storm. "I couldn't sleep."

He cocks his head. "Want to tell me why you were crying?" The look of hurt across his face is painful to see.

I drop my gaze to my feet and push back the memories taunting me from the sidelines of my mind. I sway on my feet, feeling lightheaded. I count in my head to regain my equilibrium. *Ten, nine, eight, seven, six . . .*

"Are you okay?" Josh asks, reaching for my arm. His eyes are wide with what looks like panic. "You're scaring me, Emerson."

I snap at him, ripping my arm away. "I just need you to leave me alone."

"Don't you dare say you regret what happened between us," he says in a surprisingly gentle tone. "I won't believe you, so I need to know what's going on and try to help you if I can."

"And what if I don't want to be helped?" Tears prick my eyes again, but I hold his gaze. "I don't regret what happened between us, but it can't happen again."

"Your eyes tell me a different story." His voice is calm and even.

I turn away. "My story is camouflaged, and you're only seeing what you want to see."

"Jesus, Emerson. I really don't get you at all sometimes. One moment you're taking control in the bedroom and the next you're shutting down. I'm worried if I say or do the wrong thing, you'll break into a million pieces, and I won't know how to put you back together."

Frustrated, I find myself shouting at him. "You're just someone who plays around with paint telling vulnerable sad sacks that 'expressing yourself through art,'" I say that with air quotes to drive my insult home, "will help heal them." I poke my finger hard into his chest. I know I'm lashing out, but I can't help myself. "And you know what?"

Josh takes a step back and crosses his arms over his chest. "What?"

"You're not a shrink, and it's all a load of bullshit."

He shouts and I jump. "Then tell me why you showed up to three classes if it was such a waste of your precious time!"

Without considering my words, I let them spill out. "Because I was lost and so fucking lonely." Tears slip down my cheeks. I hadn't even realised the truth in my words until I heard them said in my own voice.

Silence settles between us, and neither of us breaks eye contact. There is power, adrenaline, relief, and sadness passing back and forth between us. I can hear my heavy breaths thundering in my ears, and I know my chest is rising and falling as oxygen calms me.

Eventually Josh breaks the silence. "It's okay, Emerson." He closes the distance between us and wraps his arms around me. "I'm here."

The tears spill free as I rest my cheek against his hard chest, cocooned in his strong embrace. I'm embarrassed by my admission, but it felt cathartic. I trust Josh, and trust is not something I thought I'd ever feel with someone other than Mereki. Perhaps we found each other for a reason, and this man is allowed to be important to me. Deep down, I know I'm not a terrible person. The time I've spent with Josh has been like therapy, and it was horribly wrong of me to say otherwise. However, I know that if I care for him at all, I'll leave him alone. I need to work out my own life and complications before I drag him down any further.

"I can't come to your classes anymore," I say, pulling back from his now-soaked shirt. "I'm sorry for what I said before. I think what you're doing with your art is a beautiful thing. It's just . . ."

"That's crazy," Josh says. "You're unblocking your mind and your creativity. You can't stop now." He cups my chin with his right and tips my face up to meet his gaze. "And anyway, I'd miss you."

"I'll think about it," I say, giving him a small smile as he swipes the tears from my cheeks with his thumbs. "But no promises."

"At some stage, you need to tell me why you were crying out here all alone in the middle of the night, because I know it didn't have anything to do with what happened earlier." He gives me a small smile, and my heart aches in acknowledgement that it was the best sex of my life. *How can that even be true?* "I care about you, and I think you need to tell someone what is going on in that head of yours."

I take a deep breath, then let it out slowly. "It was years ago, and I've not spoken about it since."

"Maybe you haven't surrounded yourself with the right people then if they can't see there's a part of you that's broken and tried to help you heal."

He has no idea why his words are so crushing because I've hidden the most important part of me from him. I've hidden Mereki—my love, my life, my heart.

I shiver, and Josh places his arm around my shoulders. "Come on. Let's get you back inside."

Reluctantly, I allow him to walk me back to the house and back to his bed. I allow him to spoon me, and I allow myself the reprieve of feeling safe and wanted. After our brief talk by the lake, I feel a small amount of weight has been lifted from my shoulders. Closing my eyes and clasping Josh's hand in mine, I drift off to sleep. For the first time in five years, I don't suffer through my recurring nightmare where I replay what happened that horrible night. In fact, I don't think I dream at all.

CHAPTER

27

WAKING UP IN Josh's arms, I mentally dust off the cobwebs of my sleepy brain to assess my feelings. I should be devastated, or at least more ashamed and guilty than I am. I can't let this go any further, but for now, I snuggle closer, revel in his warmth and go back to sleep.

He shifts behind me sometime later and begins feathering kisses across the back of my neck, pushing the shirt he gave me to wear off my shoulder. I turn over to face him, pulling the shirt back up. "Morning."

"How did you sleep, beautiful?" He leans forward to kiss me, but I pull back, putting my hand over my mouth.

"Morning breath," I say. It's not a deflection technique because it's a completely legitimate concern.

He pulls my hand away and kisses me quickly before I have a chance to stop him. "I care about kissing you far more than morning breath."

"Josh," I say, pushing my palm into his bare chest, eliciting a laugh from him. "You're so weird."

I shuffle out of bed and use his bathroom. When I return, Josh is sitting up in bed.

I can't get back in that bed with him. My traitorous body wants another round of mind-blowing sex, but I've made up my mind not to let him be dragged down any further with me. I need to get back to the city and keep my distance while I work out what's going on with Ki. "I'm going to go find my jeans," I say, grabbing my dress and underwear from the floor and shuffle out of the room before he has a chance to make me change my mind.

When I'm showered and dressed, I find him in the kitchen making coffee. He's wearing a pair of baggy shorts that sit low on his hips. He's shirtless, and my mouth waters at the glorious sight. I curse my damned existence where walking up to him and slipping my arms around his waist, knowing it would be welcomed, is cruel and dragging out the inevitable.

Despite me not making a sound, Josh turns to face me and smiles. He has a smile that penetrates the wall around my heart, but Mereki is the foundation for that wall and Josh is calling its integrity into question.

"Feeling better?" he asks, turning back to finish making the coffee.

"I am. Thank you." I take a seat at the island bench and rest my chin in my hands, resting my elbows on the counter top. "I think I should get going soon."

Josh's shoulders slump slightly, and he shakes his head. When he turns, he's holding two steaming mugs, and his expression is serious. "What's the hurry? Nothing is open today, and you don't have to work." He places the coffee down in front of me and remains on the other side of the bench.

"This has been great," I reply, looking at my coffee rather than him. "I just-"

"I thought we were getting somewhere, especially after last night." There is a note of anger or maybe just frustration in his voice, and I can't blame him.

Do I tell him the truth now? Do I tell him my heart has always belonged to someone else? Do I tell him I am damaged beyond repair? Do I owe him an explanation at all? All these questions whirl around in my mind as I stare at the steam rising from my mug.

"Can you look at me, please?" he asks.

I drag my eyes up to his. Instead of feeling guilt and shame, I feel angry at him for even temporarily breaking down my carefully constructed wall of ice. In some small, rational part of my brain, I acknowledge he is innocent in his pursuit, but rationale doesn't always play a role in matters of the heart. Why did he have to be so goddamned irresistible to my fragile, attention-starved body and mind? Then I realise I'm not actually angry at Josh. I'm angry at Mereki for so many things, but mostly, I'm angry at him for leaving me. Seething, boiling, enraged, out-of-my-mind angry.

I drink my coffee quickly, scalding the roof of my mouth and burning my tongue. I want the caffeine injection, then I need to get the hell out of here, away from Josh and any further temptation. When my cup is empty and my mind is made up, I push back from the bench and stand. "I need to go."

"What?" Josh asks, throwing his hands in the air. "What the fuck is going on?"

"I . . . I . . ." I can't get the words out as I stumble backwards, causing the stool to scrape across the floor.

Josh storms around the bench and grabs my elbow. I pull away, but his grasp is firm. Until now, he's been nothing but kind, gentle, and considerate, but I've obviously pushed him over the edge I didn't even know was there. His eyes are narrowed, and the veins in his neck throb. He is intimidating, and fear pulses through me as the night I was attacked comes rushing to the forefront of my mind. I was held down by a man physically dominant over me while life as I knew it slipped away.

"Please let go of me," I say, pleading with him to acknowledge my fear.

He drops my arm as if I'm on fire. "I'm sorry." He takes a step back and swallows hard. "Please don't look at me like that."

"Like what?" I ask, holding on by a thread.

"Like you think I'm going to hurt you."

"I don't think you're going to hurt me." I pause to take a deep breath. "But I don't want to hurt you anymore." I wrap my arms around myself protectively.

"I don't know what that means. Last night meant something to me, Emerson, and I don't know what has changed since then." He runs one of his hands through his hair, then scrubs his face. He is frustrated, and he has every right to be.

"I didn't mean for this to happen, Josh." My anger has subsided, replaced with the need to end this with as little damage as possible. "I shouldn't have come out here, and I certainly shouldn't have stayed as long as I did. I should've called roadside assistance to sort out my car."

"Then why didn't you?"

"Because for the first time in a long time, I wanted someone to know me as more than just the cupcake girl or whatever other title I take on for a few months at a time."

"I thought we went through this last night by the lake. We found each other. Was that not a breakthrough that led to a connection the likes of which I didn't know existed? Was I the only one who thought that?"

I shake my head. "I was there, too, but . . ." I have to tell him, but I don't want to suffer the consequences. As selfish as it is, I don't want to lose him from my life.

"Go on."

I swallow hard, knowing I must deliver the killer blow. I should just come out and say I can't be with him because my heart and soul belong to someone else and that I'm so sorry for everything, but the words won't come. Tears slip down my cheeks. I don't even try to stop them or wipe them away. I want Josh to see how sorry I am for letting him feel something for me. I look up at him through wet lashes. "You deserve so much more than this."

"I don't even know what that means. I want you, Emerson. I want all of you, and I thought we were building something real." He reaches for me, but I take a step back. "Don't run away from this. Stay and talk to me."

Is this what I want? Is Josh *who* I want? The way my heart feels like it's being torn is both devastating and liberating. Mereki has pulled away from me for years, and I've fought it tooth and nail. It feels good to have someone want me for a change. Someone is fighting for me to stay, and it feels . . . it feels so good.

We continue to stare at each other until eventually, I can't take it anymore. With furrowed brows, limp limbs, and an ache in my chest I didn't even know was possible, I take what might possibly be my first honest step towards this beautiful man and hope desperately he will try to understand what I still need to tell him.

Josh wraps his arms around me and kisses the top of my head. "Thank you."

"Your driveway is a nightmare," a man's friendly voice

calls out from somewhere.

Spinning in Josh's arms, I come face-to-face with a man who so strongly resembles Josh, it simply must be one of his brothers.

"Luca," Josh says, holding me tightly against him. "What are you doing here?"

"Sorry for crashing in on you." Luca winks at me before turning to Josh. "I'm on my way back from Tom's bachelor weekend. I told you I'd stop in."

"Sorry, mate. I completely forgot."

Luca looks at me then back at Josh, raising his eyebrows, obviously waiting for an introduction.

"Sorry." Josh releases me, and I step forward. "Luca, this is Emerson."

"Ah. Emerson." He holds out his hand and I shake it, trying to hide the emotion I am feeling. "It's great to meet you. I've heard a lot about you."

My gaze snaps to Josh, then back to Luca. "You have?"

I can't deny the butterflies fluttering in my belly or the wide grin on my face that is impossible to rein in.

"Josh here told us about you at a family lunch last weekend."

"Shut up, Luca," Josh demands, but there's laughter in his voice. "Emerson doesn't want to hear about that."

"Don't be silly," Luca says, putting his arm around me. "I want to get to know the first girl my brother has ever voluntarily told his whole family about."

He ushers me to the lounge room and essentially forces me to sit down. I should be wishing Josh and I were still alone so I could have the hard conversation with him, but I am grateful for Luca's upbeat personality and welcome the distraction.

"How was the party?" Josh asks, probably trying to change the subject.

"Another one bites the dust. It was fun, but I couldn't help feeling like it was death row for him."

"You like who he's marrying?"

Luca faces me. "I work with Tom. He's a bit on the crazy side but a decent guy. Never met the bride-to-be, but she sounds like a looney tune to me." He rolls his eyes. "She called him about a hundred times over the weekend. Full clingy-psycho behaviour if you ask me."

"Did Tom mind?" Josh asks, chuckling.

Luca shrugs. "I think he's scared of her to be honest."

"Oh hey. Do you want something to eat?" Josh asks. "Bit of grease for the morning after?"

"Bring it on, mate." Luca rubs his stomach.

Josh disappears into the kitchen, leaving Luca and me alone.

"You and Joshy, huh?" Luca asks, smiling warmly.

"I can't believe he told you about me."

"He showed up to our family lunch last Saturday with a big bunch of flowers for Mum and a bigger smile." He taps the side of his head. "We all knew something was up."

I swallow hard, unsure if I want him to keep going, but I remain silent.

"It's a family tradition our father started," Luca continues. "That before we start a meal as a family, we each say the best thing that's happened to us since the last time we were all together."

I raise my eyebrows, knowing what he's going to say before he says it.

"He said you. He said Emerson Hart was the best thing to happen to him."

My heart clenches with the agony of knowing I could really hurt Josh if I'm unable to explain everything to him and make him understand.

Needing a moment to compose myself, I say, "Sorry, Luca. I just have to use the bathroom and pack up my things."

"No prob. I'll go annoy Josh in the kitchen then."

I leap up and scurry off to the spare bedroom to gather my purchases from the markets and use the bathroom, determined to pull myself together.

I stare at my reflection in the mirror and smile. It isn't a big smile, and it barely reaches my eyes, but for someone who hasn't been able to properly look at her own reflection for five years, it feels monumental. I had thought Mereki was my forever person, but life doesn't always work out the way you think it will. Sometimes life throws you curve balls, and sometimes, like in my case, a giant crater opens up in front of you and gives you a swift shove in the back so you plummet into its depths. I've spent enough time wallowing in the dark, and I'm now ready to clamber up the steep slope back to the light. Josh has made me see another path for my life, and I'm ready to travel it.

When I return down the hallway, I stop short when I hear Luca and Josh talking in the kitchen.

"She came here with my other art students on Saturday, and she had car trouble, so ended up staying two nights," I hear Josh say.

"Wow. So, she's artsy. Tick. And she obviously wanted to stay out here with you because she conveniently had car trouble," he says. *He thinks I made that up!* "And she's definitely a looker. I'm really happy for you, Joshy."

"I know this is going to sound crazy, but I think I'm in love with her."

I slap my palm over my mouth to stifle my gasp. There is silence between them for a few moments, and I'm envisaging Luca's face scrunched up as if he's simultaneously tasted and smelled something repugnant.

"I know," Josh says, responding to whatever Luca's expression conveyed. "It sounds too soon, but I feel like I've known her for much longer than I have, and there's just something really special about her."

"Ugh. I knew this would happen with you," Luca says. "As soon as you found her, you'd fall hook, line, and sinker."

"I didn't even know who I was looking for until she turned up on Mum's doorstep. I feel like I've known her for a whole lot longer than that."

I clear my throat before venturing back into the kitchen.

Both Josh and Luca snap their gazes to me.

"How long were you standing there?" Josh asks, guilt and possibly fear on his face.

"Not long." *Long enough.*

"Josh was just singing your praises. He says you're an amazing artist."

I smile, meeting Josh's gaze. "Thank you."

"Well, I'm going to hit the road," Luca says, picking up the egg and bacon roll Josh has made for him. "I've got a conference call this evening, and I have some prep to do."

"I'll catch up with you this week sometime," Josh says, patting him on the back.

"It was lovely to meet you," I say.

"You too, Emerson." He kisses my cheek. "Maybe I'll see

you at the next family lunch."

"Sure," I say, awkwardly.

Luca laughs. "No pressure. We're a laidback bunch of idiots."

"Nice," Josh says, shaking his head.

We all walk outside together, then Luca climbs into his silver Ferrari and disappears down the driveway in a cloud of dust.

"I like your brother," I say when the dust settles, and we turn back to the house.

"He's alright," Josh replies, touching his hand to the small of my back.

When he closes the door behind us, he is on me in a flash, kissing me hard and ripping my shirt over my head. "I want you," he says between kisses. "I need you right now."

Unable to think straight, I nod. With a groan, he pushes my jeans and underwear down my legs, then deftly unhooks my bra, letting it join my clothes on the floor. He crushes his body to mine and my back hits the door. I can feel his hard erection grinding against me, and it's driving me wild with lust.

"Are you on birth control?" he asks, his lips almost touching mine.

I nod again. "I'm on the pill."

"Do you mind if we don't use a condom?" he asks, his breathing ragged. "My last girlfriend cheated on me, so I got myself tested after we broke up. I'm clean."

I'm not cheating, I tell myself. Mereki and I have been over for a while now, and I plan to let him go. I'm confident that's what he wants anyway. I don't know why I hadn't seen that before now. My heart will never be the same, but right now, this feels so right, and I need something to feel right for a change.

I push his shorts down to his ankles, and he kicks them off his feet. He isn't wearing any underwear, so we are now both completely naked, staring into each other's lust-filled eyes. "Take me, Josh," I say, holding his face in my hands and pulling his mouth to mine.

He picks me up and my back hits the door. With my legs wrapped around his waist, he thrusts into me in one fluid motion. I tip my head back and welcome the intense sensations that dull every thought other than how good he feels filling me up completely. Josh is the missing puzzle piece I found when I wasn't looking.

We both climax quickly, releasing the built-up tension of the earlier conversation and the intense weekend. I stay wrapped around him while he carries me back to his bedroom. I don't want to let him go yet, and it certainly doesn't feel like he wants to let me go. When we've cleaned up in the bathroom, we lie on his bed, still naked, facing each other.

"There's something I need to tell you," I say, taking a deep breath.

"You can tell me anything," he whispers, running his hand along my arm and the dip of my waist, then placing his whole hand over my backside.

We're so close, and his warm breath tickles my face. I could get lost in him far too easily; I must find a way to speak to him openly.

"I think I can explain why you feel like you've known me for a lot longer than just this year."

He nods. "I can't explain it, but I felt a strong connection to you from that first moment. It was as if I already knew you, as crazy as that sounds."

I close my eyes briefly. "In a way, you did."

"What do you mean?" He props himself up on his elbow.

"Madeleine gave you a drawing five years ago."

His eyes widen, and his bottom lip drops. "What about it?"

I break eye contact and focus on the very interesting pattern the light makes on the ceiling.

"What about it, Emerson?" Josh's voice sounds strained, and I meet his gaze again.

"I met Madeleine five years ago when I was selling my art for the first time at a market stall back in my hometown."

Josh bolts up, throwing his legs over the side of the bed and pushing his palms against his knees. "It's your drawing," he says, nodding.

I crawl across the bed and kneel behind him, running my hands tentatively over his back and shoulders before hugging him from behind. I want him to be okay with this. I whisper in his ear, "I left a big piece of me on that paper, and you've been holding it ever since."

His shoulders sag, but his hands grip mine against his chest. "I think I already knew that."

"I think you did, too." I kiss his shoulder, pressing my breasts into the taut muscles of his back. "I think you saw me in that drawing, and you've been waiting for me ever since."

"What took you so long?" he whispers, picking up my right hand and placing his lips to my palm. "Five years." He kisses my palm, then pulls me around and onto his lap. "I've waited for five long years without even knowing it."

"I have so much to explain." I look into his eyes, and what I see now has changed. There is a whole new level of emotion swirling around, and I am falling.

"That drawing changed my life," he says, and I wonder if it's painful memories etching lines into his forehead. "It helped me through a really dark time, and it started a chain of events that brought you to me."

"Where is it?" I ask in a confident voice, surprising myself with how calm I feel.

"At Mum's place."

"You gave it to her?"

"I saw light overcoming darkness in your drawing. It helped me, and I wanted it to help her, too. She plunged into darkness when Dad died, and I was convinced she was going to die from a broken heart."

"Did it help her?" I ask, shocked by the idea of my own personal journey helping others.

He nods, nuzzling into my neck. "My brothers and I have our mum."

"She's still grieving though," I say, thinking back to her vacant stares and red-rimmed eyes as she spoke of her lost love.

Josh pulls back and looks me in the eye. "And she'll grieve forever, but it doesn't consume her whole existence anymore." His smile is sad, but his eyes are light. "I like to think you showed her a way back."

Something Mereki once said to me springs into my head, and I'm choked with emotion.

You're my shining light whenever the world is dark. Never let your light die because it's going to brighten more than just my world.

"I have so much more to tell you, Josh." I now know my own world is shifting and that Mereki was never my compass. I need to move out from the shadows and shine again in my own right.

Josh's right arm slips under my legs and scoops me up and

onto the bed where I find myself lying on my back before him. Pushing my legs apart, he kneels between them.

"Can it wait?" he asks, his eyes hooded and blazing with love. He grips my ankles and pushes back so my knees are bent and I'm completely open to him. I don't feel vulnerable or embarrassed. I feel ready to let him bask in my body again.

"It can wait," I say, groaning as he kisses me from my knees, down my thighs to the most sensitive part of me.

"Oh my God, Josh," I say, panting out his name as he takes me in his mouth, licking and sucking me with expert precision. My hips buck, and my head snaps back into the covers when his tongue flicks the bundle of nerves, shooting fireworks throughout my writhing body. I am open and completely vulnerable, but I feel safe and cared for. He is focused solely on my pleasure, and I'm taking everything he has to give me.

While the waves continue to crash, and I'm awash with ecstasy the likes of which I've never known before, Josh moves up my body and enters me. My eyes snap open as the new sensations take over. I am filled with him, crushed by him in the best possible way, and I wrap my legs around him, forcing him deeper, harder, faster.

"Look at me," he says, propped up on his elbows on either side of my head. He uses both his hands to push my hair back from my face, then he leaves them there, cupping my cheeks. "Feel me deep inside you."

I stare into his clear, green eyes and smile. "I feel all of you."

He thrusts again, and I raise my hips to meet him. "You are so beautiful, Emerson."

I accept the compliment with a languid smile, drugged with pleasure, but managing to somehow maintain eye contact. I run my hands down his back and over his tight backside. His physique is breathtaking, but the way he's consuming my entire being at this moment is more than just physical. I've missed being this close to a man, skin to skin. We're no longer driven entirely by lust, and I feel connected to him in every way possible.

"This has been an incredible weekend, Josh," I say when we're facing each other, revelling in our post-coital bliss. "Thank you."

He kisses me lightly on the lips. "I should be thanking you for running out of petrol."

I cringe. I hate feeling like a damsel in distress, but I have to admit, it set off a chain of events that led me into Josh's arms. "I wonder if this would've happened regardless."

"Of course it would." He waves a hand between us. "This was inevitable."

I wonder if what happened days after my eighteenth birthday was inevitable, too.

Before I can get too lost down the vortex, Josh gets up and heads for the door. I roll onto my tummy, propping myself on my elbows and resting my chin in my hands. It gives me the perfect vantage point to admire a very naked Josh walking away. The show is over far too quickly, but he returns less than a minute later holding all our clothes.

"I am one hundred percent on board with you staying naked, just so you know."

Rolling my eyes then smiling, I flip my legs over the side of the bed and reach for my clothes. "Good try," I say, chuckling. "I really need to get going now."

Josh takes my hand as he walks me to my car.

"Will you call me to let me know you got home safe?" he asks, holding me against him as if he might never let me go.

I nod against his chest. It feels like an incredible relief to embrace something real. I've spent too many years battling my past.

As I drive away, I wonder how or when I'm ever going to tell Josh the truth.

CHAPTER

28

IT'S BEEN TWO days since I left Josh's house, and I miss him more than I could've imagined and certainly more than I should. I miss having his arms around me and our bodies moving together. I hadn't realised how alone I'd really been.

I haven't spoken to Mereki, and it's better that way. I need to stop craving him like a drug-addicted junkie, always looking for another hit. I am on the right road now, and it's time to set him free, too. I know it will be the hardest thing I'll ever have to do, but regardless of what we are or aren't, we owe it to each other to part ways properly. I will keep my promise to be at our place by the river four days after my birthday, and I know he will, too. I've held onto him too tightly and I see that now.

"There's someone here to see you, Emerson," Carrie says as I pull a tray of cupcakes from the oven.

My heart seizes, hoping Josh has arrived in the city early but knowing it's unlikely. He told me on the phone last night he had plans with Todd this afternoon and would pick me up after work for an early dinner before class. I hope it isn't awkward for him to have me in his class given what transpired between us over the weekend, because I want to be there for the art as well as for him.

"Who is it?" I ask.

"Madeleine Gibson from the gallery down the road. She's having a coffee on one of the outside tables, and she asked for you." In an uncharacteristically friendly tone, Carrie adds, "It's quiet, so why don't you just finish up now and join her?"

"Okay, thanks." I remove my apron, grab my bag from the shelf, and go through to the shopfront to meet Madeleine.

"I hope you don't mind me stopping by when you're at work," she says when she looks up and sees me. "I was just hoping we could have a quick chat."

"Carrie said I can finish up now, so I'm all yours," I reply, taking a seat opposite her. "What's up?"

"I don't really know how to say this," she says, shifting awkwardly in her chair.

Her tone puts me on edge, and I swallow hard. "What's wrong?" Then my stomach clenches. "Is Josh okay?" I don't know why I ask her that, but they are friends and maybe something happened, and she is about to break some awful news to me. Tears prick my eyes, and I start to shake.

Her eyes are swimming with turmoil. "Josh is fine. This does involve him though."

I shake my head. "Please tell me what's going on. You're kinda scaring me."

She meets my gaze. "You told him about your drawing."

I nod. "I did. How did you know?"

"Josh called me today wanting to talk about your art."

I sit up straighter, not liking where this is going.

"He wants to help you, Emerson."

"I never asked for his help."

She holds her hands up in front of her. "I know you didn't, and I don't think you ever will." She raises an eyebrow. "But I've never heard him so passionate about anyone before."

"I'm only just finding my passion for art again." I cringe at my words. "I hope that doesn't sound ungrateful, but this is all a bit overwhelming."

"I'm not going to help unless you ask me directly. You're an adult, and I think there's a very good reason why you gave it up in the first place. But that's not exactly what I came here to talk about."

"Oh," I say, clenching my teeth.

"Josh is like a son to me, Emerson. I know he has romantic feelings for you, and I'm worried he's going to get his heart broken."

I open my mouth to speak, then close it again.

"Why doesn't he know you have a boyfriend?" she asks in a stern tone.

My head snaps up as my past crashes head-on into my present. "What?" My mind runs at a million miles an hour.

"You told me Mereki is here in Melbourne, so why does Josh think he stands a chance with you?"

Mustering the only shred of calm I have left, I say, "I'm really not sure this is any of your business, but Mereki and I have been over for a long time now."

"Don't let Josh be your rebound. He deserves more than that." She leans forward and takes my hands in hers. "Tell him the truth, Emerson. It will set you both free."

I nod, now realising that I will have to tell Josh about

Mereki sooner rather than later or Madeleine will. But how will I tell him? *What* will I tell him? "I don't want to break his heart, Madeleine. I care about him, and I'm in unchartered territory."

"That's all very well, but both Mereki and Josh deserve the truth."

I glance at my watch. "I'll tell him." I wrinkle my nose. "Soon."

She stands, smiling. "Good. I think you and Josh could make a lovely couple. I'm sorry it hasn't worked out with that handsome boy, Mereki, though. I only met him that one time, but there was something about him that I've never forgotten. It was like he was an old soul, and he was clearly besotted with you. I'm not surprised you're having trouble letting him go for whatever reason, but you've found another amazing man in Josh." She hugs me, then pulls back to look me directly in the eyes. "You're a lucky girl, Emerson Hart."

Lucky. Am I lucky? I give her a sad smile because I don't have the mental fortitude for anything more.

"Good luck, sweetheart," she says, placing her hand on my shoulder before floating away with her trademark grace. There really is something strangely ethereal about the woman.

I sit on my own for a few more minutes before deciding I need to walk for a while to clear my head. I am rattled by the conversation I had with Madeleine, but at the same time, I feel brave and ready to make a change.

Turning left, then left again, I make my way along the tree-lined street. I pull my phone out and send a text to Josh telling him I finished early and will meet him at his mum's house instead of at work. Josh had suggested we have dinner there as it's walking distance to the gallery, and there really aren't any restaurants close by other than very fancy ones that don't offer a quick, casual bite at six in the evening.

After taking the long way, I make my way up Sarah's path. She's at her friend's house, so I sit on her tiled steps and wait. My phone beeps, alerting me to a text.

Josh Holland: *On my way. Spare key under the black flowerpot next to the front door. See you soon. I'll bring dinner. X*

The swarm of butterflies that took up residence in my stomach the day I met Josh take flight. I'm not sure if it's the casual ease of the message or the kiss at the end. Perhaps it's a combination. The man makes me feel alive, and when you know what it feels like to be a breathing corpse, you want to hold on to that feeling. You want to hold on to it and never let go.

Me: *Thanks. I'll let myself in. x*

Is tonight the right time to tell him about Mereki? Perhaps I can play it by ear given he has a class to teach and see how it pans out. Is this cowardice or thoughtfulness? I have no idea, but what I do know is I don't want to hurt this beautiful man who has been nothing but the perfect gentleman, unaware of my situation or inner turmoil. That must change, and it must be me who enlightens him. If he hears it from anyone other than me, we stand no chance of a future together. But the only person who knows my past and present is Madeleine, and she was kind enough to warn me. And she was right. I had my head in the sand hoping I could muddle my way to the day Mereki and I would say goodbye.

Lucky. The word Madeleine used to describe me is on repeat in my head. Despite growing up with an uncaring, distant mother and a cruel stepbrother, I do feel lucky. I've developed my own resilience to outside forces beyond my control, I've found my own art, and "lucky" sounds like the biggest understatement to describe how I felt about meeting Mereki. The unparalleled friendship, the unwavering support, the beautiful stories, the love. Without him, I was a resilient warrior. With him, I was more. I discovered what it means to be loved. I discovered what it means to truly love someone with all your heart and soul.

Despite preparing myself over the coming weeks to say goodbye to him, I believe our love is unconditional. We will love each other forever, and there is a big part of me that is fearful for myself and for Josh that you can only love like that once. Josh has made me feel again, and that has given me so much hope. That fateful day five years ago ripped Mereki and me apart, and it was stupid of me to believe he'd stay when he needed to go.

Swiping a few rogue tears off my cheeks, I stand and retrieve the spare key from under the pot where Josh had told me it would be. Once I let myself in, I lean against the door for a few beats. Memories of the day I delivered cupcakes come flooding back. I was awestruck by Monet's painting hanging above the hall table.

Oh my God. My drawing is within these walls somewhere. Imagine if I'd seen it that day. I'm paralysed by the idea that it's somewhere close right now.

I make my way down the hallway to the kitchen where I've been before and drop my bag on the island bench. Looking around, I decide to wait for Josh outside where I can't accidentally come across my drawing. I know it's just a piece of paper, but it holds so much significance, both good and bad. I don't know how I'll react to seeing it again in the family home of the man I'm falling in love with.

Sitting down at the outdoor table, I contemplate my

feelings for Josh. Am I falling in love with him? Am I *already* in love with him? I shake my head, hoping to jostle the scattered pieces of my mind into some kind of manageable chaos. I can't think like this. I need to say goodbye to Mereki once and for all before I can give myself fully to Josh. If I thought I could stay away from Josh until such time, I would. But I don't want to stay away from him now that I've felt his lips on mine, his hands on my body, and his eyes stripping my shield. Instead of seeing broken pieces, he sees the warrior within.

The front door closes and the butterflies take flight again.

"Emerson?" Josh's voice calls out down the hallway.

I stand and walk back inside. "In the kitchen," I reply.

He appears seconds later, and the moment our eyes meet, I suck in a breath. He is so incredibly handsome in ripped jeans, a plain, brown T-shirt, and with his dark blond hair tied back in a short ponytail. All these superficial traits pale in insignificance to his smile reaching his emerald eyes as he closes the distance between us, barely pausing to deposit the takeaway food bags on the benchtop.

He stops directly in front of me and tucks a few loose strands of my hair behind my ears. I'm like a deer in the headlights, unable to move or respond, thanks to a heady combination of intoxicating lust, deep fear, and relief that he wants me.

Holding my face in his hands, he whispers, "I've missed you."

I smile. A genuine upturn of my mouth that gives him the green light to take what he now believes is his.

His kiss is soft at first. Our closed mouths meet in a sweet reunion of past intimacy but with the excitement of new lovers. I wrap my arms around his neck at the same time his tongue seeks entry to my mouth. When I grant it, he groans, placing one hand on the back of my head to pull me impossibly closer to him. I'm crazed with lust for this gorgeous man who has held a part of me close for the past five years and is working on the rest of me piece by piece. I wonder how he'll feel when I tell him there will always be a piece missing.

With that depressing thought, I pull back and whisper, "I missed you, too." It is the truth, and I promise myself right then and there that Josh will only get honesty from me from this point forward.

He kisses me once more lightly. "How are you?" he asks. "And more importantly, did you bring me any cupcakes?"

I scrunch up my face. "Oh, I'm so sorry. I forgot." I had selected the ones I know are Josh's favourites but hadn't taken them with me when Madeleine asked to see me.

"I can think of something else I'd rather for dessert anyway." He winks, chuckling to himself.

I roll my eyes. "How cliché of you, Mr Holland."

"Cliché?" He gasps in mock horror. "You can accuse me of many things, Ms Hart, but cliché is not one of them."

I move next to him and nudge his arm with my shoulder. "I never said you were cliché. I said that cheesy line was."

"I'm kidding." He kisses the top of my head, then proceeds to divide the takeaway between two plates. "Red or white wine?"

"White, please," I reply, moving over to the open shelves where I spied the upturned wine glasses on display.

It's turned a bit too cold to eat outside, so I follow Josh into the dining room. It feels far too formal for takeaway and ripped jeans.

"My lady," Josh says, pulling out one of the twelve

covered seats from the long, dark wooden table.

"Why thank you, kind sir," I reply, chuckling at his over-the-top chivalry. I can't deny how much I enjoy his attention.

I track his every movement, and I'm getting to know him with every gesture he makes with his brilliant hands, every smile he gifts, and every word that comes out of his beautiful, talented mouth. I'm not in love with him because I'm not ready yet, but I want to be, and that is a startling revelation.

He points his fork at the food on his plate. "I hope you're not fussy because I had no idea what to order. I just made a few executive decisions."

I shake my head. "Not fussy. I rarely get takeaway, so it's a bit of a treat."

He holds his hand over his heart. "This is the best Thai food in Melbourne. You have to try the green curry." He picks up his fork and scoops some rice and chicken drowning in some sort of milky sauce.

I open my mouth and allow him to feed me. The second the flavours hit my taste buds, I wince. "It's okay," I say, reaching for the water glass.

Josh devours everything on his plate, and I find the more of the curry I eat, the more I like it.

"You know I don't know if I can be with someone who doesn't like Thai food." He is joking, but he has put our relationship status on the table even if he didn't mean to.

"Where do you see this going, Josh?" I ask, unable to resist turning the conversation serious. I wave my hand from him to me. "Us."

He doesn't say anything, and I feel the weight of his gaze on me. I don't know if he's considering his response or analysing my question. Maybe both.

"You haven't noticed," he says. Not what I was expecting

him to say at all.

"I haven't noticed what?" I ask, confused.

He gestures to the right with his head, but his eyes never leave mine. "What's hanging over the fireplace over there."

I freeze, immediately knowing what I'll see when I turn my head. "That isn't an answer," I say, unable to hide the tremble in my voice.

"You asked where I see this going, and I'm going to tell you." He stands and walks over to the fireplace. "When my father died, I lost my way completely. I became a barely-functional shell as I tried to find reason in the mayhem. He was a young and seemingly healthy man in his prime looking forward to the golden years with the love of his life."

I push my chair back and stand. Moving across the carpet without lifting my gaze, I stand next to him. I place one hand on the mantle and the other on his arm. "It must've been really hard for you and your family."

"One minute he was here, laughing and holding Mum's hand while they watched a funny movie together on the couch, and the next he was gone. Deleted. Erased. Just . . . gone." He looks down at me with pain in his eyes. "How is that fair?"

I shake my head. "No one ever said life was always fair." I bite my bottom lip, knowing I should be trying to broach the subject of Mereki, but wanting to see where he's going with this.

"For years, I struggled to come to terms with Dad's death. I went to art school, and I owe Madeleine an awful lot for her support, but I felt adrift."

"I don't know where you're going with this, Josh."

"I'll get there. Be patient, Ms Hart."

I hold up my hands. "Sorry. Continue."

He glances up at my framed drawing. "The day I saw your drawing for the first time was rock bottom for me. I was planning to give up on my art despite having an offer to exhibit at a gallery in London. I know it sounds odd, but I felt my world shift on its axis when I opened the packaging that was protecting your drawing. It whacked me in the face with the emotion. I'd never experienced anything like it."

"It's strange for me to hear this." I glance up at it and stare, incredulous that a piece of paper with my pencil marks on it could mean so much, not only to me, but to this man, too. "I never meant to sell it, you know. For a long time, I regretted that decision so much, it consumed me."

"I can understand you not wanting to part with something that is obviously personal, but I'm really grateful you did. You see, at the time, it felt like it had been sent to me directly. Kind of like a lifeline. I didn't know you or anything about why you drew it the way you did, but it gave me something I needed."

"I'm really glad it helped you, Josh." I pause, trying to process everything he's saying. "Do you feel indebted to me or something? Is that why you want to be with me?"

He jerks back. "Why would you say that? We'd already spent the night together when I found out you were the artist. Remember?"

I drop my gaze from the drawing to my feet, feeling guilty for my thoughtless question. "I'm sorry. I'm just coming to terms with all of this."

"I still haven't answered your question."

I nod, barely remembering what it was.

"You asked me where I see this going," he says as if he's read my mind. "All I see is you, Emerson. Your drawing showed me how to find happiness in my life again, and it's you. It held me over until I got the real thing, and I'm not letting you slip through my fingers." I choke back a sob. "The light and shade, the strength, the resilience. The perfect imperfections. All you."

"That was a very long answer," I say, smiling despite my tears.

"The short answer is that I've been falling in love with you for years now, and I only see my future with you in it."

Happy tears block my vision, but I feel his arms around me, and I feel his warm breath on my neck.

"We're going to be late for class," he whispers.

My whole body tenses. I've run out of time to tell him what I really need him to know.

"What's wrong?" he asks, pulling back and holding me at arm's length so he can look me in the eye.

I chew on my bottom lip, madly debating in my head whether to broach it now. "I need to tell you something about my past."

His eyes soften. "You can tell me anything, Emerson."

I nod, still chewing on my poor, innocent lip. "We don't have time now, but I want you to know I trust you and there's something I've been keeping from you. I don't think you'll like it, but I'll need you to try to understand if you really want me in your future."

His brow furrows. "It definitely sounds like a conversation we need to have when we're not running late." Glancing up at the drawing, he sighs. "I trust you, too."

We take the plates and wine glasses back to the kitchen where he hurriedly stacks them into the dishwasher. I give the bench a quick wipe down, then grab my bag. Part of me wishes I'd explained everything to him, but we moved forward, and I will tell him soon. Josh deserves my truth, and Mereki deserves to be released from my chains.

CHAPTER

29

THIS EVENING'S ART class is different. I'm present and relaxed, able to enjoy it for what it is. Josh is a professional and gives each student equal portions of his time and attention, but he's not even trying to conceal what we've become to each other. Earlier, when he was giving me some constructive feedback on my work, one of his hands rested casually on my lower back. It felt so intensely intimate, especially when his fingers found their way under the hem of my T-shirt and made tiny circles on my skin. I was unable to concentrate nor hear a single thing he said. My whole world was reduced to a square inch of skin for those seconds, and everything else faded to insignificance.

"You and Josh, huh?" Brooke leans across and whispers with a conspiratorial smile and a wink when Josh is on the other side of the room.

"Seems so," I reply, grinning.

Her smile widens. "You go, girl. He is so hot." She wipes her brow. "I honestly thought he was taken. He didn't seem at all available, or I would've jumped his bones first night."

I shake my head, chuckling. "Shhh. He'll hear you."

She shrugs. "I'm an open book. Doesn't matter anyway. Plenty of fish in the sea."

I don't tell her I would have no idea about that. I've never been fishing. Not in the sense she means anyway.

She adds a few more strokes to her painting before leaning back and asking, "Are you free on Friday night?"

I hesitate, not because I don't want to go out and celebrate her birthday, but because it occurs to me that I'm making friends and planting roots for the first time since I moved to the city.

"Come on. It's my birthday, and we're going to Pulse for drinks and dancing." She pouts and hits me with her puppy-dog eyes. "Please."

She claps, then stands up. "I have a request." She waits for everyone, including Josh, to look at her. "It's my birthday tomorrow, and you're all invited to Pulse to celebrate . . . well, to celebrate me." She waves her hands in front of her. "I've got a bunch of my friends coming already, so just turn up anytime from eight-thirty." Then she points to Josh. "I really want Emerson to come, and I know she will if you're there."

My cheeks heat, and I can't look at him, so instead, I watch her in awe. She is so open and confident. I always had an inner confidence, but I kept it mostly hidden, reserved only for myself and, until recently, one other person. Due to my outer shield, I've been referred to as aloof, shy, vacant, and dull, but I never cared, and I never will. I rely on myself and I choose who I let in. I find love in my own way and on my own terms. And it seems I've found it again in a way I would've never expected.

When I hear a throat being cleared, I realise I've just been staring at Brooke, and I snap myself back to the here and now. I feel Josh's eyes on me, and I lift my gaze to meet his. Even from the other side of the room, his emerald eyes burn with intensity and affection.

He breaks eye contact to address the room. "Happy birthday for tomorrow, Brooke. I'll definitely try to make an appearance."

At the end of the class when everyone has gone, Josh and I are alone in the gallery. I keep working on my last painting while he packs up the supplies and returns them to the shelves.

"Will you go to Brooke's birthday bash with me tomorrow night?" he asks as he lifts the last box.

"I will," I reply, adding some yellow flecks to my sunrise.

He walks across the room and pulls out a stool. Grabbing mine, he drags me away from my easel so we're sitting face-to-face. "I want us to go together, and I want to spend the whole night with you." He reaches out and runs his hands up my legs. "I want to wake up next to you on Saturday morning."

All I can think about is how much I want that, too. Then it hits me that he might be thinking he'll stay over at my place, and my blood runs cold. I don't think I'm ready to have him there before I've said goodbye to Mereki. It isn't fair. "We could spend the weekend again at your place," I reply, placing my hands over his.

"Does it not make more sense to stay at yours tomorrow?" His hands move farther up my thighs. "Then you stay at mine Saturday night, or we could spend the whole weekend at yours."

This is moving too fast. I've barely caught my breath before I'm planning a second weekend with Josh, and I have absolutely no idea what I'm doing. All I can do, because it's all I've ever done, is go with what feels right, but this whole situation is confusing. The idea of having Josh spend the night in my home . . . the home I share with Mereki, however cold and lonely I've felt there, is wrong on every level, but I have no way of making him understand. I can't tell him everything because I don't have the right words. I don't know if I'll ever have them. Memories of his arms around me, his lips kissing me, and his whispered words making me feel whole again bombard my muddled brain. All those things felt so incredibly right. "Okay," I say, feeling anything but okay. "Sure."

He picks up my bag and throws it over his shoulder, takes my hand, and pulls me to standing. "I better hit the road. Leroy will start wondering where I am."

"Oh, maybe it's better we do go home to yours tomorrow night then. What will you do with Leroy?"

Ushering me towards the door, he says, "I'll drop him at Clare's Friday afternoon and pick him up the next day. I think he loves her more than me."

Shit.

"I'll drive you home," he says when we stop at his Landcruiser parked right out the front of the gallery.

"I have my car here. I've been driving into work Wednesdays and Thursdays for the late finish. I'm parked on Melling Street where it's not metered."

He insists on driving me to my car, then kisses me goodbye. When I'm safely inside, he drives away. Life for me is still complicated, but I'm moving forward, and that's a whole lot better than standing still and infinitely better than going backwards.

As I drive home, a memory hits me out of nowhere. My hands tighten on the steering wheel as my mind attempts to block something I don't want to remember. It was about a year before Ki and I finally got together. We must've been about sixteen at the time.

"What is your problem, Mereki?" I ask, stabbing him in the arm with my pointer finger.

He turns to face me, raises his eyebrows, cocks his head to one side, then looks away. Not a single word passes his lips, but his silence speaks volumes.

"Are you angry at me for what happened with Jacob today?" It is the only thing that makes any sense. Jacob had asked me out to dinner in front of Ki and half the school as we were lining up for lunch earlier today. I didn't say yes of course, but I also didn't want to make a big scene, so I pretended I needed to go to the bathroom and avoided responding.

He snorts but doesn't meet my gaze. I've hit a nerve. I'm sure of it. His jaw clenches, and I'm worried he's going to snap his fishing rod in two from the white-knuckled grip he has going on.

"You can't possibly think I'd go out with Jacob Smith." Gagging, my whole body shivers in disgust.

Ki reels in his line, picks up his fishing box and walks away from me and our place by the river. Seeing red, I storm after him.

"Silent treatment is so immature, Mereki," I call out. "Is it possible your maturity is decreasing with age?" Frustration and my own anger lace my tone. "Are you gonna go home and cry to your mother now?"

He throws me an angry look over his shoulder but still doesn't say anything. Mereki is my best friend. He's definitely my only real friend, but his anger management needs work. Giving me the silent treatment is never an option. Never ever. We talk, we laugh, he fishes, I do art. We have so many positive ways of communicating that this is unacceptable to me. Silent treatment never solves anything.

CHAPTER

30

"E MERSON." I HEAR my name literally screeched the second the Pulse nightclub's entrance comes into view.

Brooke bounces on the spot, waving to me, and I wave back, embarrassed by the attention I'm now getting.

"Where's Josh?" she asks, glancing around.

"Running late I'm afraid, but he'll be here." A burst water pipe at Todd's café this afternoon was, of course, a valid excuse for Josh to change our plans of meeting for dinner and going to the club together. The plumber hadn't shown up, so Todd had begged his best mate to help minimise the damage. I'd told him to give Todd a hug from me and that I'd just meet him at the club later.

Kissing my cheek, Brooke holds me at arm's length. "You look hot." I'm not offended by the shock in her voice. She's never seen me in anything other than jeans and T-shirts. "I'm so glad you came."

When I was choosing what to wear last night, I realized how few 'going out' clothes I had and that my nightclub attire was non-existent. On my lunchbreak, I walked to a clothing shop located in the adjoining suburb and found a slim-fitting black dress. It was shorter than I was accustomed to, but the shop assistant insisted it really suited me. She also managed to talk me into some gold accessories and strappy heels. My left arm is completely covered while my right arm is left bare. It creates a striking contrast, and I'm determined to own the look.

Brooke drags me through the club like a woman possessed. I direct all my focus into staying upright as I stumble along behind her. I knew I couldn't wear my trusty Chucks or even ballet flats with this outfit, but my feet wholeheartedly disagree. When we stop, I'm introduced to a large group of her friends both sitting and standing around two tables near the bar. I nod and smile, attempting to remember names. A couple of them seem vaguely familiar, and I wonder if they're actors.

"And of course you know Tennyson," she says, and I sigh with relief that I know one other person. He's walking back to the table with a tray of drinks and smiles widely when he sees me.

"Hey, Tenn," I say, my smile matching his.

"Well, aren't you a sight for sore eyes?" he says, nodding as he appraises my outfit. "Josh here?"

I can smell the alcohol on his breath. "Not yet, but soon hopefully."

"Well don't accept drinks from anyone but me. Okay?" His happy-go-lucky tone from moments ago is now replaced with a very serious expression. "What's your poison?"

I have so little experience with alcohol but figure a little Dutch courage wouldn't go astray. "Vodka tonic please."

"Coming right up." He disappears back to the bar.

Glancing around, I take in the monochromatic interiors being shot with colour in a lightshow that feels like some sort of artistic entertainment. The dance floor is heating up with semi-naked bodies, and I can't deny the surge of adrenaline the atmosphere injects into me. My anti-social instincts are being driven out by the synchronised music and lights.

"One vodka tonic," Tenn says, handing me a tall glass. "Do not put it down."

"Thank you," I say, warmed by his concern. I take a long sip and welcome the buzz.

I open my mouth to say something else, but Tenn has already turned away, beckoned by one of Brooke's very attractive, busty friends. Knowing he's in a dark place having been left by his wife, it's really good to see him letting loose a little.

I finish my drink in one long gulp, then feel a tap on my shoulder. Swivelling around, I'm face-to-face with a guy I was introduced to earlier. His name escapes me.

"Emerson." He holds his hand out, so I shake it confidently, willing his name to miraculously appear in my head. Obviously realising I don't have a clue, he saves me. "Rick. There were a lot of names for you to remember."

He's still holding my hand and rubbing his thumb over my knuckles. He's flirting with me, but I have no idea how to deal with it. "Good to meet you, Rick."

"Can I buy you a drink?" he asks, taking a step closer so he's officially in my personal space and still holding my hand.

"We need to dance," Brooke says, grabbing me by the arm and yanking me away. "Dance or throw up. That's my motto." Her long, black hair is flicked over her shoulder, and her chin tips up. She glances at Rick. "Sorry, buddy. She's taken."

One of her friends, I think her name is Taya, jumps up from her seat, and we follow Brooke to the dancefloor. I must've glanced at the front entrance a hundred times since we arrived, hoping to see Josh, but he's yet to show. The music is overwhelming, but as the beat rises and falls, I begin to relax. I want to feel completely free. Then, out of the corner of my eye, I see him on the other side of the dance floor. The music simply fades away. Like a woman possessed, I push past jostling, sweaty bodies for a closer look. His back is to me, and he's moving in the wrong direction. I can't get to him. When he turns, I stop dead in my tracks, and my heart thunders painfully in my chest. It's not my Mereki at all. Of course it isn't. My knees feel too weak to hold me up, and I can't get enough air into my lungs. Whipping around, I see Brooke and Taya still dancing provocatively, oblivious to my near meltdown. I can't think straight. Clutching my chest, I try to rub the ache away, but I need more space to breathe. "I'm going to use the bathroom," I say into Brooke's ear when I make it back to her.

"Are you okay?" she asks, shouting. "You're white as a sheet."

I nod, then rush off the dance floor.

The relative quiet of the bathroom gives me the opportunity to pull myself together. Listening to a group of drunk girls gossiping with over-the-top animation helps to get my mind off what just happened. By the time I return to the group near the bar, I'm feeling a lot better.

It's almost after ten and no Josh. I check my phone and see a text from him fifteen minutes ago saying he's nearly here. I smile at his message, then smile wider when I look up and lock eyes with him only a few feet away. My insides liquefy as his gaze carefully examines my body. Lust is clear in his eyes and determination evident in his stride as he closes

the short distance between us. I reach out and grab a
conveniently-placed handrail as my legs feel unsteady. My
angst, pain, and heartache fade to grey when Josh drinks me
in and absorbs it all.

Without caring that Brooke and her friends are right there,
he kisses me like he means to lay claim, and I let him.

"You look fucking amazing," he says in my ear.

It's the first time I've heard him really swear, and there's
something very hot about it when used so rarely and with
such passion.

"Thank you." I run my hands around his neck. "You don't
look so bad yourself." And boy is that an understatement.

The usually very casually-dressed Josh is now in dark
denim jeans that appear custom made for his incredible body,
together with a black, short-sleeved, button-down shirt. It
isn't tight because I know that's not his style, but it is more
form-fitting than anything I've seen him in before.

Brooke introduces him around, and he attempts
conversation with a few of her friends, but the music seems
to be getting louder. I can barely hear myself think.

When I next look at my watch, it's after midnight.

"Another friend of mine is DJing at the new club on Little
Bourke," Brooke says. "Do you wanna come?"

Taya bounces up and down on her seat. "Absolutely." She
turns to Josh and me. "Come on, guys. The night is young."

Josh meets my gaze, and the air crackles between us. It's
clear neither of us has any interest in hitting another club. I
hold my hands up in front of me. "Not me. I'm done."

Josh appears relieved. "Happy birthday," he says, kissing
Brooke on the cheek.

As we leave the club, Josh's hand firmly clasping mine, my
gut twists in elaborate knots while my mind leaps in a

thousand different directions. Regardless of how much I want to ignore it, my body is giving me a warning and I should be taking heed.

CHAPTER

31

W E TAKE A taxi back to my place, and my nerves reach fever pitch as we turn into my street. Despite the desperate desire I feel for Josh, the reality of being here with him is even worse than I'd anticipated, and I'm having massive regrets.

"What's wrong?" Josh asks, most likely sensing the tension I'm giving off.

With my vow to honesty, I answer. "I've never invited a guy to sleep over here before."

"Well that makes me ridiculously happy," he replies, putting his arm around my shoulders as I rummage in my bag for the keys. "No pressure. Okay? I just want to be with you. I want to be here *for* you."

His words are like a balm on my deep and painful wounds. "Thank you."

When we're inside, I don't give Josh even a moment's opportunity to take a look around. Instead, I grab his hand and drag him to the bedroom with the single-minded focus of a woman possessed, and he offers me no resistance. In fact, he's half-undressed by the time we fall onto the bed in a frenzy of lust. His hands are everywhere, and his deep thrusts remind me how much he wants me to be his.

Afterwards, Josh slips easily into a deep sleep, while I toss and turn. My body is content, but my mind grants me no peace. It's a raging inferno of yet-to-be-spoken truths and the anguish I'll feel if they ruin what I have right here in this warm bed. Eventually I drift off, my mind conceding to continue the torture in my dreams.

What feels like minutes later, my toe stubs painfully on the corner of the skirting board, and I nearly scream out, but I can't find my voice. What am I doing in the hallway?

Then I remember. I heard the front door closing, and I panicked like I've only ever experienced once before in my life. Naked, with Josh's arms still locked around me, I struggled to push him off me, then managed to slip one of my oversized t-shirts I often slept in over my head.

Everything feels too fast but not fast enough at the same time. My world is crashing in on me in the worst possible way. I exhale, now thinking it had simply been a very vivid nightmare. Obviously my subconscious wreaked havoc and made my fears seem real.

Deciding to get a glass of water to calm myself down, I tiptoe towards the kitchen. When I turn the corner into the lounge, I come face-to-face with Mereki. This time I do scream, but my hands fly up to my mouth to muffle the sound. I haven't seen him in weeks, and he looks different. He appears older, as if the years since moving to Melbourne have caught up with him all at once.

"Nineteenth of November," I say, hopelessly, holding out my hands to touch him, desperately wanting to touch him. "I was going to explain everything by the river. I needed more time."

He points to Josh's jacket and raises his eyebrows, then sits on the couch. Instead of ignoring me like he has done for what feels like forever, he doesn't take his eyes from mine. The strange thing is, he doesn't appear angry. Instead, he appears resigned and, dare I say, happy. I pinch myself to make sure I'm not, in fact, still dreaming and find I am most definitely awake.

Walking over to the couch, I sit down next to him. Oh God, I love him so much. *What have I done?*

"Will you still come to the river on the nineteenth?" I ask. It comes out in a sob of anguish.

I need him to nod. Just a tiny movement of his head to tell me he'll do what we promised five years ago.

"Please." I'm begging now, and my voice is louder and more demanding. "I need to hear your voice, goddammit. I need you, Mereki. Don't leave me. Please don't leave me." Tears are now coming hard and fast.

"Emerson?"

Hearing Josh's voice, I leap off the couch. I can't look at him. I can't face this scenario.

"Who were you talking to?" he asks, concern lacing his voice.

I glance at him standing by the doorway in his black boxers, then stare down at the empty couch. The sob that escapes my chest is not of this world. It's the unparalleled pain of acknowledging that someone you love more than your own life is dead. Mereki is dead, and there isn't a goddamned thing I can do to change that. Lord knows I've tried. It doesn't matter that I still see him, still talk to him, still love him. He's gone, and it crushes me to the bone.

I'm completely confused, I'm terrified, and my body starts

to shake uncontrollably.

"What's going on?" Josh crosses the room and stops in front of me, blocking my view of the couch. He takes hold of my upper arms. "You're scaring me. Did you have a bad dream?"

I almost laugh at his question, holding my hands out, palms up, willing the shaking to cease so I can try to explain. "I wish that's all it was." I raise my eyes to meet his concerned gaze.

He tries to pull me into him, but I shake him off. I can't handle him touching me now.

His eyes flare with confusion. "Tell me what's going on, Emerson. Please."

Like a wild animal caught in a trap, my eyes dart around the room looking for an escape. This is no one's business but my own, and now I'm going to have to verbalise something I don't think I can explain out loud.

Irrational anger swamps me, and I go on the attack. "I don't know what is and isn't normal anymore."

"Why are you shouting at me?" he asks, holding his hands up.

I feel like I'm smack bang in the middle of a train wreck, and I don't know what to do with myself because I'm both the cause and the casualty. Josh has become collateral damage. When he looks at me again, his eyes are unreadable, and I have no idea what he's thinking. I'm emotionally spent. My mind spins, and I struggle to organise any coherent thoughts in my messed-up head.

Swallowing hard, a cold sweat prickles my skin. The simple act of pushing my shoulders back gives me a little strength, and I swipe at my eye, irritated by a few strands of hair that won't behave. "I have so much to tell you, and I don't know if you're going to understand, but I owe you the truth."

Josh bristles. "Okay," he says drawing out the vowel. "I want to know everything about you. The good, the bad, and I suspect the ugly stuff have all made you into the incredible woman you are today." His hand reaches out for mine, but I still can't let him touch me. "Tell me what you've been hiding, Emerson."

Closing my eyes briefly and taking a deep breath, I say, "When I was eighteen, my boyfriend and I were mugged. The money I took for that drawing that hangs in your mother's house was stolen along with my entire world. The only reason I wasn't raped and most likely killed was they panicked when they realised Mereki wasn't breathing. He'd been knocked out trying to save me, and his head hit the pavement in just the wrong way. He died in a deserted alleyway, a few metres from where I lay unconscious." The words spill out so fast, my head spins.

The colour drains from Josh's face. "Oh my God, Emerson. You were talking to him as if he's still here." He pushes the heels of his palms into his eyes.

"Let's sit down," I say, gesturing towards the couch.

Taking a deep breath, I start at the beginning. I give him a quick summary of my first ten years and my less-than-ideal family life. Then I recount the story of how I stumbled across the market and found my love for art after running away from Jacob Smith.

Again, Josh reaches for my hand, but I don't let him take it. I am hanging on by a thread, and his touch could unravel me. "I made my first true friend a few weeks later down by the river doing my pebble art." Josh's eyes are soft and encouraging me to continue. "Mereki and I were inseparable, and our relationship turned into something more when we were seventeen, and we acknowledged we were in love with each other."

Josh sits back slightly. The movement is small, but the significance is large. No man wants to hear about an ex, let alone one on an untouchable pedestal.

"How long were you together?" he asks, his voice breaking with emotion.

He asks the one question at the heart of why this conversation is so bloody difficult. "Not long enough," I answer, truthfully.

Josh leans further back as if he has reached a conclusion all on his own. "You're still in love with him, aren't you?"

I glance around the room, looking for guidance. Maybe I'm looking for Mereki's strength. Oh, the irony. "Mereki was my whole life from the age of ten, and all the good qualities you seem to see in me are because of him."

He shakes his head. "I don't believe that."

"Excuse me?"

"You are everything all on your own."

I shake my head violently. "That's not true."

Awkward silence hangs between us, and I desperately wish my toe could actually dig a hole in the carpet to swallow me up.

"I need to tell you the rest of my story." My words are whispered, and my heart is aching.

"Can I just say something first?" he asks.

I nod, quietly relieved.

"I'm thirty-one years old, and you're the first woman I've been unable or unwilling to find a fatal flaw with. All my serious relationships ended because I've been waiting for you without even realising." He cringes. "I don't think I'm perfect by any stretch, but I was always looking for that someone who would be perfect for me. There's a difference, you know."

"At this point in my life, I'm not perfect for you and have more flaws than you can possibly imagine." I'm still whispering.

"That's just it, though." He hesitates before continuing. "Whatever you think your flaws are, I see as beautiful imperfections." He cups my face and wipes away the tears with his thumbs, just like Mereki used to do. "There's so much sadness inside you and now that I know why, I want to help. But I need to know you're here with me and not stuck in the past."

I lift my hands and cover his with mine. I committed my life to Mereki and, in a million years, I had never expected to question that commitment.

"I don't think I'm ready," I say, tears slipping down my face. "I want to be, though, and that's a big step for me."

Silence builds a wall between us, and I don't have the energy to stop it.

"Try to get some sleep now," he says eventually.

"Are you going to stay?" I ask, then chew on my bottom lip.

He nods but doesn't move, so I turn on my heel and return to my bedroom. As if my body knows I need a reprieve from reality, sleep claims me quickly. I dream of curling up by a dried riverbed, crippled with devastation. I am Miann, and my tears are going to make the river flow again.

When I wake, daylight streams in through the open blinds.

Last night's events come rushing back, and my heart clenches. Squinting, I rub the sleep from my puffy eyes and see Josh standing on the balcony. I have no idea if he slept in my bed or on the couch or if he's been awake the whole time. Even without seeing his face, I know that he's desperately sad. His back is to me and his shoulders are slumped, perhaps heavy with regret that he ever got involved with me or the fact he's getting ready to walk out the door. It kills me to know I am entirely to blame. My life began again when I met Josh, but I haven't been fair on him, and he has every right to leave me. I'm relieved he cared enough to wait for me to say goodbye in person.

As if sensing that I'm now awake, Josh turns to face me, leaning against the railing, and crosses his arms over his broad chest. My body aches, but I push myself out of bed and join him, knowing it's time to face the music.

"Did you get any sleep?" I ask. My voice is raspy, so I clear my throat.

He shrugs. "A little."

Biting my bottom lip, I'm unsure what to say next, so we stand there staring at each other.

He breaks the silence. "Last night was . . ."

"I'm so sorry, Josh." I don't try to reach out to him.

"What are you sorry for?" he asks, flatly.

"I'm sorry you had to find out like that. I'm actually sorry you found out at all."

He nods, smiling, but it's a sad smile. "You know, sometimes I talk to Dad when no one else is around. I tell him about my artworks or how Mum is doing. I know he isn't there and I've no idea if he can hear me, but when I talk to him, the void doesn't feel quite so painful." He pauses for a few seconds, and I hear him take a few deep breaths. "I know what it's like to wish someone you love was still around, but I don't know how you can be with me while you're still in love with a ghost."

Tears slip down my cheeks because I can't give him the reassurance he so desperately needs and deserves.

He holds his arms open, and I'm unable to resist his warmth. I step into him, crying five years' worth of tears into his chest with his arms wrapped around me. I think back to the grief counsellor who came to talk to me in the hospital when I'd been told Mereki was dead. She told me about the five stages of grief, starting with denial.

"He isn't gone though," I'd told her. "I saw him standing right next to my bed."

She had tried to explain that I'd been in a drug-induced state and he wasn't real. Instead of believing her, I took denial to a whole other level and fought tooth and nail to stay in that stage forever. I believed if I let go of denial, I'd be letting go of him. Whilst I was only just treading water, I wasn't drowning in my devastation. I can't keep treading water forever though, and it's time for me to swim again.

Eventually, I pull away from Josh. "I think we need some space for a while."

He shakes his head. "I don't want space." His brows furrow. "I don't run when things get tough."

"I love that about you, but it's important I face up to this on my own. I just need a little time and space to sort myself out properly."

His eyes harden. "What the hell does that even mean, Emerson? You were happy to lead me on while I was in the dark, and now I know the truth and don't do a runner, you push me away? What the hell is that? How much time?"

Walking past him, I lean against the railing. "I'm heading

back to my hometown for the five-year anniversary of Mereki's death. It was a pact I made with him when we were eighteen that we'd return to our clearing by the river at sunset on the nineteenth of November every five years. It was meant to be something we did together, but I plan to uphold our pact and say a proper goodbye to my best friend."

Josh places his hands on the railing next to me, and I glance up at him. His face is a myriad of warring emotions. I know he wants to understand so we can find a way forward, but this is obviously testing his staying power. I don't blame him at all. "This is pretty fucked up."

I nod. "I'll call you when I return, but I completely understand if you rethink this." I wave my hand from him to me. "Rethink us."

Josh hangs his head. "I hope you get the closure you need." He pauses for a few moments, then raises his eyes to meet mine. "It kills me to say this . . ." He steps forward and kisses my forehead. "Goodbye, Emerson." And with those words, he goes inside and leaves my apartment.

Staggering back inside, I crumple onto my bed, unable to stand. My heart splinters with a new wave of devastation, rejecting my decision to push Josh away while I confront the mess I've made by holding onto Mereki. The irony isn't lost on me.

I don't leave my house all weekend. In fact, I barely leave my bed, and I allow myself to wallow in self-pity before I have to pull myself together again.

On Monday morning, I go into work and give Carrie my four weeks' notice. She isn't happy but doesn't ask for an explanation. I am replaceable, and she sets about finding a new employee. If she'd asked and I thought she'd care, I would've told her it was time I stopped hiding from life and pursued my passion for art. Ever since I met Josh all those months ago, I've slowly opened my heart again to love, but also to art. The memories that have flooded in since have reminded me that when I found my passion, I also found a gateway to my inner strength. I found my wings then and I'm so close to finding them again, I can feel the sun's warmth on my face and the cool breeze kissing my body.

That would've no doubt been entirely too much information for Carrie, and she would've cut me off with an eye roll, a shake of the head, and the sight of her walking away. But that's what I know in my heart, and that's what matters now.

CHAPTER

3 2

~ Six Weeks Later ~

TOMORROW WILL BE five years since Mereki was killed. I ended up working beyond my four weeks' notice because Carrie only found a replacement a few days ago. Meg, however, is experienced and enthusiastic, so I'm handing over my apron to a much worthier employee for Carrie's high standards of baking and passion for cupcake designs. I'm leaving town today to return to my hometown to say the goodbye I should've said to Mereki a long time ago. Josh is always on my mind and I miss him desperately, but the space has been good for me and when I return, I'll make contact, with the hope we can find a way forward together.

As I hit the freeway, I open the windows to enjoy the warm breeze as I sing along to the classic hit, U2's "With or Without You." When I pause to listen to the lyrics, I promptly change the song because I don't need Bono telling me he can't live with or without someone. It's too personal and completely counterproductive for what I am doing tomorrow.

I leave home at lunchtime and drive all afternoon, only stopping occasionally to fill up and grab snacks, arriving in the town I avoided for five years just as the sun dips below the horizon. Rolling slowly through the quiet streets, my emotions leap from one extreme to the other. A part of me is thrilled to be back here where I do have many wonderful memories. I relish the idea that being here will bring many of them to the forefront. However, a bigger part of me is filled with anguish.

Parking my car outside the familiar house, I take a long time to make it to the front door. I'm stuck somewhere between wanting to laugh nervously and cry inconsolably. Plucking up the courage I've been mustering for the past few weeks, I knock lightly.

The door opens, and I sway with the weight of emotion crashing down on me.

"Emerson," Adina says. "It is so wonderful you're here."

"I . . . um . . ." I stutter, step inside, and literally fall into her arms. The devastation and joy at seeing Mereki's mum is completely overwhelming.

"Oh, sweetheart." She hugs me tight to her ample bosom.

She is the closest thing I have to a mother. I haven't seen her in five years, and my decision to leave without looking back weighs heavily.

Mereki's father appears from the kitchen, and our eyes meet. "Hello, Emerson," he says, giving me a small smile.

Adina releases me, and I walk slowly towards the only positive father figure I ever had and stop in front of him. "Hello, Warrin." My voice breaks as I say his name.

Tears pool in the corners of my eyes, and I rub my chest in an attempt to ease my aching heart. He looks so much like his son, and it rips me apart. A million emotions pass between us without another word being spoken. It's all so horribly unfair.

"Hello, Emerson." His voice is strained with emotion, and I fall into his open arms. "It's so good to see you."

I pull back and look him in the eye. "It's so good to see you, too." A few tears slip down my cheeks.

"I'm so sorry, but I have to go into work now," he says. "I'm on the night shift, but you're staying a few days at least, right?"

I nod, swiping at my cheeks. "Just a few."

"Then we'll be able to catch up properly."

After he's gone, Adina puts her arm around my shoulders and ushers me towards the kitchen. We sit at the small table and I glance around, comforted by the familiarity of this room.

"It's really so wonderful seeing you again," she says. "We both missed you."

"I missed you, too." I thought seeing Ki's parents would hurt too much. Instead, my heart swells with love. "So much." I shake my head and fiddle with a loose thread on the tablecloth. "Do you ever see my mother or Trent?"

"She left town soon after you and, last I heard, Trent's in rehab. Adelaide, I think." Her eyebrows knit together. "Developers bought your old house and demolished it. There's a new housing estate out there now."

I don't want to talk about them. I don't even know why I asked. I'm here to apologise to the woman who was the closest I had to a real mother. "Adina," I say after taking a moment to organise my thoughts. "I should've stayed longer after I was discharged from the hospital. I should've been here for you and Warrin." I swallow hard over the lump in my throat. "But I couldn't stand being here without Ki."

She reaches across the table and takes hold of my hands. "You'd become each other's whole world. We understood you wanted to get far away from here."

I nod. "I couldn't stay. It was too hard to confront reality, so I escaped from it instead." My words come out quickly as if they've been trapped inside my mind for too long, begging to be let out. "The whole time I was talking to the police, I was thinking there had been some sort of huge mistake and Mereki was going to show up at any moment."

"You were dealing with far too much. I wish Warrin and I'd insisted you stay, but we weren't coping either." She squeezes my hand. "You have to know we love you like a daughter, and you're always welcome in our home."

I nod but can't find any more words.

After a few moments of silence, she stands, walks to the oven, and pulls out a baking dish. "I made lasagna. Are you hungry?"

"A little," I reply, not wanting to be rude despite my churning stomach.

After we've eaten, we move to the lounge room and sit next to each other on the couch. I look at the woman who I'd hoped would be my mother-in-law one day, and I see the toll losing her only child has taken. She appears to have aged far more than the five years it's been, and the worry lines around her eyes are deep grooves of emotional toil.

"Are you doing okay?" I ask.

She shuffles closer to me. "We're finding peace one day at a time. I'm more worried about how you're doing."

"I'm still finding peace, but I'm closer than I've ever been before."

She nods. "There's no timeframe or road map for the

grieving process. We all do it differently, and no one should judge anyone else for finding their own path."

We sit in silence for a few moments.

"I hate that justice was never served," I say in a whisper. "I can't believe no one was ever charged."

"I know, but it wouldn't have brought him back."

I nod. "That's true, but the idea that he's dead and no one . . ." I can't finish the sentence. The fact that Jacob and Trent had rock-solid alibis when the attack happened meant I'd had nothing to offer the police to help with the investigation. There were so many out-of-towners there that night for the live music that, without any witnesses, the case was a dead end.

She sighs. "I spent years feeling angry, resentful, and bitter, but then I realised I was letting strangers steal my life, too. I was focusing on something I couldn't change, however much I wanted to. It was killing me, and I think it was doing the same to you." She stands and moves over to a wooden desk in the corner, piled high with papers and books. Opening a drawer, she pulls out a stack of opened envelopes, then returns to the couch. "Thank you for sending me these," she says. "The last one particularly brought me so much joy."

A few times a year, I sent them a letter to let them know I was alive. I never had a lot to report, but I wanted to keep in touch in some small way. The most recent one I sent only a few weeks ago and was a drawing I did of Mereki fishing.

"He was with me when I wrote those letters," I say quietly, handing her the letter and pointing to the drawing. "I know it makes me sound crazy, but I felt his presence so strongly for so long, and it stopped me from grieving. I knew I was in denial, but I didn't care. I could see him so clearly. It was as if he was holding on for me."

Tears escape her eyes, and her hands cover her face. "Oh, Emerson. I wish you would've talked to me sooner."

"He stopped showing up recently, and I hated it. I tried to pretend he had good reasons for his absence, but I know now I was letting him go."

"I'm envious of you," she says through her tears. "On my darkest days, I would call out to him, begging for a sign that he could hear me. I felt ridiculous, but I just wanted to see him again. I wanted to hold my son and tell him I loved him. I wanted him to tell me one of his wonderful stories and for me not to tell him they were all nonsense."

I nod, tears streaming down my cheeks. "I loved his stories, too. Did he ever tell you about the girl who made the river flow again?"

She shakes her head. "He didn't, but he wrote them all down in a journal, so I've read the story of Miann and Iselele."

My eyes widen with joy, and my hand covers my mouth. She stands again and disappears down the hall, returning a few moments later holding a cream-coloured book. When she hands it to me, I bring it up to my nose, eager to smell the pages. It's an instinctive reaction to something that Mereki once held and obviously treasured.

I open it and start flicking through the pages, overjoyed to find all the stories he told me and some he didn't.

"You can keep it," she says. "I think he would've wanted you to have it. I'm sure you were the inspiration in one way or another for every story he wrote since the two of you met."

I nod, clutching it to my chest in gratitude. Later in bed, my eyelids become increasingly heavy reading about Darlizabeth, the fearless warrior, defending her children against the killer serpents of the Red River of Sythe. As slumber claims me, my last thoughts are of Mereki, the first great love of my life, the benchmark for all other men, and how he taught me about the infinite length and breadth of my heart. I wake up, however, thinking about Josh.

CHAPTER

33

I SPEND THE morning with Adina, going through her old photo albums and reminiscing. When Warrin wakes up late morning, we have lunch together, and I fill him in on what I've been doing for the past five years and the news that I've started drawing again. I even tell them about Josh, and they seem genuinely happy I'm finding a way to love again even if it's all up in the air. Being with them and talking openly about Ki is therapeutic and something I should've done a long time ago.

"I think I'm going to take a walk," I say, placing my plate in the dishwasher. "I have some things I need to do." I pick up my handbag and sling it over my shoulder. "Is there anything I can get for you at the shops?"

"No thanks, sweetheart," Adina says. "Enjoy your walk. We'll be here when you get back."

I hug them both, then head out the door. It's a warm, clear summer's morning, and I'm glad I'm wearing my favourite yellow sundress. I chose it specifically to wear on this day, as it's going to one of the hardest of my life.

There are two ways to walk from Mereki's home to the centre of town, and I could've easily taken the other route, but that's not what today is about. Instead, I turn left at the end of Murchison Street towards the old milk bar where my life all but stopped five years ago. Despite the warm temperature, I shiver when I reach the entrance to the alleyway. So little has changed since that fateful night, and I wrap my arms around myself as it replays in my mind.

Fuck! Let her fucking go!

It's okay, Kalimna.

Don't touch her. Please don't touch her.

I'll save you, Kalimna. I love you.

Ki!

Standing in the place where I was snatched away from Ki's arms, I acknowledge what I know. My best friend and first love of my life never left this town. He was supposed to be an engineer building enormous skyscrapers and coming home to me each night. Instead, by the time someone found us, I was unconscious, Mereki was dead and so were our dreams.

"It shouldn't have happened," I whisper to the empty alleyway, overgrown with weeds and overlooked by time.

A small amount of closure lightens my step as I continue towards the centre of town. My next destination is likely to be just as unpleasant, but equally important.

The first thing I notice when I reach the main street is how many new shops there are. Some of the clothing chains have opened stores, and I'm tempted to check out a fancy homewares boutique, but this isn't a shopping trip and I know it would just be postponing something I need to do. Today is about confrontation, not avoidance.

When I reach the other end of main street, I stand in front

of the shopfront that used to be Smith's Jewellers, Jacob's family business. It's still a jewellery store, but it's now called Proudman's, a national chain, and it's been completely renovated. I'd hoped someone here would help me locate Jacob, but that now seems unlikely. I still harbor resentment towards him and have questions that, five years ago, I couldn't face asking. But I'm determined to ask them now, so I'll continue my search.

A bell rings as the door to the shop opens and the man I came here to see walks out, head bowed and eyes focused on the pavement. He doesn't look up, and I don't think he's going to notice me.

"Jacob."

His eyes snap up, flash with what appears to be panic, then he simply stares. "Emerson," he says eventually. "What are you doing here?"

"Right now, I'm here to see you." I'm enjoying his discomfort.

Perhaps to alleviate the tension in his clenched jaw and raised shoulders, he shoves one hand in his pocket, pulls out a packet of cigarettes, removes one, and lights it with a Zippo. "Was wondering if you'd ever show up," he says after blowing smoke in the air between us.

"Did your father sell the business?" I ask, waving the smoke away from my face.

Glancing at the sign above us, he shrugs. "Turns out he was leveraged up to the eyeballs." He takes another drag of his cigarette. "It was a forced sale a few years back, but the new owners let me keep my job."

I have nothing to say to that. He'd been so arrogant about how wealthy his family was and how he was going to be running the business when his father retired. Perhaps a little humility would've served them well.

"I need to ask you something." I change the subject to the reason I'm here.

"I'm about to meet my wife for lunch," he says, glancing up the street again. "Can you come back later?"

"You got married?"

"Had to," he replies, flicking the end of his cigarette to get rid of the ash. "Accidently knocked her up. Her parents said they'd buy us a house and help with our living costs if we got hitched."

"I need to ask you about the night Mereki was killed." I'm done with small talk. I've got questions, and I'm not remotely interested in his love life.

"What about it?" He fixates on the cracks in the pavement.

"I know you and Trent had alibis, but did you tell anyone that I had cash on me? You were the only ones who knew, and I always wondered . . ."

"You think we set it up? You think we'd tell a bunch of out-of-towners to attack you and kill Mereki?"

My blood runs cold. "Out-of-towners, huh?"

His eyes dart to the ground, then he whips his clenched fist up to cover his mouth and coughs loudly. "Everyone thought it was out-of-towners."

I take a step closer to him. "Look. I know you weren't there. I know you didn't attack me or kill Ki. I'm sure he would've shouted out names if he'd known any of the men. I just want to know what happened that night. I never believed it was a random mugging gone wrong. It might give me some kind of closure if I have a better understanding." I wait until he looks me in the eye. "Perhaps you have something to get off your chest."

He drops his cigarette to the ground and stubs it out with his shoe. His chin drops to his chest. "Trent and I saw you get the cash from that old lady," he begins. "After we left your stall, Isaac and Troy were drinking with a whole group of rough dudes I'd never seen before." He glances up at me but can't seem to meet my eye for more than a second. "Trent was going on about his 'bitch of a stepsister,'" he says with air quotes, "getting a whole lotta cash for some stupid artwork."

"You think it was those guys who attacked us?"

"When you walked past with Mereki a short time later, a couple of the out-of-towners were checking you out and saying they'd like to hit that." He pauses. "Trent told them you were his 'bitch of a stepsister,' and the rough dudes disappeared after the music had finished."

"That's it?"

He shrugs. "I've no idea if they were the ones who did it, but I felt guilty, and I know Trent did, too."

"So guilty neither of you visited me in hospital or told the police what you just told me?"

He shakes his head. "Trent freaked out when news spread. He thought he'd be charged as an accomplice or something even though he didn't actually know if the guys he told were the ones who did it." Lighting up another cigarette, Jacob begins to pace. "We didn't want to take the risk."

"I knew you weren't my biggest fan, but did you ever consider warning me?" I ask, holding my hands out, palms up. "Trent had my number. You could've sent me a message." *It could've saved Mereki's life.*

After a long silence, he raises his eyes to mine, regret written all over his features. "I was drunk and stupid."

"Sounds like Trent still is."

275

Jacob nods. "He hit the bottle even harder after that night and did a stint in jail about a year later for hitting an old man on a pedestrian crossing. His blood-alcohol was three times over, and his license was already suspended for previous offences."

I hadn't noticed a woman approaching until she was standing by Jacob's side. "Chelsea?" My eyes drop to her very pregnant belly.

"Emerson?"

I glance between her and Jacob. "You're married?" I ask incredulously.

They both look at me and shrug before Chelsea pats her belly and says, "Number two is due in January."

"Well good luck to the both of you," I say with as much sincerity as I can muster. "It was . . . real."

Jacob gave me what I came for. Nothing is bringing Mereki back, and justice will never likely be served to the men who killed him, but I need to move forward with my life regardless. It's time.

CHAPTER

34

A S THE LATE afternoon sun dips behind the trees, I make my way down to the river alone. It feels completely surreal. For eight years, I made this trek almost every day, and so many memories hit me full force. Unlike the town, the riverbank remains largely unchanged as if time has skipped over it completely. I'd worried there might be some kind of development in the area.

When I arrive at our clearing, the whispered questions in the back of my head grow louder. *Do I want to see what's left of the pebble art? Do I want to see it destroyed when I came here to heal?*

Gravitating towards the river's edge where I'd watched Mereki fish so many times, I smile sadly, remembering the best and worst day of my life and the pact we made.

"Let's make a pact to come back here on this day at sunset every five years, no matter what," he said, staring at the burning orange ball descending towards the horizon. *"November nineteenth. I would say every year, but I think that's unrealistic, and I don't want to come back here that often. Do you?"*

"Wouldn't you want to visit your mum and dad?"

He shrugged. "They can visit us in the city."

I remained quiet for a few moments, deliberating. Three little words. They could have meant nothing, but in that moment, to me, they meant everything. "I don't like how you said 'no matter what,' as if there might ever be a reason we wouldn't be together."

"Is that what you thought I meant?" he asked, shaking his head. "Of course we'll be together. I just meant that who knows what we'll be doing or where we'll be in five years. We'll be twenty-three years old and probably finished with our studies by then. Hopefully I'll be kicking arse at a big engineering firm, and you'll be working on a major exhibition."

I laughed at the beautiful picture he'd painted. "Well when you put it like that . . ."

"I just think we should always remember what this place means to us and come back to where it all began. We'll tell the river about all the exciting things we've done since we left."

I pushed up onto my knees and threw my arms around his neck. "That's a wonderful idea. Let's do it." I kissed him hard on the lips before pulling back to meet his gaze. "So, four days after my twenty-third birthday, we'll both be right here watching the sunset, no matter what."

Nothing and no one would ever come between us.

Taking a deep breath, I mumble, "No matter what."

Despite my attempted composure, the tears come. Swiping them away, I push my shoulders back, determined to be strong for my beloved Ki. When the words come again, they're said with confidence. "No matter what."

The breeze picks up and I hear his voice, swirling around me. *No matter what.*

He appears out of nowhere, and I sob with relief. I feel lucky and blessed to see his beautiful, kind face again even if

I know it's for the last time. His dark eyes are soft with understanding.

"Don't look at me like that," I say, tears streaming down my face. I reach out and touch his face. I can feel him with every single part of me.

I can hear what he wants to say because it's exactly what I would've said to him if it had been me.

"Say it with your whole heart and mean it. Say it because it's your greatest gift to me, to our memory, and most importantly, to you."

Shaking my head vigorously, a loud sob escapes my lips. "I don't think I can."

"You can, Kalimna."

I meet Mereki's gaze. He tilts his head, then walks towards the very spot I've been avoiding. I need to see what's left of the pebble art that changed my life. With him, I can do this. I *want* to do this. Glancing briefly at the gathering clouds above, I follow him, my heart rate spiking with adrenaline. When he stops, I do, too.

He whispers to me, and I swear I hear his reassuring eighteen-year-old voice. *"I'm here, Emerson."*

With his encouragement adding steel to my spine, I look down and gasp. Collapsing to my knees, I cover my mouth with my hands, overwhelmed by nostalgia, devastation, and a strange kind of joy. Like looking in a mirror to my soul, I can see the damage. Some pebbles are broken, dislodged, and eroded. Others have disappeared, washed down the river and lost forever. However, the big picture is largely intact. Maybe more than ever, it reflects the strong and resilient girl I've always been inside, weathered by circumstance and time.

Darting my eyes around, I find Ki standing by the river's edge, and my mind catapults back to the hundreds of times I sat in this exact spot and watched him fish.

Brushing my hands down my thighs, my heart sinks knowing it's now time to do what I came here to do. I push up to stand and shuffle towards him, stopping when I'm close enough to feel his presence.

His smile threatens to derail me, and I commit it to the part of my memory reserved just for him. The part of my memory that I will never let go. I can still hear his voice in my head.

"I don't want to let you go." Even though I hate the weakness of my words, my mind speaks the truth.

Ki lifts his fingers to his lips and blows me a kiss. The pain is still crippling, but I can hear him. *"Moving on with your life and loving someone else is not letting me go. We had our time and it was perfect, but there's more to your love story. and you don't want to miss it."*

My sobs are uncontrolled as I listen to the words in my head, in my heart, and swirling in the breeze. My heart explodes with agony and hope all at the same time.

"You take this next chapter with both hands, bright eyes, and an open heart."

"I want to be happy again, but I can't fathom my life without you standing beside me." Shivering, I clutch my heart, knowing that's exactly where he is. "My happiness has always been so tied up in you."

Closing my eyes, I can feel his embrace. In this moment, I reflect on his friendship, his love, his absolute belief in all that I am, and it wraps around me until I'm no longer cold. Squeezing my eyes shut tighter, I want to freeze time.

"Say it, Emerson." He's whispering in my ear. *"Say it, knowing I will always be in your heart like you are forever in mine."*

Taking a shaky breath, I open my eyes and walk ever so slowly towards the river, still feeling his presence all around me.

I try to smile, but desperate sorrow is still my overriding emotion when I pick up his fishing rod and fight away the dread, knowing what I'm about to do. "Everything I am, I learnt from you," I say, looking into his loving eyes.

"Live and love for both of us, Kalimna."

I concentrate to still my shaking hands and get ready to cast the line. This is when I expect him to stand behind me to guide my movement. When I look to him, he shakes his head with the tiniest of movements. I nod in understanding, absolutely gutted nonetheless.

The sun touches the horizon, and evening mist settles over the gently flowing river when I tear my eyes away from Ki.

"Say it, Kalimna." It no longer sounds like his voice in my head. It is only the whisperings of the wind, lapping at the water and the rustling of the leaves in the trees.

Panicking, I whip my head around. Relief overwhelms me when he's still there, but he's fading. He's melting into the mist, and he appears irrefutably happy. I'm shocked to find my heart isn't completely broken. If anything, it feels hopeful. I want happiness for him as much as he wants it for me.

"Say it, Kalimna." The windswept words settle around me, and I smile through my tears.

With newfound determination, I firm my grip on the rod, swing it back, and cast it out in a smooth arc, exactly the way he'd taught me so many times. He's no longer guiding my every movement, but he's with me. He'll always be with me.

"Goodbye." I say the word I've refused to say until now for fear of really losing him. "Goodbye, my first friend, my first love, my first everything. I will never forget you, and I will always be grateful for the time we had." Despite the lightness seeping into my heart, my shoulders slump and tears stream relentlessly down my cheeks. "Goodbye, Mereki."

The Mereki I've clutched to for years swirls away with the mist. Unable to hold the rod now, I reel in the line and know I need to leave it behind, too. Without any further thought, I prop it in the dirt just like Ki had done all those years ago when he'd go in search of pebbles for our art work. Taking a few steps back, I can almost see Ki standing next to his rod smiling at me. It's different though now. It's simply a memory, and I fully acknowledge he's no longer a physical part of my life other than the permanent place he will always have in my heart.

My shoulders slump, but my heart is full. I continue to stare at the river for a length of time I can't begin to measure. It might be minutes or hours. It might be days, months or years. For the first time since I was just shy of ten years old, I'm facing life without him, and I'm determined to live for both of us.

"Emerson."

I hear my name, and for a few moments I wonder if I really am crazy. I turn around and find Josh standing a few feet away. His hands are pushed into his pockets and his shoulders are hunched, but what I see in his eyes is enough to steal the breath from my lungs. They're filled with sadness, longing and bone-deep love.

"What are you doing here?" I ask, swiping at my tear-stained face. "How did you know where I'd be?"

He edges forward, pulling his hands from his pockets as he halves the distance between us. "You told me the date and, the way you talked about Mereki's parents, I suspected you'd be staying with them." His shoulders rise and fall with each breath. "I asked around when I arrived a couple of hours ago and found their house without any trouble." I don't interrupt him primarily because I'm speechless. I can't believe he's here. "I wasn't sure how they'd feel about a stranger turning up on their doorstep asking for you, but they welcomed me into their home." He eyes search mine. "You told them about me."

I nod. "I did."

The corners of his mouth rise, but he's cautious. "I have a present for you in my car. I wanted to give it to you on your birthday but knew you wanted space, and I was trying so hard to respect that."

"What changed?"

He sighs. "Honestly, Emerson. I tried to talk myself out of coming, knowing you wanted to do this alone, but I couldn't stay away imagining how hard this was going to be." He cocks his head and points over his shoulder. "I've been up by that tree pacing for the past hour, unsure if I should be here or not but unable to walk away. I needed to know you were okay." He runs his hands through his hair, and I see his pain etched into his features.

"I'm here for you as a friend at the very least." Another step forward and he glances behind me to the river, breaking our gaze for a split second. "I'm so sorry for everything you went through."

I edge forward, and he does the same.

"Tell me to go—"

"I'm really glad you're here, Josh." I take a small step, and we're now so close that if we both reached out, we could touch. I gasp. The air crackles between us and wraps me in a warm blanket, stitched with Josh's soothing presence, empathy, and love. My eyes dip, but Josh grips my chin, forcing my gaze back to his.

"Look at me, Emerson," he says, with a firm tone. "I need to see your eyes when I say this to you."

I swallow hard, surprised I have any tears left to shed, but I can feel them regrouping in the corners of my eyes.

"I broke a promise to you and that's on me."

I shake my head, and his hand drops from my chin. "You didn't break anything. I broke you."

"No," he says. "Please let me finish."

"I saw you right from the very first moment I laid eyes on you." He reaches out and pushes my hair behind my ears, then steps into my personal space. "I saw you, Emerson, and I knew there was something you were hiding. I promised you I wouldn't push, and instead of honouring that, I let you into my heart and my bed."

The tears I was trying so hard to detain slip free. "I was there, too, Josh, even though I wasn't ready to let go of my past and move forward with you."

"I should've been your friend and waited until you trusted me enough to speak freely about this." He grazes his knuckles across my right cheekbone with such tenderness, I am at a loss for words. "I should've pushed harder for your art, not your body, and certainly not your heart. A little voice told me it wouldn't be smooth sailing for us, but who listens when it's saying the opposite of what you want to hear?"

"You're right about so much, Josh, but if you hadn't pushed me, I'd still be living my life in limbo, fearful of looking backwards but unable to move forward. I was barely living at all until I met you."

He pulls me into his arms and groans when I wrap my arms around his waist, snuggling into his firm chest. "I missed you more than I thought possible."

"I missed you, too," I say, knowing I'm speaking the truth.

He pulls me back and holds me at arm's length. "We need to talk about this, Emerson. I need to know you're going to be okay. I won't be asking for anything other than your trust and your friendship until you're ready for more."

I nod. "Thank you." I feel his lips on the top of my head, and I try to get closer to him.

"Do you need more time here or are you ready to leave?" he asks.

Reluctantly, I pull back so I can look into his eyes. "I'm ready to leave, and I'm ready to live."

EPILOGUE

~ Five Years Later ~

UNACCUSTOMED TO PUBLIC speaking, let alone coupling it with my debut art exhibition in my hometown, I take a deep, calming breath in a bid to relax my frayed nerves. I've worked too hard though, and I refuse to allow a few butterflies to take this away from me.

"Good evening, ladies and gentlemen," I say in a confident voice. "I'm Emerson Hart, and I'd like to thank you all so much for being here this evening."

A light round of applause affords me a few moments to take a quick sip of water and to glance around, marvelling one more time at the fact that my art adorns the walls. The fact that at least fifty people, including a few I recognise from school, are in attendance, blows my mind.

Removing the microphone from its stand, I move to the side of the podium. "I found my love of art right here in this town when I was ten years old. It gave me a way to express how I felt about everything and everyone around me. It was a gift and a lifeline. I attended a travelling art show as a teenager, imagining what it would be like to be an exhibiting artist." I take a few steps closer to the first drawing and sense the eyes of everyone in the room on me. I turn to face them. "As some of you would know, days after I became an adult, I lost my best friend and, for a long time, I was unable to find peace with it. He had shown me how to love and be loved." A sense of deep calm washes over me, and I know whatever the response to my work is doesn't matter. My plan is to finish my speech, mingle for a few hours, then head down to the river to tell Mereki all about it. He won't be there like he was for so many years, a real-to-me figure that I could latch on to. But he'll listen, and he'll be proud of me and that's enough. "Thanks to the help of some very special people I met five years later, I was able to find peace, partly through art and partly through remembering how to use my wings. I'm strong and resilient in my own right, and I'll fly high enough for him and for me." A louder round of applause startles me and I smile appreciatively, waiting for quiet before continuing. "What you're seeing here tonight has been a beautiful kind of therapy for me, and I sincerely hope you take something for yourself from my journey." A lump forms in my throat, but I swallow past it and smile. "Thank you so much for being here this evening. It means a great deal to me. I'd be happy to answer any questions you might have as you take a look around." I smile while the audience applauds.

I'm blocking the first painting, so I move to the side as the crowd hustles towards it.

A woman with greying auburn hair and squinty blue eyes studies it for a few moments before saying, "You appear so lonely."

I've admitted my work is autobiographical, so of course she assumes the girl in the painting is me as a child. I'm walking down an empty street in a non-descript country town, dressed in dirty, ragged clothing. On my head, I'm wearing bright orange antennae attached to a headband—the one Jacob cruelly ripped off and trampled on. There are other people in the painting, but all their backs are turned to the little girl.

"I was lonely," I reply candidly.

"Why are you wearing antennae?" she asks. "Is it an existential metaphor?"

I smile, shaking my head. "It's quite literal, actually. I always felt like an outsider, so I pretended I was an alien adventurer from another planet where no one questioned appearances because we all looked the same."

"I see your loneliness and fear, but it makes me feel hopeful." The auburn-haired woman waves her hand in a sweeping motion over the top of the canvas. "The colours in the distance are brighter. You're walking towards the light."

I smile at the woman. "Loneliness, fear, and hope. Three emotions I'm familiar with."

"Hope is a dangerous emotion," she says. "It can be just as destructive as fear and hate."

"That's very true, but what do we have without hope?"

She appears to contemplate my words, then says, "Well, I'm intrigued to continue your journey."

I wave my hand in front of me, indicating she should move on to the next drawing. "Thank you for taking the time to really look."

She smiles. "Thank you for sharing your talent with us."

A waiter walks past and I refuse the champagne, opting instead for a mineral water. I smile over the rim of my glass when I see Zoey on the other side of the room chatting to Eric, Kaye, Tenn, and Brooke, who is now a huge star thanks to her role as the sexy artist's muse. I'm so touched they made the journey. Zoey's floral crown is bursting with colour this evening, and I can't see any missing petals. It fills my heart with joy seeing her look happy and relaxed in her own skin. She makes eye contact with me and waves.

"You did it, sweetheart."

I smile as I turn around and step straight into Madeleine's embrace. "I was a nervous wreck," I reply as I pull away.

"I know, but you owned it, and I'm so proud of you."

My eyes sting with overflowing emotion. "Thank you for everything. I couldn't have done this without you and—"

"This is amazing," Zoey says, cutting me off with an excessively tight embrace. "*You* are amazing."

"Thank you," I squeak.

Mercifully, she releases me and I drag in a breath.

"Zoey," I say when I've composed myself. "You remember Madeleine?" I wave my hand between them. "Madeleine. Zoey is one of my friends. She was in that first art therapy class I took in your gallery."

They shake hands warmly.

"Well if you'll excuse me," Madeleine says, placing her hand on my shoulder. "I've just seen John Foster. He said he wants to discuss exhibiting your work in Sydney. I better go and say hello." She turns to Zoey. "It was lovely to meet you."

"Thanks again," I say, sincerely. "This is beyond my wildest dreams."

"It's no more or less than you deserve, my darling."

With that, she floats away. My guardian angel is the most elegant, selfless and genuinely kind woman I've ever met and, when I count my blessings these days, she's one of the many I count twice.

"I cheated a little," Zoey says, scrunching up her nose.

"What do you mean?" I ask, tearing my gaze from

Madeleine's retreating form.

"I skipped over the first paintings, looking for the ones I might recognise."

I laugh. "That's totally fine. They don't have to be viewed in any kind of order. They can be standalones, too."

"I'm so happy for you, Emerson." She shakes her head, smiling. "We all knew you were destined for greatness."

"Sure you did," I reply, chuckling.

"We did!" she retorts firmly, with a gentle push on my shoulder.

When I've put in another hour of mingling, I slip out the side door. Madeleine saw me and nodded, so I know she'll cover for me if necessary.

The warm November air wraps around me as I walk away from the gallery. It's still light, but the sun is low on the horizon as I head out of town and down the once familiar path to the river. I had specifically asked for the exhibition to be held on November the nineteenth for this very reason, and as the river comes into view, I see the loves of my life.

"Hey," I call out, and the most handsome faces in the world turn to the sound of my voice.

"Mama." My little boy calls out and runs towards me. "Caught a fish, Mama."

The excitement in his voice and on his face nearly brings me to my knees. I scoop him up when he reaches me, and he kisses me on the cheek. "Where is it?" I ask, turning my free palm up.

"He made me kiss it, then we let it go," Josh says, scrunching up his nose and making Ky belly laugh. "How did it go, gorgeous?" he asks me, taking Ky from my arms. "I can't believe you wouldn't let us come."

I look him in the eyes and smile. "It was perfect. I know

you wanted to be there, but I would've been too emotional. I needed to know you'd be down here waiting for me."

"I'll be wherever you want me to be, my love, but wild horses won't keep me from the next one."

"Deal." I reach up and place my lips on his, closing my eyes as I feel him press into me.

"No kissing." A little hand pushes us apart. Josh tickles his sides, turning our three-and-a-half-year-old into a squirming tornado.

"We'll give you some privacy?" my thoughtful, gorgeous husband says.

I nod. "Stay close by. Okay?"

"Of course." He kisses the side of my head, takes Ky by the hand, picks up the fishing rod, and moves a little way along the river.

The second Josh places Ky down, he grabs the rod. Watching them bait the hook, a deep sense of calm washes over me. Turning away from them, I stare out across the slowly flowing water. Despite the decade that has passed since Mereki died and the five years since I found peace with it, I can still see him, and I still love him in my own way. I had thought once I said my goodbyes, it would be over and he'd be completely gone from my life.

It was Josh who suggested I keep this pact to come back here every five years. "He was the most important person in your life, and he is a part of who you'll always be. There's no reason to try to forget him as long as you don't let his memory stop you from moving forward," he'd said.

It was Josh who made sure I talked about him. I've even found him reading Mereki's stories to our son. I asked him once if he ever felt threatened by Mereki's ghost, and he shook his head and said, "I'm grateful to the boy who offered you friendship when you needed it then loved you the way you deserved to be loved for as long as he could." He'd picked up my hand and kissed my wedding band. "Mereki and I are the lucky bastards who know what it's like to be loved by Emerson Hart." He'd looked at me with love in his eyes. "I'm not threatened by a ghost. He's the best man I never knew."

I close my eyes and smile as the breeze picks up around me. I whisper, "Hey, Mereki."

Rustling leaves, the occasional bird call, the whirr of the fishing line as it's cast into the water. These are the sounds I hear, and when I open my eyes, I see him. He's smiling at me, as handsome as ever, holding up his right hand in a wave.

"Another five years, but you remember what we agreed?" I raise my eyebrows. "No matter what." I pause. I had a whole speech planned out, but now I'm here, I can't remember a single thing I wanted to say. I glance over at Josh and he meets my gaze, nodding his encouragement. I bite my bottom lip, then turn back to the river, to the first love of my life. "I got married, and we have a son." I hold up my left hand and stare at my wedding band. I refuse to wear anything too extravagant, so it's a simple gold band, but its significance is my whole world. "Our son's name is Ky, and he's a keen fisherman. I like to think you're watching out for him and maybe giving him a few tips." I tuck my hair behind my ears and take a deep breath. It feels so good to talk to him again, and now I don't want to stop. "Your mum and dad are so amazing with Ky. They're teaching him all about your culture, and he adores them. We try to visit as often as we can." I shake my head. "Nope. I still have no idea where my mum is, but honestly, my life is so full, I wish her well and hope she found happiness. Sometimes I think you have to find your own family." I look over at Josh and Ky. I think about his family and how completely they've embraced me. I think about Mereki's parents who have always treated me like the daughter they never had and that I've given them a grandchild with another on the way. I pat my still-flat stomach knowing it won't be that way for much longer. "I think this one's going to be a girl." I smile at the memory of Mereki's nickname for me. "Her name will be Kalimna or Kali for short." I stand up taller and push my shoulders back, not wanting to cry but knowing it's inevitable. I could blame early pregnancy hormones, or I could acknowledge that I'm about to tell him exactly what I know he'd want to hear. "I'm really happy, Mereki. I'm loved and I love with all my heart. I've even achieved my dream of being a working artist, but I know ultimately, what you wanted was my happiness." I swipe both happy and sad tears away from my cheeks. "I miss you so much, but I'm in love and I'm loved." I blow a kiss across my upturned palm, then raise my hand. "See you in five years."

I turn, knowing Josh and Ky are approaching. "Are you okay?" Josh whispers.

I nod, giving him a smile that can't quite reach my eyes.

"I love you," he says when he reaches me.

"I love you, too," I reply, wrapping one arm around his waist and the other around our son's shoulders.

"I love you three," Ky says, giggling.

We walk away from the special place by the river, but I'll be back in five years' time to tell Mereki all about how I'm living my life for the both of us. As I always knew it would, our love transcended all.

This is love, my way.

THE
end

OTHER BOOKS BY
kate sterritt

The Fight for Life Series (Romantic suspense)
Collision (Book 1)
Impact (Book 2)
Levitate (Book 3)—not yet released

Standalone
The Holly Project (Contemporary romance)

ABOUT THE
author

Kate Sterritt lives in Sydney, Australia with her husband, three young sons and highly energetic German Shorthaired Pointer puppy.

When she's not madly juggling the logistics of soccer trainings, play dates and volunteering at the school, she can be found at her laptop, writing the types of novels she loves to read. Her characters are inspired by her own experiences, blended with her imagination and a healthy dose of wishful thinking.

Connect with Kate

www.katesterritt.com

Facebook.com/authorkatesterritt

Twitter.com/KASterritt

Instagram.com/katesterritt

kate@katesterritt.com

Facebook readers group Kate Sterritt's Hummingbirds

ACKNOWLEDGEMENTS

Writing this book was an extraordinary labour of love. It stretched me beyond where I thought my limits lay and, as always, I'm so grateful to my steadfast support network.

A huge thank you goes to my husband, the greatest man I've ever known. I'm so lucky to love and be loved by him. Regardless of how hard he works and how long his hours are, he kisses me when he gets home and genuinely cares how my day was. That's real life romance right there. He and the kids are the centre of my world, but I believe I'm a better wife and mother because of my writing. The creative outlet feels necessary to me now and I will continue to write forever, published or not.

Thank you to my dad for brainstorming this book with me and for always being a fantastic sounding board. Thank you to my stepmother for her insight into the art world and for lending me her books. Thank you to my sisters (including Jen – the sister I chose) and friends, both in my everyday life and the online community. I'm so grateful for your love and friendship. Kell Donaldson, Christine Maree and Darlene Avery, I needed to single you ladies out to thank you from the bottom of my grateful heart for your unwavering, unparalleled support, both personally and professionally.

Soon after I started writing this book, I was lucky enough to attend a writer's retreat organized by Simon & Schuster Australia and Christina Lauren. This wonderful group of women I'm proud to call my friends, inspired me to pursue this story and to keep following my dreams. Anabel, Lauren, Jay and Ryn, thank you for taking time out of your very busy schedules to support me, for believing in this story and my ability to tell it. You all had a profound impact.

To all the authors who've supported me both personally and professionally, I value you so much. In particular, ES Carter (my northern hemisphere twin) and GJ Walker-Smith. I don't know where I'd be without the two of you and I hope I never find out.

To the members of my readers group, Kate Sterritt's Hummingbirds, a special thank you to you. To have a group of readers there to support my journey means more than you could ever know.

To all the bloggers and loyal readers who took the time to read advanced copies and promote "Love My Way," I am so thankful. I know there's a lot of choice out there so I'm grateful you chose my book. Helping me spread the word is such a gift and it's never taken for granted.

To you, the reader, I sincerely hope you enjoyed Emerson's story. I might never become accustomed to the idea of people around the world reading my words, but I continue to strive to give you the very best of me.

And finally, a very special thank you to my friend, Lauren McKellar. Aside from her first class editing and writing skills, she's quite simply one of the greatest friends I've ever had. We get each other. She makes me smile every day and I hope I do the same for her. I'd move heaven and earth for her and I know for a fact she'd do the same for me. I'll be forever grateful for her support throughout the writing and publishing of "Love My Way."